BOOK TWO O
MW01037747
THE SEEKERS OF
KNIGHT
T.C. EDGE

Copyright Notice

This book is a work of fiction. Any names, places, events, and incidents that occur are entirely a result of the author's imagination and any resemblance to real people, events, and places is entirely coincidental.

First edition: October 2016

Cover Design by Laercio Messias

To hear about the author's latest discounts and new releases, sign up to his newsletter at www.tcedgebooks.com

Table of Contents

1 Stranded....5
2 An Unseen Danger....16
3 A Welcome Face....25
4 A City Subdued....35
5 Fifty Fifty....47
6 In Our Blood....59
7 The Titan's Hand....68
8 Professor Lane....78
9 Links to the Past....91
10 The Grid....99
11 Phase Three....108
12 Suspicions Rising....118
13 Back in the Game....129
14 The Coronation....137
15 Expelled....148
16 The Cabal....156
17 A Legend Awakes....168
18 Time Grows Short....179
19 The Secret Base....188
20 Battle Begins....198
21 Face to Face....210
22 The World Burns....221

23 Mercator....230
24 Defence to Attack....243
25 Preparations....253
26 Attack on Titan....265
27 Decoy....275
28 Showdown....285
29 Battle Royale....293
30 Lambs to Slaughter....303
31 The City Falls....313
32 A Final Secret....320

1
Stranded

The desert is endless, vast. It stretches out ahead of us as far as the eye can see, spreading on all sides towards the horizon.

Shimmering on its surface, a wave of heat hovers, the day growing increasingly oppressive as we travel across the open plains of this incessant wilderness. We're crossing an area known as the *empty plains*, lifeless and desolate and caught between the Western hills we've come from, and the taller peaks of the mountains in the East where Petram dwells.

And it's to the great city of stone that we're headed.

Behind, many miles away now, the burning remains of Baron Reinhold's compound lies. For a time, the towering column of smoke sent up by the inferno was visible, the secret base coughing up its black fumes. Now, however, as I turn to look back, I see no sign of it, the Western hills now far in the distance.

On the dirt bike behind me, Velia sits, clutching tight at my chest with her weary fingers. Grinding along the dirt and sand, we're rushing as fast as possible, no time to lose in our mission to reach Petram and deliver the file.

The Seekers of Knight...

Hidden safely in my bag, the file is precious cargo. Who knows what secrets it will reveal, whether it will contain more of Knight's legacy, more of the grand plan the Baron is determined to carry out. It's imperative that we reach the city and get in contact with Drake. Right now, nothing else matters.

Under the directions provided by Velia and Vesuvia, we make good progress. Even here, in this sparse and empty land, they seem to know where they're going, plotting our course ahead when we stop to take drinks breaks.

By the time the afternoon begins to evolve into evening, however, the strained, chugging sound of a spluttering engine signals danger. It's Ajax's bike that's the first to go, his heavier weight forcing it to work a little harder than mine.

I share a concerned look with him as his bike begins to fail, grunting loudly like a dying beast. A few minutes later, my own transport starts to suffer the same mechanical affliction, coughing wildly as we pull to a stop in the hard dirt.

We all look to one another, our eyes growing hooded.

"Fuel's out," I say, putting words to the obvious.

I kick out hard at the bike, knocking it off its wheels in frustration.

"How the hell didn't we think of that," I shout, mainly to myself. "How could we be so stupid…"

In our rush, thoughts of running out of fuel never even entered my mind. Whether it entered the minds of the others I don't know.

Velia comes over to me and rests a calming hand on my arm.

"There's nothing we could have done about it anyway," she says. "It's not like we'd have found extra fuel in the compound, the whole thing was destroyed…"

I take a few deep breaths as I re-gather my focus. Then I turn back to the others.

"OK, we've got no choice. We have to continue on foot."

Ajax raises his eyebrows, sweat dripping off them in the burning heat.

"On foot?" he says, looking around.

"What alternative do we have?"

No one can offer an answer.

"How far is it to Petram?" I ask, turning to the girls.

Now it's their turn to share a look. They confer as only twins can, using a few telepathic eye movements and other gesticulations, before Velia speaks.

"Too far to walk. Not out here, not without more water. We'll need to find another settlement."

The mention of water makes me suddenly aware of how little we have left. I ask the others to get out their bottles and take account of their stores. Some worried looks are spread around.

"We have maybe a day's worth of water left," says Velia, "and in this heat we'll dry up quick."

The tone of her words are matter of fact, but ominous. These two girls know what life is like out here, how much water you need to survive, and how quickly your life can be taken without it. It's something that Ajax and I, living in Lignum, have always taken for granted. Over in the woods, you could subsist forever on the dew twinkling on the forest floor each morning, or the rain gathered in leaves and hidden in roots. Here, such a thing isn't possible.

"So, which way?" I ask.

There's a rare show of concern in the girls' eyes. In this vast wilderness, how could they possibly know which way the nearest signs of life might be?

"There are hills to the North," says Velia eventually. She doesn't sound confident. "We'll never make it to Petram on foot, and the desert stretches too far that way to the East. Our best bet is to go North and find shelter among the hills. And," she says, sweeping her eyes across the landscape, "we have to hope that we pass by a well along the way."

With no better options available to us, we gather up our bags and begin marching northwards, altering our course as we drag our bodies through the sands and dried desert earth. I know that there are wells dug across the wilderness, built over the years for travellers who might find themselves in such a predicament as ours.

My father even told me once of his own pilgrimage across the Deadlands, when he led thousands of refugees to Petram in the early days of the War of the Regions. It doesn't fill me with great joy when I recall his words: each well they passed, he had told me, had dried up as a result of a particularly hot summer.

And this summer grows hot.

The sun's scorching rays begin to fade as the evening deepens, giving us some respite from the heat. On several occasions, I see Ajax taking out his bottle and preparing to take a long swig of water, only for Vesuvia to catch his arm and tell him 'no'.

"We need to ration now," she tells him. "Little sips, on the hour. Drink when I drink."

Ajax defers to her greater knowledge of life in the desert and does as ordered. Yet it's a habit that dies hard, and Vesuvia is forced to keep a constant eye on him to make sure he's not drinking when he shouldn't be.

Soon, the sunset is approaching fast, and the colours of the world turn beautiful once more. There's a charm to this place, despite its hazards, that is impossible not to admire. I stop for a moment, watching the colours change from yellow to orange to red, their hues deepening by the minute, and imagine that in other circumstances, this might be quite nice.

Velia comes to my side and smiles at the look on my face.

"It's beautiful, isn't it?" she says. "I guess I forget sometimes. It's nice to see it through your eyes."

I look at her and know what she's talking about. Sometimes you get so used to seeing something, no matter how beautiful, that it loses its wonder. The woods of Lignum are one such place, a place that I now appreciate more than ever; that I yearn to see again.

But not yet.

We chug on, the night air cool as the day is hot. Sometimes the evenings remain humid and close, at others they carry a bite on the breeze. Tonight is the latter. It's refreshing, and helps to keep Ajax's mind from wandering back to his thirst for water. But when the morning comes, we know that our appetites are only going to get more pronounced.

Night-time in the desert is rarely as dark as the woods or cities. Unless there's cloud cover, the sea of stars and bright moon above paint a constant glow on the world around us. We take advantage of the light and are able to continue on into the evening for many hours, working our way towards the sight of the rising earth in the distance.

There, far to the dark horizon, it's clear that the world grows a little in altitude, signalling the start of the hills that Velia had mentioned. Out here, in these unforgiving lands, altitude often means life. Plant life and animal life and people themselves all seek the higher passes in their attempts to ease away from the burning desert floor.

On the flatlands, however, and with the skies dark overheard, perspective is a fickle beast. Velia tells me that the rising lands are still miles and miles from where we are now, and that there may not be any settlements or little oases for many more miles after that.

"Until the ground grows high enough," she says, "we're unlikely to find anything." Then she repeats what she said earlier, her words more anxious this time: 'We have to hope that we pass a well."

On we go, our legs growing weary. Ajax, it seems, begins to suffer first, his body growing weak through lack of food and water. It's often the largest men who are hit hardest, their dietary requirements greater than the rest. And if he's struggling, I'm sure I won't be too far behind.

He soldiers on, of course, not wanting to draw any attention to himself. Weakness for Ajax is unthinkable, something his father would never permit. But this isn't weakness, this is reality. Weakness would be ignoring his obvious signs of distress.

"We need to rest," is Vesuvia's assessment as Ajax's pace begins to slow.

His eyes sweep over us and he shakes his head.

"Because of me? You're kidding. Let's keep going."

Vesuvia stops him as he tries to pace off quicker than before.

"No...because of me," she says, taking his ego out of the game. "*I* need to rest."

We all agree that a few hours worth of rest would be the best for everyone, and set about finding a suitable rocky outcrop to find some shelter from the blowing sand. I scan the horizon and spot a square shadow under the glowing moon. When we reach it, we find that it's a small wooden structure with an old door leading in. The door is barred with crumbling planks, several of them covering the opening.

Ajax's eyes light up. "A well..." he says, moving forward with haste and easily discarding the planks with his mighty paws.

The girls don't seem so taken by the place, and move towards the door with more caution. Inside, we take out our torches and find a short stairway leading underground into a little cave. In the centre of the cave is an old rudimentary lift with a pulley system designed to send it into the depths. The sight only serves to strengthen Ajax's thoughts that we've found a source of water.

It's Velia's voice that holds him back as he tries to work out how to work the lift.

"It's not a well," she says. "It's a mine. You won't find water down there."

"How do you know?" he says, turning to her. His eyes are more fierce than they should be. His thirst is clearly getting to him.

"You get them around here," adds Vesuvia, taming Ajax's temper with her soft words. "When they're used up, they're left out here in the desert. Velia's right…we won't find water here."

Ajax frowns and finds a rock to sit on, shaking his head.

For my part, the thought of finding water down there also entered my mind. I ask the girls again, just for confirmation, and they tell me unequivocally that we won't.

"The place was barred, and clearly hasn't been used in years," says Velia. "If there was a well here, it would be open. Travellers would use it regularly when moving through these parts. Trust me, this place is dead."

I take her word for it, although can't help but take a few moments to inspect the pulley system and the lift itself. I look down into the darkness, and see that the lift is actually broken, hanging awkwardly to one side and unable to take any amount of weight. It puts the entire prospect of searching below to bed.

Instead, we find our own positions to sit and get some rest. Vesuvia goes over and offers Ajax a little of her own water. When he says he can't, she tells him that her requirements are much smaller than his, and that their rations shouldn't be the same. He thanks her with a silent smile as he takes a refreshing gulp, before laying his head down to rest. She stays near him, happy to play nurse, her fingers lightly stroking his dark hair.

As I sit and watch from the other side of the cave, Velia comes over and sits beside me.

"He's not looking good," she says. "I think the last few days, at the Watcher Wars, and the compound, have taken it out of him."

I nod, staring at my friend.

"He's strong. He'll get through it."

It's a naïve comment. Whatever we've been through over the last few weeks and months, this is a whole new challenge. And it's one that will test the two of us far more than our new companions.

"We should rest for a couple of hours only," she continues. "It's best to continue before dawn, and put some hours in before it gets too hot."

I nod. "If you think that's best," I say.

She smiles, happy perhaps to be in charge. I shift my bag off my back and put it to one side. Her eyes drift to it and reach forward. I don't stop her as her fingers slide in and draw out the file.

Shining her torch on it, we both look at the front once more, our eyes resting on the words, 'The Seekers of Knight'. Then she opens it up and the face of the ex High Chancellor greets us again. Until this point, we haven't gone any further. We share a look and I nod, and then she turns the page once more.

Frowns drop on both of our faces at what greets us. It's all random, seemingly written in some sort of code. We flick through a few pages and can work nothing out. There are endless paragraphs of writing, as well as tables and formulas and other such documents inside. But none of it makes any sense.

I shut the file and put it back into my bag, knowing that it's no good wasting energy trying to figure it out. When we get to Petram, we can pass it on to someone who will be better equipped to find out if it holds any secrets beyond what we've already discovered.

I shake my head. *If we get to Petram,* I muse negatively.

Velia seems of the same thought. Right now, there are more pressing matters to attend to.

Because that's what this desert can do to you. One moment, we're cruising across it, desperate to pass on what we've discovered. The next, we're in the middle of the wilderness, sitting in an abandoned mine, our throats growing drier by the second.

And suddenly, we're in another fight for our lives. Only this time, it's with a very different type of enemy.

2

An Unseen Danger

I'm woken by the sound of a loud rattling. My eyes open quickly, and I peer towards the faint light coming down from the short wooden staircase ahead. Down the rocky passage comes the glow, now much darker than it was. And it's from the passage, too, that the heavy sound of rattling is coming.

As I stand to my feet I notice that the others are also waking, expelled from their short slumber by the racket. I feel exhausted, my legs hardly able to activate, as I wander through the dark cave towards the source of the sound. Into my ears, the whistling of a loud wind grows, and as I look up the stairs and to the door, I notice that it's banging hard against the wooden entrance to the mine.

It opens suddenly on the harsh wind, and slams shut just as fast, before performing the same routine again and again. And each time it opens, I feel the sharp spit of sand being thrust into my face, the billowing wind outside swirling it around and tossing it in all directions.

"What's going on?" I hear Ajax ask.

I don't answer, but move up the steps towards the

door. I hold it shut, and look out through one of the cracks, and am greeted with nothing but a wall of dark, churning sand.

Behind me, Ajax gets his answer from Vesuvia.

"It's a sandstorm," she says, clicking on her torch and shining it up the passage. There's a clear tension in her voice. "We should block the entrance."

I turn and move back down the short staircase. "Block the entrance? But we need to get moving."

"We can't," she says. "Not in this. It's much too dangerous."

"But…it's dangerous staying here too," I say. "We can't stay..."

"We have no choice," comes Velia's voice. She moves forward, carrying her bag and mine, and walks past me up the stairs. She fixes the bags against the door, holding it shut. "We have to wait this out, and hope it doesn't last long…"

She comes back down the stairs and gathers her sister and Ajax's bags, adding them to the others. The rattling stops, replaced by the incessant howling of the wind, and the spitting of the sand as it beats against the blocked wood.

Velia moves back down and takes her position over by the rock wall. We all do the same, returning to where we were sleeping.

"We might as well try to get some more rest," says Velia. "We can't have been sleeping long…it's not yet dawn. Hopefully the storm will blow over quickly."

Ajax's voice comes from the other side of the cave.

"And how long do these storms normally last?" he asks irritably.

Velia's answer doesn't come immediately. She delays a second, unable to find a clear response. "It depends," she says. "Some can last hours. Others can last days. We just have to hope it's the former..."

Her words put an end to any further speculation.

I lie back down where I was before, my mind still foggy and tired. But I know that it'll be hard to sleep with the howling outside, knowing that every hour delayed will worsen our condition. With all of our torches turned off, and the moonlight blocked now by the storm, the cave plunges into a deep darkness. And in that darkness, my mind starts to tumble back into a restless and uneasy sleep.

It's cracked and broken, and I find myself constantly waking with blurred images lingering in my mind. I forget them as soon as they come, however, nothing sticking out here in the desert. Soon enough, when I wake for a final time, I see cracks of yellow light creeping in from outside as the sun rises. But still, the howling wind remains, the door still being ceaselessly attacked by the brutal sands.

When the others wake, I see the same disappointment descend over their eyes. The storm hasn't abated. If anything, it's grown worse over the last few hours, the wind battering harder and wailing louder as its assault continues.

As the morning draws on, my mind starts to turn to the prospect of getting down into the mineshaft.

"Maybe there's another way out," I say. "A way up into the hills?"

The girls don't consider such a thing likely. Still, they humour me, perhaps in a bid to keep my mind busy, and help me to set about repairing the lift. Using some old pieces of rope, we fix it together, making it sturdy, before I test it with my weight. I climb on as it hovers precariously over the dark abyss. It cracks and creaks, threatening to give way.

I see it coming just before it breaks apart, the wooden slats snapping and dropping into the darkness. Clearly, Ajax does too, his strong arms reaching out and grabbing me as I leap to the side. He pulls me back up to safety, just as the sound of the broken lift clatters down the wall of the tunnel, hitting the earth with a loud thud that echoes up to our ears.

It sounded like it was a long way down.

In the end, our efforts were in vain, and only served to waste good energy. Before long, our remaining water stores are starting to run dry, a problem most keenly felt by Ajax who is growing weaker by the hour. As he sits to one side, the rest of us gather together, whispering our way towards a solution.

"This storm isn't letting up," says Velia. "We're going to have to chance it out there, break to the other side and hope it's not too far."

"We know there's higher ground close by," adds Vesuvia. "We were getting near before we stopped here. The storm should be kept mainly to the plains. If we reach higher ground we can escape it."

I have little to add, and find myself looking from one girl to the next thanking the heavens for their presence. I consider myself an assertive young man, but this landscape is alien to me, and the threats that it brings are those I've never encountered. Without these girls, Ajax and I would surely die out here. Not even our Watcher powers could prevent that.

Feeding Ajax up with a little more water from their stores, the girls set about preparing us for departure. We fetch our bags once more, fastening them to our backs and discarding anything we don't need to lessen their weight. I ditch half of my clothes, keeping only a couple of garments, mainly to use as wrapping for the file.

Velia fetches an old rope from the lift, stiff in places and rotten in others, and begins wrapping it around her waist. She then moves to her sister, wrapping it around hers, before doing the same with Ajax and then myself. All linked together into a chain, she turns to us before leading us out.

"If one of us falls, we'll all feel it," she calls. "The rope will keep us together out there. Look after each other and we'll be fine."

She speaks like a natural leader, her hazel eyes firming up as she looks to each of us. We nod in response, our bodies wrapped up tight in our cloaks and masks and goggles. Pulling her own mask over her face, she nods to us one final time before turning towards the stairs and leading us out into the raging storm.

From my vantage point at the back, I see everything unfold. As soon as Velia steps out, she braces herself for a barrage from the right. The wind hits her hard, almost knocking her down as she crouches low to give her a more stable body position.

Following behind, Vesuvia does the same. When Ajax steps forwards, he goes low too, having to fight harder than he normally would due to his weakening body. At the back, I adopt the same pose as we enter into the deafening shroud.

At the front, Velia quickly becomes enveloped by the swirling sand, her body little more than a blur. Even Vesuvia, only metres away, is hard to see. Only Ajax, right ahead of me, remains clear enough to fully make out.

We turn left, and begin moving across the desert, working our way past the entrance to the mine and back on the path we'd previously set. Now, however, the girls are going to find navigation impossible. Should they lose their bearings out here, they'll never find them again, and we might find ourselves re-treading our steps.

All we can do is use the mine as a landmark and continue in the direction we were going when we stopped. We march on, led by Velia, the rope between us sometimes slackening and sometimes growing taut as we each alter our pace. I stay as close as possible to Ajax, watching his step closely as he lumbers on, battling the winds.

Somehow, it keeps my mind focused, keeps the same weariness and exhaustion from taking me. I watch him, step for step, and keep note of his stride as we go, passing across the flat desert sands as our bodies are continually buffeted by the bitter winds.

By my reckoning, we're keeping a fairly straight path, only deviating when we need to pass by or around a rocky outcrop. The land rolls and undulates slightly as we go, sand dunes built up by the wind as it alters the landscape. Keeping to a straight path, we're forced to climb a high, slippery knoll, Ajax and I struggling along through the soft surface due to our heavier weights. The girls find it easier, their feet not sinking as deep, pulling us along with the rope as we work as a team to clear the summit.

Yet there are dangers out here that even Velia can't see.

With the sandstorm still obscuring our visibility, she doesn't see it coming, all of our ability to search the Void limited in these conditions. Perhaps she wouldn't even on a clear day, a trap set by the desert itself to consume any passers by foolish enough to enter its fatal web.

As Velia steps forward at the summit of the dune, I see her begin to sink quickly into the earth. Attached by the rope, Vesuvia jolts forward, pulled on by her bodyweight. And as their momentum passes down the line, Ajax and I find ourselves being pulled suddenly on as well.

Instinctively, I hold back and take the strain. Ajax, too, mustering his strength, fixes his feet into the sand as both of the girls begin to get enveloped into the earth.

"Quicksand!" I hear Ajax cry on the wind, suddenly alert and alive and heaving with all his might.

I lean back with my full weigh, gripping the rope tight and anchoring the four of us in place as Ajax's powerful arms begin drawing the rope in. Through the roaring wind, I can barely hear Vesuvia screaming out as Velia continues to disappear before her eyes. Soon, through the mist, I can only see the top of her head sticking out of the yellow surface of the dune.

I grit my jaw at the sight, and call forward to Ajax: "On three…HEAVE!"

I see him nod ahead of me, and begin to count down, and when I reach 'three', we pull together with all our might. Inch by inch, I see Velia emerge from the sand, unable to do anything but hold on for dear life. Vesuvia, too, half her body stuck, can do little but hope we're strong enough to save them.

Once more, I call for us to heave, and once more we haul the girls further out. Soon, Vesuvia is back on solid earth, scrambling out and adding her strength to the cause. With a final roar, we all pull together, my legs and arms burning as I empty the tank and feel Velia come free of the desert's grip.

As we pull, however, I feel my body give way. Ahead of me, Ajax too begins falling backwards, his momentum carrying him right into me. He hits me hard, and together we go tumbling backwards, rolling over and over down the side of the hill, our bodies battered as we go.

I don't know how long it lasts for, but it seems to be forever. Down we go, thirty, forty, fifty metres back. We don't stop, caught in a tumble dryer as we continue down the seemingly endless hill, nothing arresting our momentum.

Then, suddenly, the ground evens out, and we smash right into a large rock fixed to the desert floor. I feel the wind knocked right out of me, and look to see Ajax lying prostrate on the earth, a cut oozing blood on the side of his head.

My mind stars to blur, my vision losing all shape. I feel for the rope that continues to connect us, and lift it up to find a frayed and broken end hanging off the front of Ajax's stomach, the connection to Vesuvia severed as we pulled the girls out.

And as I feel the dry and broken fibres, I begin to drop to the floor, my vision turning to nothing but mud before me.

I sink into the sand, unable to stop the flood of darkness from swamping me. And slowly but surely, the howling wind fades away, and a blackness descends down over my eyes.

3
A Welcome Face

I taste dirt.

Sand covers my lips, some getting into my mouth. I gasp and breathe in a full gulp of air and lift my head from the desert floor. In my ears, I hear no howling anymore. On my face, I feel no blistering grains of sand assaulting me.

Instead, I hear a voice, shrouded in mist, filtering into my ears: "Theo…Theo…"

My senses are blurred, my mind shrouded. I feel the sensation of a hand on my shoulder, gently shaking me. My body is pulled up out of the sand, and my eyes begin to open.

Light spills in. Bright light from the sun, my goggles discarded during the fall. I squint and see a shadow right above me. And behind, two others step into view.

"Theo, are you all right?" comes the voice again.

Slowly, a face begins to take shape. Sharp features, keen eyes, a fierce countenance I've come to know well.

"Athena?" I whisper.

I see my mentor's thin lips spread into a smile.

"Welcome back, Theo," she says.

I'm lifted up further, and the two other shadows come into view. Velia and Vesuvia stand ahead of me, watching with worried eyes. In Velia's hand I see a bottle. She steps forward and puts the opening to my lips, sending cool water down my throat.

The effect is immediate. I feel life beginning to fill me again.

My eyes open fully now, and I take in my surroundings. I'm sat next to a rock, the long sand dune rising up ahead of me. The storm has receded, the air now calm and hot under the morning sun. I turn to my side and see an area of messed up sand. In it is a patch of blood.

"Ajax!" I say, my memory flooding back. I turn to Athena. "Where's Ajax!"

"He's fine," she says in her customary calm manner. "He's in the jet getting attention."

I look over her shoulder, and see that her jet plane is parked nearby on a patch of harder earth. The ramp is down, footprints trailing back and forth from where I'm sat.

"What happened?" I ask, racking my brain for further details. "How did you find us?"

"I've been searching for you for the last couple of days. Ever since you failed to appear in the area for your final fight. I had a vision of you out here…thankfully the girls were able to flag me down as I wasn't sure exactly where you were."

"You were there?" I ask. "In the arena? I thought I

saw you…"

She begins nodding, and a smile of pride appears on her face. "I told you, Theo, that I'd be watching. I had to stay incognito, but I saw you all fight. You were all impressive out there."

She turns to the girls, who smile at her. It's obvious that they know each other a little, most likely through Troy. In some ways, they remind me of her, both of them assertive and strong willed, particularly Velia.

A sudden thought enters my head, and I reach behind my back to find that my bag is no longer attached.

"My bag!" I say.

Velia calms me. "It's OK, it's on the jet. The file is safe."

I let out a sigh of relief as I turn to explain everything to Athena. She doesn't need my explanation, the girls have already told her.

"I know, I know," she says. "I was alerted to the column of smoke coming from Baron Reinhold's compound. I knew then that something was going on. I went there to find you but found nothing but a ruin. It's a miracle I found you all out here."

"The file…you know about the file?"

"The girls told me," she says. "We'll get it back to Petram and take a closer look. You can fill me in on everything else along the way."

Weakly, I stand to my feet, and together we move

towards the jet. Inside, I find Ajax at the back, lying down on a medical table, his head being sewn up by a doctor. His eyes are open, though, as I walk over to him and lay my hand down on his arm.

"Looking good there, AJ."

He smiles up at me.

"That was a close call, huh…"

I laugh. "Sure was. How's he doing, doc?"

The doctor continues to work and talk at the same time.

"He'll be just fine. The cut's deep but it'll heal up nicely. Bit of concussion, but no permanent damage."

"You don't know him like I do, doc," I laugh. "He's been damaged since birth."

The doctor raises a smile as he adds the finishing touches to his work.

"OK, all done," he says as Ajax sits back up, a bandage now wrapped around his head.

"Another scar to add to your growing collection," I say. "You'll catch up with Link soon."

The mention of his father brings an immediate reaction to both of us. We walk briskly back to the front of the jet, where Athena sits speaking with the pilot.

"You boys ready to go?" she asks as she sees us enter.

"Have you heard from my dad?" Ajax asks

quickly.

"And Drake?" I add.

She shakes her head. "I've been off comms channels for the last few days. The last I heard they'd had no tangible success. But that may not matter now with what you've learned. Come, let's talk it through."

She gives the order to the pilot to take off as she leads us back into the main cabin. We all take seats and, for the next half hour, explain exactly what we know.

I take the lead, covering everything from our meeting with the girls, to the journey to the compound, and the discovery of the clones. Her eyes grow increasingly dark as I speak, the mention of Augustus Knight bringing up old memories from two decades ago.

"Four clones you say?" she asks, a deep and anxious frown hovering over her eyes.

We all nod together.

"Knight's Terror has been training them for years," I say "The way he spoke about them…they sound unstoppable."

"And Knight's Terror? The Baron? What happened to them?"

"Theo killed the Watcher," says Velia.

Athena's eyes widen as she looks at me.

"You killed Knight's Terror?"

“I got lucky,” I say. “He had us all beat…but your gift, the dagger, it saved me.”

“Well done,” she says. “All of you have done more than we could ever have asked or hoped for. And…the Baron?”

“He escaped before the compound was destroyed. We have no idea where he went.”

She leans back, processing everything. Meanwhile, I reach over and draw out the file from my bag and hand it to her. Her eyes scan the front.

“The Seekers of Knight,” she says. She lifts her eyes to us. “This is referring to the clones?”

We nod. “The Baron talked about Knight’s legacy…how his death was never going to stop him. He wants to bring this world down, Athena, create chaos. These Seekers are at the heart of it.”

She flicks through a few pages and comes to the same conclusion as Velia and myself. “We’ll get this to Petram and see if we can decipher it. But you’ve helped our cause tremendously, all of you. I’m proud to call you my students.”

I can’t help but smile, my own actions, and those of the others, having a tangible impact on our cause. But it’s short lived as the simple realisation dawns: we’re just scratching the surface, and truly, we have no idea as to what is going to happen next.

As the journey continues, I find myself asking Athena question after question about what’s going on elsewhere in the country. Unfortunately, she’s typically brief with her responses, partly because that's her way, and partly because she's been under radio silence for a few days while she tried to track us down.

I do get some comforting news, however, about my parents back on Eden. Last she heard, they were perfectly safe, although knowing my dad, he won't want to be sitting around doing nothing. His instincts will be to get out there and help, no matter what the danger might be. As he's so often told me: "We need to stand up for what's right, whatever the odds against us."

He's uttered that to me over and over again down the years, and now it is more pertinent than ever. Perhaps, subconsciously, that's why I always rebelled against them and was adamant that I'd develop my powers – because for me, that was the right thing to do, and it didn't matter what anyone else said, I knew it needed to be done.

Now, it seems, my own instincts have proven correct.

I speak a little with Velia, too, wanting to know exactly what happened after Ajax and I tumbled down the dune.

"You disappeared straight into the storm," she says. "We had no idea which direction you'd fallen or how far. We tried to find you but couldn't…not until the storm started to clear. Then, we saw Athena's jet and flagged her down. It was too close for comfort, Theo…"

Sitting together quietly at the back of the jet, I see her hazel eyes glisten slightly. She looks at me for a moment and then kisses me gently on the cheek.

"What was that for?" I ask, my face growing hot.

"For saving my life. Vesuvia and I would have died in the quicksand if it wasn't for you and Ajax."

"And we'd have died a dozen times over if it wasn't for you," I say. "We'd have never made it out of the storm without you."

"Then I guess we're even," she says. She taps her cheek with her finger. "Maybe you could return the compliment…"

I quickly lean in and graze my lips against her cheek. It's soft, her skin warm. I feel her face liven into a brief smile, before she quickly douses it once again.

"I should save your life more often," she says, before stepping away towards the front of the plane.

The journey back to Petram flashes by as we all exchange information and ponder the last few days. All we know now is that the foes against us are more powerful than we could have imagined, and more hell bent on destruction than we thought. What started as a spate of assassinations has morphed and evolved into something far greater. The entire country is once again under threat.

It's a sobering thought, yet I'm glad to be in the centre of it. I was, perhaps, naïve to wish to be involved in such a thing. For years, I've imagined what it must have been like for my parents and the others, fighting evil and changing the world. They always told me that it wasn't as glamorous as it sounded, that people died and suffered and had to endure terrible things.

Now, I'm beginning to understand where they're coming from. Yet still, if I have this power, and can do anything to help, I will. I feel it's my responsibility, my duty, to serve. Whatever happens next, whatever threat we may face, I'll stand ahead of it and look it in the eye…and I won't back down.

No matter what.

The plane sweeps around the mountains, rising back into the cool air up in the high passes. Through a clearing in the clouds, the grand plateau greets my eyes again, the city of Petram awaiting our arrival.

This time, however, we won't be sneaking in the back. That time has passed by, our identities well known by the enemy. No longer are we going to be hiding in the depths of the mountain. I will not keep to the shadows any more.

As we glide towards the landing pads in the corner of the plateau, I scan the outside of the city and see that it's quiet, life strangled by the new threat.

"It's what terror does to people," says Athena, looking out next to me. "Most people hide from it. They stop living."

"Not me," I say, gritting my teeth. "I'll face it head on."

Behind me, the others gather. And one after another, they all repeat the same words: "Me too."

Athena looks upon us all, no longer just kids. Her sleek, fox-like eyes inspect us as she's prone to do, before sweeping back down to the plateau as we start our descent.

"Good," she says, looking out of the window, "because I've got a feeling we'll need all the help we can get…"

4
A City Subdued

The city is quiet inside and out. When we enter through the large arches and into the mountain interior, I notice that the streets are more subdued than the last time I was here. That was several months ago now, when the city was mourning the death of its great leader. I turn my eyes down to Velia and Vesuvia and see that theirs have grown small. I'm sure they're thinking of the same man as I am: their father, Troy.

Of course, the funeral of Troy was as much a celebration of his life as a lamentation of his death. The party before we left was wild, the people seemingly defiant against the threat lurking in the shadows. Now, however, fear appears to have taken a tighter grip, strangling any joy from within the great chamber.

As we move inside, we find the new city Master, Markus, coming towards us, flanked by numerous guards. I spy their eyes more closely now, knowing that there are other Watchers among us trained by Athena. By now, I'm finding it easier to tell who has Watcher powers; my own senses becoming more attuned by the day. More difficult, however, is determining the depths of a person's abilities, something only a few can do.

Markus approaches quickly down the central street, people closely monitored and brushed aside by his men as he comes. As he nears, I see his eyes passing over all of us, before sticking closely to Athena. So far, I've found him to have a warm and open countenance. Today, however, his eyes are wary.

"Athena," he calls out as he approaches. "It's good to have you back. Where have you been?"

She steps towards him, leaving us in her wake. We follow closely behind as the two city leaders meet.

"I have plenty to tell you, Markus," she says. "But not here. There are too many eyes and ears."

Markus nods.

"Of course. Come this way."

They begin moving off, and we find ourselves following. Only when we near a passage leading from the main chamber does Markus turn before entering.

"Perhaps we should speak alone," he says, looking towards myself and Ajax and the girls.

"Not at all. Really, it's them you need to speak with."

A frown falls over his eyes, but he doesn't argue. We move down the passage, the walls growing smoother and more sleek as we go, the rock cut into the shape of a corridor. At the end, a large door looms, heavy and wooden and guarded by two further men.

When we reach it, Markus orders his men to stay outside as the rest of us enter. The room beyond is long and rectangular, set with a table in the middle and several paintings on the walls. To the left hangs one of Eden, the ocean raging around it, the sky dark and filled with lightning.

As Athena closes the door, Markus looks to us.

"This is the City Master's room," he says. "During the war, we'd use it to plan and form our strategies. Your parents were often here, their opinions counting just as much as anyone else's, despite their age at the time. I think it's quite fitting that you should all be in here now."

He takes a seat and invites us to do the same.

"Now tell me," he says, "exactly what's been going on."

For the next few minutes, we go over what we've been doing, leading all the way back to Eden and the plan Drake came up with for us to train with Athena in the depths of the mountain. We each offer our voices, adding them when needed, until Markus has a full picture of the current situation. By the time our tale has been told, Athena has withdrawn the file and passed it down the table to the City Master.

Markus' expression has turned stark. He eyes the first page of the file, and the image of Augustus Knight, with revulsion.

"I'm sorry to have kept you in the dark about

this," says Athena. "However, Drake thought it was best if as few people as possible knew."

"Well, it's clearly paid off," says Markus. "Drake always had a profound intuition about these things. Perhaps he knew that you would all have a part to play in uncovering this mystery. What's crucial now, however, is to try to decipher all of this. There might be details of Baron Reinhold's plans in here…"

"That's what we thought, or hoped for," I say. "That's why we were so desperate to get that file out of there."

"Well, I'll get my best people on it as soon as possible. See what they can dig up. In the meantime, you four look like you could do with a wash and a rest. I'll have some rooms set up for you."

"Thank you, sir," say the girls.

He looks at them fondly. "You've really grown up, ladies," he says. "The last time I saw you, you were down around my hip. Your father would be proud of what you've done."

I see their eyes firm up. I've discovered that it's something they do in order to prevent the show of another emotion. In this case, to stop any tears from welling. Like Athena, these girls have lived a hard life out in the desert. They've been bred into hardship, a strength inside them that goes right to their core.

Before we're sent off, we ask once more about Drake and Link, Ajax in particular wanting to know if there's any news about his father. Markus merely utters the same as what Athena told us, saying that they haven't been heard from for a few days. Link's eyes darken at his words, a look of concern passing over his face.

"Don't let it worry you," says Markus. "If they've gone quiet, they've done so for a reason. They're probably chasing down a lead as we speak. If there's anyone we needn't worry about, son, it's your father."

He raises a smile and temporarily sets Ajax's concerns at ease. Yet, in his mind, I know that those worries are only going to build the longer this lack of contact goes on. I, too, feel a stab of concern at the fate of my grandfather, knowing now who they're up against. Should they encounter the Seekers, I suspect even someone as powerful as Link would come off second best.

We're led out of the room and down the passage by Athena, before being taken back to the same chamber we stayed at previously during our last visit. And, once more, we're given the same accommodation as before, the four of us taking up residence in a comfortable house built into the rock wall. Up on the first floor, Ajax and I share one room, and Velia and Vesuvia another.

We part ways with a weary smile, my eyes tracing Velia's steps as she follows her sister into their room. She turns to me once more just before she enters, and I find myself averting my eyes out of instinct and quickly retreating to my own chamber.

The sight of a comfortable bed is truly one for sore eyes, the air fresh and cool up here in the mountains. After quickly washing my body of days worth of accumulated sand and soot, I drop onto my bed and fall fast asleep. Never in my life have I dropped off quicker.

The following morning, we're left to our own devices, our exhausted bodies given a chance to rest and recover. Sleeping in until mid afternoon, I wake to find myself alone in the room. When I leave, and step out onto the landing, I hear voices coming from the kitchen below.

I go down to find the others already there, now snugly dressed in winter gear. I can't help but stifle a smile at the sight of the girls, tightly squeezed into several thick layers.

"Hey, it's freezing up here," says Velia, hitting me in the arm. "You try living in the desert your whole life and then coming to this."

"Well, I can see why you chose not to live here now," I laugh. "Have you visited much?"

"Not for years," she says. "Mostly, dad would come to the West to see us. We wouldn't leave our mother."

"And what about now? Is your mother back home?"

She nods. "We had to leave to go to the Watcher Wars. We needed to find out what was going on…she understood."

"And, she knows you have powers?"

"Of course. She's proud of us," says Vesuvia. "No one where we come from has stood up to the Baron for years. If ever they did, they'd disappear like that." She snaps her fingers, loud in the little room. "We trained so we could do what the rest couldn't…"

"Yeah, we just didn't realise things were this bad," says Velia. "I mean, the Baron's been running the show out in the desert for a long time, but no one thought he was cooking up something as big as this. These clones…I just can't get my head around it."

"There's a lot of that going around," growls Ajax. "The worst thing is the waiting. The not knowing. I wonder when they'll strike next…and where."

"Could be anywhere," I say. "Eden is in lockdown, and so are we here. All the important figures are well guarded. I don't know, maybe they'll try to lure us out into the open or something."

I see Ajax's eyes turn stark.

"Maybe they already have," he says coldly.

The girls look at each other.

"You mean Link and Drake?" asks Vesuvia quietly.

Ajax continues to stare, his head slowly nodding.

"I just have this feeling," he says, his words fading. "I can't explain it."

"I'm sure it'll be fine," says Vesuvia, always the first to comfort Ajax when needed. "We've heard the things your dad has done. And President Drayton too. I don't care where these clones got their DNA…they can't be that strong, can they?"

She looks up to me, eyes asking for support I cannot give. My eyes tell their own story, because my words stay locked inside. They say that I have a terrible feeling too. That I, like Ajax, have a knot in the pit of my stomach that refuses to unravel.

It's Velia, instead, who breaks the silence. She claps her hands together, paints a smile on her face, and says: "So, who's hungry?"

Clearly intent on keeping our minds off what we can't control, the girls set about gathering together some food that they find in the larder. I stand to help them, and together we fashion a picnic that we take through into the cosy sitting room.

Inside, several comfortable armchairs sit, with a table in between. We pile the table with food, and I set myself the task of lighting up a fire. Soon enough, the flames are rising nicely, and the cold room is growing pleasantly warm, sufficiently so for the girls to discard one or two of their layers.

We sit in a little circle and eat and talk, turning to less depressing subjects. It's hard, really, given the few days we've had, but we try all the same. The girls talk about where they live, a small settlement on the edge of the desert, the coast not too far away. I tell of Lignum and the woods, of the days Ajax and I would spend hunting and dreaming of adventure.

"Well, you got your adventure," says Velia flatly.

“And who knows...maybe you’ll get the hunt of your life,” adds Vesuvia.

Sitting furthest from the fire, Ajax stays quiet for the duration of the meal. Sunken into his chair, he remains consumed by his thoughts as the rest of us talk, his presence keeping us from lightening the mood for too long.

I don’t blame him one bit. As much as I love my grandfather, nothing compares to the concerns Ajax now has to bear. He may have a tough exterior, but inside he’s got a sensitive side; a deep caring for his family and friends that would see him do anything to keep them safe. Sitting here, not being able to help or do anything, is excruciating for him.

In the end, he excuses himself and heads back upstairs to our room.

He taps the bandage on his head as he goes and simply says, “I’m tired,” before disappearing around the corner. Vesuvia watches him go. I can see she wants to go with him, a natural caring streak running through her own blood.

“Don’t,” says Velia as she makes a move to follow. “I think he just wants to be alone right now.”

She looks at me for confirmation, and I nod.

The evening drags on, a sombre mood beginning to descend. We try to lighten it on occasion, speaking once more of normal things, but everything seems to link back to something serious.

We talk of friends, and the girls tell me about a close friend of theirs who fell to the Baron’s drugs, eventually succumbing to an overdose. We talk of family, and our minds immediately switch to those we've lost or those we're worried might suffer the same fate. We talk of our passions, our future, and realise that all of us have wanted for nothing but to develop our powers and use them for good.

When I listen to their reasoning, however, it makes me feel stupid. They only wanted to develop their powers to help their people, to one day sink the Baron's operation and, latterly, avenge their father. My motivation was always different. Sure, I wanted to help people, but I only considered such a thing with a selfish mind. Really, I just wanted to be known and adored, to free myself from my parents' shadow, to do great things as they did.

I was selfish, but now my mind has changed. Now I want to help because it's the right thing to do. I want to help because it is my duty to do so; not for fame or fortune or the adoration of the people, but because I don't want evil to once more consume this world. When I look at people like Velia and Vesuvia, their father dead, and think of my best friend upstairs, worried that his father may have befallen the same fate, I merely think: *I want to help. I want to make a difference. I want to see them all happy.*

With the hour growing late, Vesuvia is the next to depart. She kisses her sister goodnight and I hear her feet creaking away on the stairs and floor above. I share a smile with Velia when we realise she's gone towards mine and Ajax's room, no doubt keen to make sure he's OK. Moments later, however, her footsteps take her back in the opposite direction.

She must have thought better of it, or found him asleep.

As the fire dies, I sit across from Velia in silence, merely happy for her company. Slowly, we allow the flames to fade and become nothing but a small blanket of glowing embers. I watch them die away and think once more of the inferno that engulfed the compound, it's own sea of ash still burning out there in the desert.

I think again of the training room where we fought Knight's Terror. Of the lab and the tubes and shadows. Of the boys' faces, kids who were grown in those tubes, who lived and died in those tubes. Only four made it through the gruesome process, only four managed to get out. And after living in that subterranean facility for so many years, now they've finally been unleashed.

And all they know of the world is what they've been taught by the Baron, by Knight's Terror. They will hate us with a passion, programmed to kill and destroy and cause utter chaos. Bred for a single purpose: to destroy this world of ours, to carry out the final wishes of their 'father'.

In the dim light, Velia's soft voice brings me back out of my thoughts.

"What are you thinking?" she asks.

I look into her hazel eyes, orange firelight reflecting on their surface, and a smile naturally rises on my face.

"Nothing," I say. "Just…I'm glad we met you."

"We?" she asks, half smiling.

"Me," I say. "I'm glad *I* met you."

She stands and moves over to me, bends down, and kisses me once more on the cheek. "Me too, Theo Kane," she says. "Me too."

And with that, she turns and disappears up the stairs, drifting away into the darkness. Leaving me alone once more with only my thoughts for company, and the gentle crackling of the dying fire in my ears.

5
Fifty Fifty

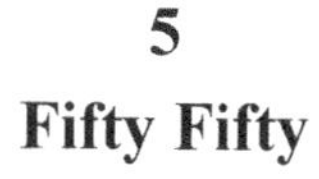

I wake in the darkness of the sitting room, the dying embers of the fire just clinging to their final moments before fading out. I sit up in the comfortable armchair, my body aching all over from the numerous battles I've had to face in recent days and weeks. From training in the cave, and fighting in the stadium, to facing the savage storm, I've barely had a chance to recover. I feel like I could go back to sleep and not wake for a month.

I stand, thinking it best to head upstairs and climb into bed for the rest of the night. As I do, however, my ears are drawn to several noises coming from outside of the house in the quiet residential chamber.

I hear voices whispering harshly, people moving about. I stand and wander to the front door, and peek out to see several soldiers being mobilised and moving up towards the passage that leads to the main chamber.

I watch them as they go, and as I do feel the urge to follow. Quietly, I open the door and shut it without a noise, not wanting to wake the others upstairs, before moving off down the street towards the exit.

As I walk up the passage, I continue to hear voices speaking and feet rushing. It seems there's some sort of commotion that's leading them towards the central city chamber.

Reaching the end of the passage, I scan the great cave ahead, searching for the source of the activity. I walk towards the main street, silent now at this time but for a few guards and other sentinels, and see that a small crowd of security forces are gathering towards the main archways leading out onto the plateau.

I move down the street towards them, and see Athena amid the rabble. Then, coming from a side passage, I see Markus, looking weary and flanked once more by his personal guard.

I don't try to hide my presence as I approach. Instead, I move straight towards the gathering, keen to discover what's happening and, if needed, offer any aid I can. It's Athena who spots me first, her eyes sweeping towards me as if she knew I'd be coming.

She steps out of the crowd, her eyes alert.

"Theo, what are you doing up at this hour?" she asks.

"I heard a commotion," I say. "I wanted to know what was going on?"

Clearly she sees no reason to keep me in the dark, an explanation being quickly offered.

"Our scouts have reported a vehicle coming up the mountain. It appears to be a merchant, he says he has an injured man with him." Her eyes narrow. "We think it might be Link."

"Link?!" I say. "How do you know?"

"He's been stopped at the tunnel checkpoint, and our guards have passed on a description. There aren't many men who look like Link."

At that point, Markus appears, the news already having been delivered to him by his guards.

"How close are they?" he asks.

"Just coming through the tunnel now," says Athena. "They'll be at the main gate any moment."

"OK, let's go."

The two turn and quickly begin marching out onto the plateau and towards the grand city gate. I follow in behind, joining the guard of Watchers protecting the city Master. Around, other soldiers on duty watch as we pass by, whispering among themselves as they speculate as to what's going on.

We're at the gate in moments as it begins to draw open, grinding on heavy gears. Ahead, a merchant vehicle appears, driving quickly forwards. Armed soldiers surround it as it skids to a halt in the dirt, and a man jumps out with his arms up in surrender.

Athena and Markus rush forwards, and I follow right behind.

"Lower your weapons," calls Athena, approaching the man. "Where is he?" she asks quickly as she reaches him.

He leads us around to the rear, where he opens up

the back of the vehicle. Inside, lying in a pool of blood and surrounded by hanging collections of clothing, is a towering man I immediately recognise.

And so do the others.

"Right, get a medic here NOW," shouts Athena, moving in and pressing her fingers to Link's neck. I watch her eyes narrow, then widen. "He's alive…his pulse is faint, but he's alive."

She turns to the merchant as a medic comes pouring forward, several soldiers behind him carrying a stretcher. He quickly sets his own fingers to Link's neck, before scanning his body to perform a quick diagnosis of his injuries. I look at the great man and see several holes and cuts leaking blood, his skin growing paler by the second as the scarlet liquid drains from his body. Clearly, however, the merchant has attempted his own rudimentary treatment, applying bandaging and tourniquets where needed.

As he's loaded on the stretcher and rushed inside, Athena begins her questioning.

"Where did you find him?" she asks, her voice rushing.

"A way down to the East," says the trader. "I thought this would be the closest place to bring him…and the safest."

The middle aged man watches as Link is carried off inside. I can see that he knows who he is. Most people do.

"Down to the East?" asks Athena. "Where

exactly?"

"Nowhere near anything," says the man. "I was just travelling through the scrubland, heading back to the regions, when I saw an old car, and a trail of blood leading out of it. I followed it and found him among some rocks, passed out. He must have driven from wherever he was…I don't know how far or which direction he'd come. I just put him in the car and brought him straight here."

Athena's hand drops to the man's shoulder as he looks once more to see Link being taken off.

"You did the right thing," she says. "You might have saved his life."

"Might?" I ask.

She looks across at me. "We can't know yet, Theo. Where's Ajax?"

My thoughts rush to my friend, back in our room. I grimace at the thought of him finding out.

"In bed," I say.

Then, my mind takes another step forward, and a single name comes crashing out of my mouth.

"Drake! What about Drake?"

I look at the man, who shakes his head, looking confused.

"I only found Link," he says. "There was no one else."

Markus, who has stayed quiet up until now, adds in his voice as he turns to Athena.

“Athena, take this man and go and inspect the site where Link was found. It might offer us some clue as to where he came from. Take my Watchers with you.”

Her eyes narrow and she nods.

“I’m coming too,” I say suddenly. “I can help.”

They look at me together. Markus shakes his head.

“No, you’ll stay here where it’s safe.”

“I’m stronger than most of these Watchers,” I say defiantly. “Athena knows. I can help.”

Markus looks to Athena.

She nods. “He’s right, Markus. Theo can hold his own against most. He and Ajax are the most gifted of those I’ve trained. I can vouch for him.”

Markus looks at me once more. “So be it,” he says. “I know from experience that age counts for nothing if you have such power. I will go and inform Ajax of the news and bring him to the medical chamber. You two, take some of my guards and inspect the site.” He turns to the merchant. “Can you lead them back there?” he asks.

The man nods. “I know these lands well,” he says. “It shouldn’t be a problem.”

“Good,” says the city Master. “Now go, and good luck.”

With that, he marches off, leaving several of his personal guard behind, all men and woman who have been trained by Athena in the Watcher arts.

We're quick to act, no time to waste. Leaving the merchant's car where it is, we rush inside towards Athena's jet and climb aboard. The merchant looks quite out of his depth, most likely never having stepped foot on such a transport. At Athena's order, he takes up a position in the cockpit alongside her and the pilot, quickly summoned from his bedchambers. I hover in the doorway, listening in.

"Will you be able to navigate your way back from the air?" Athena asks.

The man looks unsure. "I haven't flown before. I can try my best."

"That'll do," says Athena. She turns back to me. "Theo, take a seat in the back. It won't take long to get there. And try not to worry about Drake…I'm sure he's fine."

Her words do nothing to comfort me. In fact, she should know better than to utter them at all. Frankly, they're the sort of words you'd tell a child who'll just believe anything you tell them.

Truthfully, my mind has already turned to the prospect that my grandfather is dead. If he was with Link, and they could do that to him, then what hope would Drake have? It's a painful thought, but I have to use logic and be realistic. Link escaped, and Drake was killed. That's the only conclusion I can come to right now.

I take a seat as ordered, and stew on the prospect of another major casually. This time, it's far closer to home, my own blood. I grit my teeth and stare out of the window at nothing, my hands shaking as the thoughts tumble through my mind. And before I know it, we're sweeping down low to the ground, zipping through the air in search of the site where Link was found.

I hardly know how much time passes as I sit and stare blankly outside, the world rushing past in a blur. The only sign of passing time is the light. When we left, it was still dark. When we touch down on the sand, the sun has already risen, the open plains now painted yellow and brown.

We're led out into the burning desert by the merchant, the Watcher guards clearly well trained and immediately forming a protective cordon as we go. Immediately, the sight of the abandoned car appears. We rush towards it and begin a quick inspection.

All over it are bullet holes, the interior splattered with blood. It's an old vehicle, fairly non-descript, the sort of modified desert jeep you see around these parts all the time. It looks as though Link was shot through the door as he made his escape from wherever he happened to be.

The only indication of the direction of travel comes from the position of the car. It appears to be pointed towards Petram, Link perhaps attempting to get to the city himself before he stopped. Both the merchant and Athena are able to attest that there's little in the opposite direction, nothing but long swathes of empty land before reaching the old remains of Knight's Wall, and the regions beyond.

"Why did he leave the vehicle," I say out loud, my

eyes searching the trail of blood.

"I suspect he ran out of fuel and sought refuge in the shade of the rocks," says Athena.

She begins following the blood to where the merchant found him, a large pool gathered in the shadow of the little outcrop. Other than the drops of blood, there are no trails; neither footprints nor tyre tracks from the car. Out here, the blowing winds tend to scatter any such thing before they can settle.

"Anything else you can tell us?" Athena asks the merchant. "Anything at all?"

He racks his brain and shakes his head.

"I'm sorry. I just found him here and brought him to you."

"And he was unconscious when you found him?"

"Just about. His eyes flickered a bit but then he passed out."

"OK," says Athena. "We'll do a quick sweep from the air, see if we can spot anything of interest. Other than that, we'll just have to wait for Link to wake up so he can tell us what happened himself."

She says it with conviction, not allowing herself to even consider the thought of Link not making it. Ever since the war, the two have been on many missions together and share a close bond. Even though she's not showing it, I know that she'll be feeling all of this inside.

The faces of the other men show that they're feeling something too. It's a concern, a fear even, something that Watchers aren't meant to let in. But right now they can't help it, and I know just where their thoughts are leading them.

If Link can be beaten, then anyone can...

We rise back into the air, hovering slowly off in the direction the jeep seemed to come from. Soon enough, we have a long aerial view of the area, no clouds hindering our sight below. Athena moves around, handing out telescopic goggles.

"Put these on," she says. "They'll allow you to see much further. Scan for anything suspicious."

We put on the goggles as the jet hovers ever higher, giving us more desert to inspect. From the naked eye, there's little to see below. When I put on the goggles, however, I find my eyesight magnified a hundredfold, my vision stretching off for miles in every direction. Suddenly, what was merely a dot on the desert floor becomes a detailed view of the jeep once more. I slide my finger along a little touchpad on the side of the goggles, and my vision dives even deeper, the tiniest details appearing clear before my eyes.

With orders to search, that's what I do, all of us scanning the world below for any clue as to where Link might have driven from. I look forward and push the telescopic goggles to their limit, looking as far ahead as possible. There, many miles from where we are, I see some of the old ruins of Knight's Wall, the old dividing line between the Deadlands and the regions.

If he was coming from that direction, it's possible

that he was attacked somewhere over in the regions themselves. Frankly, it could have been anywhere; a mile from here, two miles, ten, a hundred. The jet sweeps around for a while as we continue to scan the world below, but no one comes up with anything of interest. In the end, Athena calls a close to the brief investigation, ordering the pilot to return to Petram.

We arrive back quickly, and I waste no time in darting down from the jet and rushing into the city. Athena accompanies me, the two of us hurrying down to the medical chamber to get an update on Link's condition.

When we arrive, we're told by Markus that Link is currently in surgery, the doctors doing everything they can to help him.

"Right now," says Markus, "it looks like a 50-50 shot at best. They'll be working on him for a while. Did you find anything at the site?"

Athena shakes her head, her eyes hooded. "Only that Link seemed to have come from the direction of the regions. Nothing much to go on."

Markus curses quietly under his breath, equally frustrated as the rest of us.

"Did you tell Ajax?" I ask him.

He nods solemnly, and raises his eyes down the passage. "He's down there, outside the surgery room. Poor kid."

"Thank you, sir," I say.

Then I turn and move down the passage, and find

Ajax standing in a corner, his eyes dark. Ahead of him is a door, beyond which his father's life hangs in the balance.

I move over to him and lay my arm around his broad, muscular back. It's tense and hunched, his arms folded and chin embedded in his neck. I look into his eyes and see that there's a slight redness around them, his jaw so firmly clenched shut you'd need a crowbar to open it.

"I'm sorry, AJ," I say. "I'm sure he'll be OK."

He nods slowly, and raises his eyes.

"Drake?" he asks softly.

I shake my head. "He's…missing," I say.

"Sorry…" he says. "Whatever happens, we'll find him."

"I know we will, AJ," I say. "I know we will."

The words come out, because they're all I can say at a time like this. There is no space for doubt, even for logic. Not here, not now.

Link will be fine. Drake will be found. Neither of us can consider any other option right now. Neither of us have a choice.

6
In Our Blood

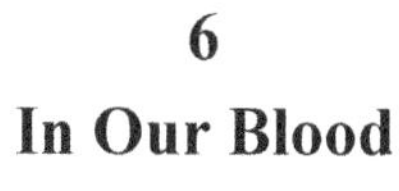

I stay with Ajax for hours in that little room, waiting for the doctors to emerge. Here, in Petram, I never knew provisions even existed for such delicate work. Yet they do, and for many hours the surgeons do their best to patch up Link's wounds and refill his body with blood.

The girls come to join us at one point, Vesuvia immediately moving in to give Link the sort of embrace I can't offer. She hugs him tight, his eyes set firm, as Velia steps in beside me.

"We heard about your grandfather," she says. "How are you?"

"I'm fine," I say, looking forward. "Just…trying not to think about it, I guess."

She nods and takes my hand in hers for a brief moment, before letting it slip away again.

We stay there together as a four in silence for a time, Athena or Markus coming in regularly to check if anything has happened. Mostly, we have nothing to tell them except for what one of the doctors tells us: that they're still working on him, and he's not yet out of the woods.

Each time, it's the same man who comes out of the room. And each time, his words seem to grow a little lighter. Then, after many hours of waiting, and with evening now dawning, he appears with a small smile and addresses Ajax.

"Your father is stable," he says. "We've managed to patch him up as best we can, but he'll need to be transferred to Eden for proper monitoring and recovery."

"Thank you, doctor," says Ajax, taking the man's hand. "Thank you so much."

"Now you need to be aware that he's suffered significant trauma. We're going to have to keep him in a coma for a while as his body recuperates, and watch closely for infection. There is a chance that he may be a different man when he wakes up."

Ajax's eyes narrow. "A different man…what does that mean?"

"It simply means that he may not be as strong as he was. We all know what your father can do. However, those days might be behind him. Time, I'm afraid, will tell."

Ajax nods, accepting the doctor's words. "Can I see him?"

"Of course," he says. "Come this way."

The doctor leads Ajax off into the room, leaving the rest of us outside. As we wait, Athena comes sweeping in from the corridor, Markus alongside her.

"What's the news?" she asks quickly.

“He’s out of surgery,” I say, raising a half smile. “But he’s in an induced coma while he recovers. They say he’s going to be OK.”

Athena and Markus look at each other and let out a collective sigh of relief.

“Well, that’s some good news at least,” says Markus. “We need something to go our way.”

“The doctor did say something else, though,” I add. “He said Link might never fully recover. His days as a Watcher might be done.”

The relieved expressions on Markus and Athena suddenly drop once again. If what the doctor said was true, we might just have lost our most powerful warrior. And with Drake missing, our numbers are quickly dwindling.

“We need to keep our heads up.” It’s Velia’s voice, strong and firm, that comes from behind me. “The good news is that Link is alive. We can’t know what happened to him, but we do know he was strong enough to get away. If anyone can recover from this, it’s him.”

Athena smiles at the young girl, perhaps seeing a reflection of herself in her. “You’re right, Velia,” she says. “There can be no space for negativity now. We are on the ropes, but we’re still in this fight. Now, we just need to find an opportunity for a counterpunch.”

As we speak, the doctor comes back out of the room, Ajax still by his father’s bedside. Markus addresses the man.

“We need to speak with Link,” he says, “to find out what happened to him. Is there any chance we can bring him out of his coma for a few minutes?”

The doctor considers it, and then begins shaking his head.

“I’m not sure that’s a good idea, Master Markus. He’s very weak…”

“But can it be done?” asks Markus firmly. “He might hold information we could use.”

Again, the doctor hesitates, before eventually speaking again. “We can try, but only for a minute. Don’t expect to get anything out of him, though.”

Markus nods. “Do it.”

A few minutes later, we’re gathered around Link’s bed, all of us with our ears primed to hear what he might have to say. I look down at his large frame, covered in bandaging and hooked up to various tubes, and think of how strange it is to see him laid low like this.

Ahead of us, the doctor holds a syringe, which he sinks into Link’s mighty arm. Slowly but surely, I see Link stir, his eyes beginning to open up, weak and blurred and confused.

“Dad…dad,” says Ajax, leaning in.

Link’s eyes remain half open, his lips opening and closing silently.

“Link, it’s Athena, can you tell us what happened?”

We all hold our breath as Link’s eyes flicker, his

light breathing carrying indiscernible words.

"Link," says Athena again, "where were you? Who did this?"

She's speaking loudly, forcefully, trying to pull Link from his stupor. Again, we turn silent as his lips continue to flutter, and out of them we hear a single word.

"Knight..."

Then, his eyes close once again, and he falls back into the blackness.

We all look at each other, and at that moment I know that he must have come face to face with the Seekers. That he will have seen them first hand, these clones of the evil Chancellor, the spitting image of their long deceased father.

The doctor steps forwards again, breaking the silence.

"OK, he needs to rest. Everyone out unless you're family."

We shuffle out of the room, and I look down at Ajax, still sitting by his father's side.

"You staying?" I ask.

He merely nods.

Later that evening, we convene once more in the Master's chamber. As per the doctor's advice, Link is to be transferred to Eden, with a medical transport coming overnight to collect him.

"It will arrive in the morning," says Markus.

"We'll send some of our best Watchers back with him. Cyra is there also, and we know what she can do."

Velia looks at me.

"Your mum? Is she off her meds? I heard she was suppressing her powers."

"She was, and now I understand why. But yeah, she went off them a month or two ago now when I left Eden to come here to train. I'm just hoping she's got all her powers back."

Velia smiles. "Yeah…your mum is a legend. We could really do with her help right now."

Across the table, the conversation continues, Ajax the only one absent. Ever since Link was brought in, he's been by his side. I'm not sure he'll leave him until he wakes.

"I reckon Ajax will go as well," I say. "He'll want to see his mum and stay with his dad."

"I'm sure of it," says Markus. "And you, Theo, will be accompanying him."

"Me? But I want to stay here and help. What about the file?"

"Oh, that's precisely it. The file is going to Eden too, and I want you taking it."

"It's going to Eden…why?"

"Because I've had my smartest people working on it and no one can figure it out. We need Eden technology to decipher it. There's only one person I can think of who might be able to crack open its secrets."

"And who's that?"

"A woman called Professor Lane."

"Professor Lane? I had no idea she was still alive," I say.

"Yes, well, she's been keeping a low profile for a while, working down in the depths of Eden. Take the file to her, and see if you can figure it out together."

"Yes, sir," I say. "Whatever you need from me."

"Good man."

"And what about us?" ask Velia. "We wouldn't mind going to Eden too, hey Vesuvia?"

"Oh yeah, we've always wanted to see it. Maybe we could help too?"

"It's up to you, girls. You've earned the right to go wherever you want."

They look at each other and smile. "Eden, then," they say.

Velia smiles at me, and I can't help but smile back. Frankly, the four of us have been through a lot already and have become a bit of a team. I wouldn't want it broken up…

"What about you, Athena?" I ask.

She speaks without hesitation. "I'm sworn to protect this city, its people, and its Master. My place is here," she says.

"But shouldn't we all stay together?"

"And put all our eggs in one basket?" she says. "No, that wouldn't be smart. It's best I stay out here and search for the Baron…"

"You kidding," I say. "Talk about not being smart. You've seen what's happened to Link. You can't go out there alone."

"I won't be alone," she says. "I have my Watchers. I'm going to gather as many as I can muster and we're going to comb these lands for that coward. I can't just sit in this mountain, Theo. That has never been my way."

I make a move to cut in, but she holds up her hand.

"I'll be fine, I can assure you of that. Just concentrate on breaking open that file, OK. And if you find anything, don't hesitate to let me know."

With that, she glides quickly out of the chamber and down the passage, no goodbye dropping from her lips. Markus, meanwhile, sits in his chair smiling as she departs.

"Athena was born for battle, Theo," he says. "She relishes this. Not once in her life has she shied away from a fight, no matter what the odds."

"Yeah, but usually the odds are in her favour. They're not anymore."

He nods, his smile fading. "I know. But regardless, we can't just hide here. You weren't here twenty years ago when Augustus Knight's army was on our doorstep, starving us out. We went to war then, and we're going to war now. It's only the numbers that are different."

He stands and moves over towards the painting of Eden, hanging behind his chair on the wall.

"Eden," he says. "It's a wonderful city…but this mountain is my home. This desert is my home. It's the same for Athena. We'll stay here and fight whatever comes our way. That's what we do…it's what we've always done."

His eyes fall to Velia and Vesuvia. They stare back at him and nod. I don't know what it is, but there's just something in the water around here. Despite it being so arid and barren, the people born here have a deep love for these lands. A love so deep they'd put their lives on the line to defend it.

And when I think of my own home; of the woods and streams and hills, I suppose I can understand that. Our homes are in our blood. As much as the people in our lives, as much as our families and friends, where we live is a part of who we are.

But right now, it doesn't matter where you live, where you come from. Lignum or Eden or the Deadlands or Petram. All of them are under threat from a hidden enemy. And if we don't work together, we might just find all of our lands in ash and rubble.

Because that's all Knight's legacy is: chaos.

7
The Titan's Hand

The rumble in the air indicates the arrival of the medical transport. We stand beside the landing platforms out on the plateau, watching closely as the plane emerges from the thick, white clouds.

There are a number of us there. Ajax, the girls, several Watchers trained by Athena. Link lies before us on a trolley, the doctor standing next to him, ready to pass him onto his new Eden carers. Beside his father's bed, Ajax looks exhausted. He hasn't slept since yesterday morning when Link was brought in.

Markus and Athena are there too, officially sending us on our way. As the medical aircraft descends, and Link gets loaded up onto it, Markus offers me a few words of goodbye.

"Take care, Theo, and stay vigilant." His eyes look to the bag on my back. "Is it safe?" he asks. I nod. "Good. Take it to Professor Lane, and figure this thing out. Good luck."

He shakes my hand as Athena steps forward, having said goodbye to the others. As they all board the plane, we find ourselves alone. She peers deep into my eyes, searching them as she often has.

"You've come a long way in a short time, Theo," she says. "But there's a long way yet to go. Take these." She lifts up her left hand, and in it I see a pair of telescopic goggles. "They may come in handy," she says, without further explanation.

"Thanks, Athena…for everything you've done."

"No, it's you who we should be thanking. You've been thrust into the middle of this and you haven't missed a step. You have your father's clear head and leadership skills, and your mother's passion and power. It's a potent mix."

She draws me into a rare hug, and whispers into my ear.

"When you get to Eden, keep training. There's more potential in you, I know it. You have to unleash it."

She draws back, and fixes me with another customary stare, before her eyes rise to the plane behind me.

"They're ready to go," she says.

"Will I see you again soon?" I ask.

She smiles. "I hope so, Theo. Now go, there's no time to waste."

I take a couple of steps back, still looking at her, before turning and boarding the plane. It's larger than Athena's jet, fitted with medical equipment and supplies. Already, several doctors and nurses are hooking Link up to various machines to monitor him during the journey. Ajax looks on, sitting as close as he can, his posture sunken and drained.

I take a seat across from the girls towards the front of the plane. Behind, the space is filled by the half dozen Watchers accompanying us. Velia shuffles towards me, leaning across the gap and whispering: "Do you think we can trust them?"

Her eyes gesture to the four men and two women we don't know. Watchers have a tendency to appear untrustworthy on the outside, their experiences typically hardening them and turning their eyes narrow and sleek. It's something that comes with the territory when you spend half your life seeing visions of pain and suffering, and the other half continually focusing and searching the Void for danger.

I nod and respond quietly. "If Athena trained them, and trusts them, then that's good enough for me. You know how she can read people."

"Yeah…I guess I'm just being paranoid."

"That's not surprising at a time like this. Let's just keep our focus on the real threat."

She nods and slinks back towards her sister, the two of them entering into a private discussion, whispering back and forth. I'm quickly reminded of how they did the same thing when in the chamber beneath the stadium, hidden behind their black masks. It's bizarre to think that I met them only a week or so ago. So much has happened since then.

Something else I find strange is how accustomed I've become to aerial travel. For years Ajax and I would get excited when we saw a jet pass by overhead back home, wondering what it would be like to fly in one.

'Up there, so high, we'd be able to see the whole world,' we'd say, yearning to be set free from those quiet woods.

Now, we've seen more of the world than we could ever have hoped. And we've seen a whole lot more besides. Sitting on a plane, gliding through the sky, has quickly become a mundane and familiar experience.

As we go, however, I find myself drawing out the telescopic goggles Athena gave me to pass the time. The sky is clear, the vast world below barely more than an orange and brown blur. Yet with the goggles set to my eyes, everything changes.

Their range is quite staggering. I don't know how far we're up, but it's got to be at least a few miles. Yet even from this height, I can make out clear vehicles and structures on the ground as I gaze towards distant settlements. I see people going about their quiet lives, seemingly undisturbed by the recent violence, unlike in the major cities. I suppose, for them, little ever changes. Whether back during the time of Knight, or during the last two decades of peace, their little lives subsisting on the Deadlands have been unaffected by any changes in regime.

It's odd, I guess, that some people can go on, living for years, without really knowing much of what's happening elsewhere. Many of these people live off the grid, untangled by the net that envelops the rest of us, the systems of society that spread from Eden to Petram and beyond. Mostly, the major towns and cities and other settlements have a symbiotic relationship, relying on each other to grow and expand and create prosperity and peace. Yet still, there are pockets here and there out in the vast wilderness where none of that matters; where the people get by in their little groups, year after year passing by with little influence from the outside world.

As I look out, however, fewer communities appear as we cross over the flatlands, endless swathes of wasteland too relentlessly oppressive for even the hardiest of desert dwellers. Somewhere down there was where Link was found, his torn up jeep still sat in the sand. I spend some time searching for it, but find the task impossible and end up giving in fairly quickly.

Soon enough, however, the old dividing line of the nation grows in the distance, the skeleton of Knight's Wall cutting a line across the earth. Mostly, it's been dismantled, but even where it has been completely removed there are signs that it was once there. The earth remains discoloured, a darker brown staining the ground where the structure once stood.

I fix my telescopic goggles once more to my head and turn my eyes down below. Occasionally, at points between where the wall used to be, gigantic mounds of rock offer a natural barrier to the lands beyond the regions. Knight was smart enough to use the landscape when designing his wall, linking the man-made structure between the impassable mountains.

One particularly interesting outcrop catches my eye. I fix my gaze on it, zooming out with my goggles to take in its full picture. From the earth, five jagged peaks rise, each spread out and pointing to the sky in the shape of a giant hand.

I recall legends about it from my youth. The people would say that a giant was encased within the earth, only his hand reaching beyond its surface. When the world would shake with earthquakes, they'd say it was the giant waking and trying to break free. The lands, they said, were cursed. It was somewhere that they'd never go.

The Titan's Hand, I think to myself, staring at it in wonder.

As I look at it, movement at its base draws my eyes. I run my finger along the touchpad at the side of the goggles, and begin zooming in closer. There, where the titanic thumb explodes from the earth, I see a portion of Knight's Wall still being dismantled. There are workers there, taking down the final stretch of wall for many miles in either direction.

It's hard to see from up here, hard to make out much. But as I look, I think I see the sight of a weapon glinting in the sun as it catches the light. Perhaps, even down there, they have guards protecting them from this fresh threat to the world. Or maybe the people have taken it upon themselves to carry arms. Frankly, I wouldn't blame anyone for that.

With the plane rushing fast, however, I don't get

much of a chance to look any closer. I zoom back out, and take in The Titan's Hand once more, marvelling at the natural formation. And then, before long, it fades again before my eyes as we enter a soup of white cloud, heading straight for the ocean.

The weather only gets worse as we get closer to the coast. By the time we reach it, the clouds outside have turned black, pouring rain from above. Strikes of lightning burst from out of them, reminding me of the picture that hangs on the Master's chamber in Petram. As we begin to descend, the rough seas only add to that image, Eden sitting there like a giant metal fortress, even the most powerful storm and waves having no impact upon it.

I stand and move up towards the cockpit, wishing for a better view than through my little window. The pilot barely seems to notice as I gaze over his shoulder at the enormous platform. Seemingly, he's too busy on the radio.

"Identify yourself," says a crackling voice.

I look at the dashboard of the plane and see that some sort of weapons detection system has gone red. Below, I look down to see one of the giant cannons on the side of the city turn in our direction, ready to spray anti-air missiles right at us.

"Jeez," I whisper, "don't they know it's us?"

I was mainly speaking to myself, but the pilot hears me and turns with a frown. "You shouldn't be here," he barks, before responding to the man on the radio with his flight identification number.

“Don’t they know who we are?” I ask again, taking no notice of the pilot’s irritation at my presence.

The radio crackles once more. “OK, copy. The hanger door is opening. Medical staff are waiting for the patient. Stand by.”

The pilot begins hovering towards the city walls as one of the mighty hanger doors begins to slide open. As he does so, he deigns to answer my question.

“The city is in lockdown, kid,” he grunts. “They’re not taking any chances.”

That becomes even more evident when we land. Within the hanger, numerous guards and soldiers are ready to receive us, all heavily armed and armoured. It’s actually quite comforting to know how impenetrable this city is right now.

I step out of the cockpit as the pilot sets us down and lowers the ramp. As Link is rushed straight off by the medical staff, Ajax follows closely behind. I watch them from the plane’s exit and see Ellie coming forward. She wraps her arms around her son as my eyes scan the mess of people below.

There, walking towards the plane, I see my parents. I’m quick to dart down the ramp and into the large hanger, all of us quickening our step as we approach each other. It’s my mum who reaches me first, her own arms gripping tight and half suffocating me. My dad stands by, smiling and waiting for her to let go. Then he takes his turn to deliver a more reserved embrace.

"You have a lot of explaining to do, Theodore," says Cyra, glaring at me as she has so often. Yet in her eyes I see a toughness that I've never seen before. They're not the soft motherly eyes I've known all my life. There's something more in them now. They're the eyes that tell me one thing: her powers are coming back.

I nod my head, knowing this would be coming.

"I can explain everything. Grandfather…it was his plan…he foresaw it all. We had to keep you in the dark. I hope you understand."

Cyra looks at me and begins nodding. To her side, Jackson does the same. In their eyes I don't see the typical looks of admonishment that I'd get when I'd come back late after hunting, or return home having suffered an injury seeking some dangerous adventure. No, this is different. I see in their eyes a measure of pride.

As they nod, my mother speaks again.

"We do understand," she says, her voice calm amid the rushing bodies around us. "We understand everything, Theo. My father is missing. Link is badly hurt. And now…now the spectre of Augustus Knight is upon us again. Oh, we understand this all too well. This is war now. And we all have to do what we must."

I can hardly believe what I'm hearing, what I'm seeing. Ahead of me, stand two legends, now come back to life. And for the first time, I don't look upon my mother as I always have: a timid woman, hiding from her powers, hiding from her fate. I see now a warrior, a fighter, a woman who will do anything to protect the people she loves.

I see, for the first time, the Golden Girl return to the world.

8
Professor Lane

Security in the city is even tighter than before. Now that the revelation of our adventure at the Watcher Wars and the Baron's compound has come to light, more soldiers and guards have been deployed, the ways in and out of the city being more closely monitored.

Trade has been largely suspended, the walls only opening if absolutely essential. Martial law has been put into action, the people advised to obey the new curfew in place. For all intents and purposes, it appears as if the city has retracted to how it was in the days of Augustus Knight. The irony, I'm sure, isn't lost on anyone.

Nevertheless, they're necessary measures to ensure that the people are safe. While most don't know the full details of what's going on, they do know that the city's security protocols have been dialled up to eleven, and that another terrorist attack or assassination is considered imminent.

We move through the city in our convoy of hovercars, Jackson driving ours with Cyra next to him, heading towards our new accommodation. Next to me in the back, Velia and Vesuvia sit, their eyes open wide and marvelling at the wondrous sights around us.

I can't help but smile when looking at them, knowing that I was doing precisely the same thing only a couple of months ago. They do look quite comical, their eyes bigger and brighter than I've ever seen them, their mouths slightly agape.

Cyra looks back and offers her own smile. "Quite a place, isn't it girls," she says.

They turn to her and nod silently, their faces equally star struck as they look at her. Only a few minutes ago, they'd greeted my parents like giggling children, losing their cool for the first time. Above all others, my mother's name became the symbol of the rebel cause during the war, her visions forging the path to Knight's eventual defeat. Clearly, the Golden Girl is well known and admired, even as far away as the Western coast.

We move towards the centre of the city, and the convoy comes to a stop outside the main Senate building where the city leaders reside. Outside, a number of guards stand, protecting the entrance. We climb out and pass through, before moving straight up towards the stairs ahead. The last time I was here, Ajax and I were rising right to the summit of the building for President Stein's wake. It was then that Drake took Link and us to one side, and our secret pact was formed.

It didn't work out so well for them, I think to myself, shaking my head.

Ahead, at the top of the stairs, a large set of double doors block our path. Jackson pushes them open, and leads us in towards a large open hallway, beautifully furnished and adorned with fine art hanging on the walls. When my father shuts the doors, there are only five of us inside: my parents, Velia and Vesuvia, and me.

Cyra turns to address us.

"This was, until recently, President Stein's home. Now, it officially belongs to Drake. Given his temporary disappearance, we'll be keeping the place warm for him." She grimaces slightly as she vocalises her father's current fate, but maintains her composure. "There's plenty of space here, and it's well protected. Girls, you'll be sharing a room, as will you, Theo, with Ajax. Ellie is also staying with us, although I suspect she'll be spending a lot of time at the hospital. It's important, right now, that we all stay together, and stay strong. OK?"

We all nod, before we're guided through the sprawling level towards the bedrooms on the East wing at the rear, pretty much as far from the front as possible. Inside, the rooms are large and overly luxurious. I don't look at them with any pleasure, not at a time like this. If anything, such a state of living will make us weak.

I bring that concern immediately to my father.

"It's not where you lay your head that makes you weak or strong, Theo," he says. "We're here because it's the safest place in the city. And we're here because it's where Drake would want us to be. The size of your bed is irrelevant."

Down the corridor, Cyra appears, having shown

the girls to their room.

"Do you know who once lived here, Theo?" she asks me.

I shake my head. "I guess saying President Stein is too obvious?"

"Actually, it was your name-sake," she says.

"You mean…Theo Graves?"

She smiles, remembering the young man who saved her life, and my father's too. "You're a student of history, so you'll know that his parents were Councillors…Priscilla and Emerson they were called. Both turned on Knight right at the end. Without them, and their son, we'd have lost the war."

The Graves family is well known throughout the country. The two elderly Councillors were extremely close with Knight until his twisted mind took things a step too far. In the end, they helped free the city from his grip, and for several years before their deaths they were instrumental in reforming the country as it is today, working alongside the likes of Aeneas Stein and my grandfather, among others. Time and illness, unfortunately, took them both, long after their son, Theo, had been killed during the war. And with them, the name of Graves was lost.

"I came here the evening Theo and I were paired," continues Cyra. "It was so awkward. We hated each other back then, and had to dance in front of all the parents." Her face slowly darkens as she speaks. "It was the same night I met the High Chancellor as well. I'll never forget that first meeting."

Everything goes silent as she speaks, disappearing into her own mind. She just stares forward as my father and I stand there, her eyes starting to burn.

"I'm not surprised that he had clones made of himself," she continues. "He always wanted to live forever. The day he died, he did so with a smile on his face. I suppose, maybe, he knew what would happen. He must have had this plan in place all along." Her eyes turn to the floor. "He's down there now, laughing up at us."

Jackson steps forward, right ahead of her, and lifts her chin back up.

"He's not laughing, Cyra, because he's dead. And soon enough these clones, these Seekers, will be dead too. We'll wipe all memory of him off the map. And then," he says, sweeping his eyes around his family, "we can all go home."

Down the corridor, the girls come out of their room, apparently far more excited than I am by this luxurious new residence. Their sudden presence lifts us out of our discussion, their voices carrying down the hall.

"This place is amazing," says Vesuvia, turning to us with a beaming smile. "Can we explore the city?"

They come towards us, and I watch as Cyra's face works up a smile.

"Well, girls, I'll let my husband answer that one. He's in charge of security now."

We turn to Jackson, who also appears somewhat lightened by the girls' energy. "I don't see why not. I'll have someone take you around."

"Thank you, Governor Kane."

"Please, girls, if we're to live under the same roof, let's forget any formalities. Call me Jackson."

"OK. Thank you…Jackson," they say.

I stand silently, watching the exchange, looking at Velia's eyes light up bright and beautiful. It's nice to see them so excited, so innocent even, the burden of what we're facing fading away, if only for a few fleeting moments.

After briefly being shown the rest of our new quarters, we return outside where Jackson sets about recruiting someone suitable to show the girls around the city. Some of it will, of course, be off limits, the upper deck level providing the majority of the tour.

It's no surprise that it's Leeta who is summoned, her own role as Chief Secretary to the President continuing to blur now that Drake has gone missing. She rushes in to greet me as she did before, with a hug, before performing the same routine on the girls. Then, under orders from Jackson, she moves off with them, accompanied by a couple of guards, to show them around the deck.

Alone with my parents, Cyra now sets about meeting the new Watchers trained by Athena. By the looks of things, they're to stay in the adjoining building to ours, and will be tasked with front lining the defence of the city leaders. They meet Cyra with a great deal of reverence, her status once more preceding her.

I stand to one side with Jackson, several questions bubbling up in my mind.

"So…do the Senate know about this?" I ask.

He turns to me with a frown. "You mean, the fact that there are Watchers out there?"

"Yeah, and that Athena's been training them in secret, with the support of Stein and Drake. It's illegal, isn't it?"

"Well, technically it's not. From what I've heard, Athena saw to this on her own. Stein and Drake's involvement is something that cannot be proven. In any case, perhaps now the Senate will realise that having a few extra Watchers on hand might be a good thing."

"Well they'd be stupid not to, with everything that's happening," I say. "What about mum…are her powers coming back?"

We look at her again, keen eyed and assertive, talking quietly with the Watchers who she'll most likely take under her wing.

Jackson nods.

"Her visions have been returning slowly, but they're blurred," he says. "It may take time for her powers to fully return. She's been suppressing them for many years now."

"That's what I thought would happen. And Ellie?"

"The same, although as you know she could never

see into the Void. I hear from Athena that your own powers are growing significantly, Theo? How was your training with her?"

He offers me a knowing look, perhaps aware of the brutality of Athena's methods. He reaches forward with his hand and brushes a lock of blond hair from my forehead, revealing a couple of scars around my hairline.

"I guess these aren't the only ones you received?"

I shake my head, knowing how many other marks of battle now litter my body.

"Athena did what she had to do in the short time we had," I say. "Her training was tough, but she prepared us well. We'd have probably died in the Watcher Wars if it wasn't for her."

"Well, you'll have to tell me all about it sometime. Your mother and I had no idea these Watcher Wars even existed. There's a lot coming to light that we're just catching up on. And right now, there's one thing that we need to see to immediately."

He leads me towards Cyra, interrupting her conversation.

"Cyra, I'm taking Theo down to Underwater 3. We'll be back a little later."

"OK," she says. "Good luck."

We climb into a nearby hovercar, and begin working our way towards the perimeter. I can't help but think of my previous journey to Underwater Level 3, when Ajax and I secretly unleashed our powers under the genetics scanner. I don't have to ask why we're returning. Jackson is quick to fill me in as we approach the perimeter and move towards the lifts.

"Professor Lane has been operating down on Underwater 3 for many years now, and she's been doing a lot of great work," he tells me. "It was her and her team who developed the suppressor medication for your mother and any others who wanted it." He taps his bionic arm. "She also built this for me, for which I'll be eternally grateful."

We enter the lifts, and begin plunging down past the surface levels and beneath the waves. Outside, I suspect the storm is still raging, but within this metal fortress you'd never know. We step out onto Underwater Level 3 at a very different point to my previous journey here. Beyond the perimeter wall, I see labs extending far into the distance, all with clear, see-through walls. Inside, scientists work on various projects, bright lights creating a constant yellow glow deep into the level.

Jackson leads me around towards a large entry door and opens it using a keycard. Beyond, an endless corridor stretches into the distance, labs on either side. We begin walking down it, passing rooms marked with their specialisms: illness prevention and cure; agricultural science; biomedical research. Here, it seems, engineering also plays its role, new modes of transport being developed and tested. I even spot a sign for weapons development, something that makes me hope that, down there, they've cooked up something that might even the odds against the Seekers.

Then, I consider that, if the Baron is able to create clones, he's probably got a team of scientists of his own who are able to do just about anything else. Perhaps he too has more secrets that we've yet to uncover.

Soon enough, we're moving towards a part of the level that isn't so busy. Some labs now remain dark and unused, seemingly surplus to requirements. I suspect it's also possible that, given the current state of play in the city, not all projects are being considered a priority.

Before long, we reach another door, marked with an extra layer of security, and enter an inner level within the level. Inside is a larger, open space, filled with machinery and screens and lab equipment. Here and there, technicians and scientists go about their work. And from the front, standing by a series of giant computers and glowing screens covered in data, an elderly woman turns to look upon us.

She works her way towards us, her body slightly bowed by the years, a pair of spectacles nestled on the end of a pointy nose. Her eyes, however, remain bright and untarnished, inspecting me closely as she approaches.

"Jackson," she says. "I assume this is the prodigal son?"

"Yes, Professor," says Jackson. He turns to me. "Theo, meet Professor Lane."

I reach out my hand and take her spindly fingers. Her grip is stronger than I'd have expected. "A pleasure to meet you, Professor Lane," I say.

"Likewise, young Mr Kane," responds the old woman. "Now, I hear you have something for me?"

I nod and swing the bag from my back. My hand dips inside and pulls out the file. Eagerly, the Professor takes it from me, eyeing the cover with great interest.

"Hmmmm," she says. "The Seekers of Knight. What has Augustus been up to now…"

She turns and begins walking back towards her computers. Jackson and I follow as she gently lowers herself into a chair and opens the file. She quickly flicks past the picture of Knight without so much as a flicker of the eyes, before passing over page after page, only stopping a second to inspect each one. After a few moments, she looks back up to us.

"This might take a while," she says. "The coding looks to be quite sophisticated. Tell me, Theo. Where exactly did you find it?"

"In Baron Reinhold's compound," I say. "There was an underground lab and training area through a secret tunnel at the back of the main house. It was where these clones were grown and trained. The file was in a locked drawer. There were lots of others, but we didn't have time to retrieve them."

"I see. Well, you've done extremely well to get it to us. We just have to hope it offers us some clues. If it is merely dedicated to the Baron's cloning experiments, I fear it may be of little use. As I see it, these clones are already fully mature and wreaking havoc. Knowing the science behind their development won't change that."

"Well, Professor, I'm sure you'll find something important that we can use," says Jackson. "Get working on it, and we'll return soon."

"Of course. I'll put it as a top priority."

"Thank you," says Jackson, turning me towards the door.

We begin walking away, heading for the exit, as Professor Lane starts barking orders behind us, gathering her own troops for their assault on the file.

"So…what now?" I ask my dad as we make our way back to the level.

"Now," he says, "we can only wait. This is a game of chess, son, and we have to be patient. We'll make our move when we have to. But right now, we can do little from the confines of this city."

I hate the thought. That, out there, the Baron is holding all the cards. That he's planning his next assault on God-knows-where and God-knows-who, while all we can do is stay here and hide.

But maybe that's my biggest failing. Like my mother, I've got an impulsive streak that's hard to suppress. I look at my father, a born leader, and realise he's right. That we have to wait, and be smart, and gather our own resources.

Because right now, we're losing this fight. And if we don't consolidate what we have, the whole world might just collapse from under us.

9
Links to the Past

That evening, I return to our quarters to find the girls chatting with Leeta around a large table in the kitchen. She appears to be cooking, and telling them stories of the old days when the world was so very different.

It's interesting, looking upon the frumpy old woman from Eden and the two young girls from the far side of the Deadlands. Such different backgrounds and experiences, but now a shared goal: to see the Baron pay for his atrocities; to once more wipe the lingering evil of Augustus Knight from this world.

I join them, and listen to Velia and Vesuvia excitedly talk of the city. For them, the bustling energy of the place is so new and enticing, the same as it was for Ajax and I only months ago when we first came here.

Soon enough, such a thing will fade when reality sets back in. For now, though, it's nice to see them smiling and happy, their expressions usually perpetually dominated by frowns and grimaces.

As we sit there, we hear the sound of footsteps behind us, and turn to see Cyra and Jackson return, this time accompanied by Ellie and Ajax. Leeta is quick to step away from her cooking duties to offer her condolences to the two of them, although is typically upbeat with her assertion that Link will be 'just fine.'

The looks on their faces suggest otherwise, forcing me to ask how things are.

"He's stable," says Ellie. "But…the doctors are unsure as to how long he'll be under."

The energy in the room is immediately expunged, the frowns returning to the girls' faces. We eat dinner under a heavy weight, talking through the events of the last few days and once more trying to bring things together in our heads. Ajax stays quiet throughout, the girls and me doing the talking for our part of the story.

Aside from the concerns about Link, we turn our attention to the fact that Drake is missing. Naturally, no one makes the assertion that he might well be dead, even though it's probably what we're all thinking.

With President Stein having died so recently, and the new President missing in action, I begin to wonder just who is in charge in the city. I pose the question, and get an ambiguous response.

"The Senators are deliberating on that very topic right now," my father says. "There is no protocol in place for this eventuality. The leading candidates will be Senator Alber, who heads the Defence Council, and Senator Doryen, who is in charge of the Trade Council. They're the most powerful offices behind the President and Vice President."

I hear Leeta huff at the end of the table.

"I hope it's not Senator Alber," she says. "I don't want to work for *that* man."

"Why's that?" I ask.

"Ah, he's just a horrible man. Rude and entitled. After working for Aeneas for so long, I can't imagine a man more opposed to his philosophy on life."

"Which was?" asks Velia.

"Oh, just to be the most delightful person you can be, I suppose. He was so welcoming, so charming and friendly. I think all who knew him would agree?"

I see the heads of my parents nodding, along with Ellie's

"Yes, I'd have to admit that Senator Alber is a difficult man," says Jackson. "I've dealt with him before and he doesn't have too many endearing qualities. Not, as Leeta says, like Aeneas."

"You've dealt with him?" I ask.

"Yes, on security and military matters," says Jackson. "As head of the Defence Council, all regional Governors meet with him to discuss local security."

"So, how do they decide who takes temporary charge?" asks Ellie.

"They'll vote in the Senate," says Jackson.

"Obviously, Drake has only just gone missing, and we don't yet know his fate, so the vote his been delayed."

"But he's been off hunting clues for months," I say. "Why didn't they have someone in place before?"

"As I say, no protocol was in place for that. Whilst Drake was in contact, his position wasn't in doubt. Now, though…"

"Can we please change the subject…"

All eyes sweep towards Cyra, who's maintained a stoic silence throughout much of the conversation. However, speaking about her father in such terms has clearly got to her.

"You're right," says Jackson. "I don't mean to speak so flippantly about Drake's disappearance. You know how much he means to me."

"I know, Jack," says Cyra. "But all this speculating…I think we've had enough of it for one evening."

Several heads nod, and the conversation breaks down as the dinner concludes. As soon as it does, Ajax and Ellie rise again and tell us they're returning to the hospital. As they leave, I rush to my friend's side.

"I'll come to the hospital tomorrow, AJ," I say. "OK?"

He nods and moves off as Leeta begins clearing the table. I add my hands to the task, and together we make light work of it.

"That was delicious, Leeta," says Jackson before he departs. "Thank you. It's important that we stay together at times like this. Your wonderful cooking helps to ensure that."

She smiles at my dad, half blushing through the praise.

"If only you could be President," she says. "You have a lot of Aeneas in you."

He nods to her in thanks, before moving off with Cyra to perform a few security checks outside. I watch them as they go, proud to see my mum now fully committed to her role.

Now back with only the girls and Leeta, I sit at the table and our discussion resumes. Mostly, I want to know more about these Senators, Alber in particular.

"Well, Senator Doryen would be far better to work for," says Leeta. "He was a merchant for years, and knows trade and the economy inside out. He's not a man of war like Alber. Sometimes, they can be less pleasant to deal with."

"So, has he been around for a long time?" I ask.

"Alber? Oh, quite some time, yes."

"During the reign of Knight?"

She nods. "Yes, he was on the Junior Council, as it was then if my memory serves. He'd probably have graduated to become a full Councillor at Knight's table had certain events not taken place."

"You mean the war?" asks Velia.

"Yes, indeed."

"And...are there lots of Senators who were once under Knight's thumb?" I ask.

"A few, perhaps," she says, peering at me. "I wouldn't put much stock on that, though, young Theo. Lots of people were around during Knight's rule. That doesn't mean they were loyal to him. As much as I dislike Senator Alber, he's done better under this new regime than he ever did, or would have done, under Knight. Back then, the High Chancellor made all the calls. It was nothing but a dictatorship. Now, a politician can havc ambitions of being President. It's a better world for everyone."

"Not everyone," says Velia quickly. "What about all those who were driven out when Knight was defeated. The likes of Baron Reinhold, and others across the Deadlands?"

"Well, of course there were some. But...none left in Eden. Not after so long, anyway."

"Yeah, well after what's been happening, I think you'll excuse us for being suspicious," I say. "I mean, President Stein was killed, and now Drake's missing. Maybe all this was a set up?"

Leeta shakes her head, and rises from the table, the suggestion seemingly making her uncomfortable.

"I wouldn't let your thoughts run away with you like that, young Theo. Now, it's getting rather late, and I have a very early morning." She turns to the girls. "It was lovely to meet you, ladies. I hope to hear more of your stories from the Deadlands sometime."

"And you, Leeta," comes their reply, before she scuttles off out of the kitchen.

"She's easily rattled, isn't she," say Vesuvia, watching on as she disappears down the corridor.

"Head in the sand mentality," I say. "Most people don't want to believe what's happening right now."

"Yeah, but come on, Theo…you think this Senator is on the Baron's side?" asks Velia.

"Maybe, maybe not. I'm just saying, anyone who was close to Knight in any way needs to be considered as a possible threat. At least, we should be wary of them."

"I think you're reaching," says Vesuvia. "All this mess has come from the Deadlands. I think we can discount a Senator who's been working under this new regime for 20 years."

I let out a breath, and then offer a shrug.

"I dunno…maybe you're right. Let's just wait and see how the vote goes first. I'm not gonna trust anyone right now."

"Except for us?" asks Velia with a smile. "You trust us, right?"

I glare at her, and closely consider the question.

"Hey!" she says, slapping my arm. "I think your mum's right. Enough speculating, hey? My brain's starting to hurt."

"Fine. I'll give it a rest," I say. "Just to spare your

poor brain."

She crinkles her nose at me as we stand and leave the kitchen. Once more, I part with them down the corridor to our rooms, and step into my own, vast and empty after the various places I've slept in recent months.

I settle into the bed, my mind so filled with questions, and look up at the ceiling. And slowly, as the room fades to darkness, and I fall into an uneasy sleep, flashes of carnage come to me.

Raging fire, consuming buildings. Screaming people, cut down by guns and shrapnel. Images of death and destruction on a grander scale than what I've seen before.

I don't know where it is, and I don't know when. But I do know one thing: soon, the Seekers are going to strike again. And this time, it's not going to be quiet assassinations.

This time, I'll be terror.

And chaos.

10
The Grid

I wake in a cold sweat, the morning light emerging through the window. In a flash, my mind reawakens with the images that filled it as I slept, forcing me straight to my feet and into my clothes. I rush out of my room and down the corridor to where my parents sleep, before knocking loudly.

When no one answers, it's a clear indication that they're already up. I open the door to double check that they're not there, before heading towards the kitchen. I find them both there preparing their morning coffee.

It's my mum's eyes that find me first. Immediately, she knows something's up.

"What is it? What have you seen?" she asks.

"Destruction, death," I say breathlessly. "Somewhere…in a city. Buildings were on fire. People were being killed. I don't know when…"

My parents forget their coffee, and come straight towards me.

"The buildings," says Jackson. "What did they look like?"

I shut my eyes and think. "I don't know. Just

buildings."

"Think, Theo," he says loudly.

"I don't know! It was blurred and rushed. It could be anywhere."

"Leave it, Jack," says Cyra. "I know what it's like. When you can't see it, you can't see it. We'll have to search for more. I'll talk with the Watchers, see if they've seen anything."

"And Ellie…Ajax," I add.

"Ellie's visions are still weak, like mine," says Cyra. I see her grimace in anger, unable to utilise her full strength. Her visions were always the clearest, the most wide ranging, of everyone's. "I'll talk to her, though," she says. "Stay here, I'll be back soon."

As she leaves, my dad continues to question me on what I saw. I have nothing else to say other than what I've already told him.

"Trust me, dad, if I had any clues, I'd tell you. I've been having visions for months now. Not once have I known exactly where they were or when. It's not as easy as that…"

He places a hand to my shoulder. "I understand, son. It's just, we've had nothing for months, no sign of any threat. And now this. It has to be another attack." He takes a quick glance at his watch. "Look, I've got some things to do. Stay here and wait for your mother."

He picks up his coffee to go, and leaves the other one for me. I take a sip before realising I hate the stuff, sending the rest down the drain. Then, I remember that there are two other people here who might have seen something.

I jog back through the residence towards Velia and Vesuvia's room, and knock lightly. A louder knock yields better results, and I hear one of them answer, I can't tell which.

I open the door to find them both sitting up in their beds, their eyes sleepy.

"Theo," yawns Velia. "What's up?"

"You two didn't see anything last night did you? Any visions?"

They look at each other.

"No, why?" asks Velia. "Did you?"

"Get dressed, and I'll tell you about it in the kitchen."

Five minutes later, the girls and I are back in the kitchen, the two of them now garbed as I am in more appropriate Eden clothes rather than the desert outfits we arrived in. I quickly tell them what I saw, and see their eyes shrink.

"Do you reckon it's soon?" asks Velia.

"I have no idea. Probably."

"And what about your mum? She didn't see anything?"

"No. Her powers are weak at the moment because of the medication. No one really knows how long its effects last."

"That's not good."

"Tell me about it."

As we speak, the woman herself comes marching back into the room.

"No one saw anything much," she says hurriedly. "One of the Watchers says he saw blurred flames, but that's nothing to go on. Probably from the same event, but his abilities are weaker than yours."

"And Ajax?"

"He still hasn't slept," says Cyra. "He's been too worried about Link. Ellie too. But their minds are primed now, particularly Ajax. It's in times of stress like this that we often see the clearest visions."

She comes straight for us, closing us into a circle.

"All three of you need to focus when you fall asleep. Make sure that your minds are ready and free to explore. I know it's not pleasant, but think of things that make you sad and upset. Any loved ones you've lost, or things that you're afraid of. Fracture your minds and they'll search deeper." She looks directly at the girls. "Have you had any training?"

"A bit," says Velia. "Our dad trained us when he could."

"Troy?"

They nod.

"Well, he's clearly done a good job. I've been told you can see well into the Void. However, we have provisions here to extend your training. I think it's time that I revisited a room I know well. All of you, come with me."

We follow my mother through the city and into the perimeter wall, dropping right down further than I did the day before with my dad. Soon enough, we're at Underwater 5, stepping out into total silence, the world dim and empty. To the left and right, the entire level looks completely abandoned.

"What is this place?" asks Vesuvia. "Leeta didn't show us down to these levels yesterday."

"Well, no one has access here any more," says Cyra, walking us down a long corridor into the interior of the level. "This place was always quiet, even when I came here over twenty years ago. Now, it's totally dormant."

"This is where you trained?" asks Velia.

"Yes," says Cyra, reaching a large security door. "Right through here."

I see her take a breath as she inserts her keycard, the large door opening up before us. Beyond, a long, black hall stretches into the distance, immediately reminding me of the training room we found beneath the Baron's compound.

Cyra steps in, as stale air pours out. She looks around for a moment, before calling: "Eve, give us some light."

Immediately, the room begins to glow, bringing its darkest corners to life. To my sides, the girls cough from the dust, drifting around in little clouds.

"Eve, clear the air in here," calls Cyra once more.

Again, the reaction is immediate, the air being quickly conditioned by large filters that appear on the walls. Within only a few moments, the entire place smells fresh and clean, the air pure.

"That's better," says Cyra, stepping in a little deeper. She turns to me. "I'll bet you've always wanted to come here, haven't you Theo?" she asks.

I nod, staring around and whispering: "The Grid..."

"The Grid?" says Vesuvia.

"This is where I learned to be a Watcher. I was trained here by a man called Commander Ajax. You may well have heard of him. It's where you new friend got his name."

She turns and continues to walk deeper into the room, looking around as she goes.

"I saw unimaginable things in here," she says quietly. "This room, it carries a lot of terrible memories. It can morph and change at will, bringing to life your darkest fears. Through that fear, your abilities are nourished."

She turns to us again, and inspects us one by one.

"That's what we all endured when we first trained here. But you are all far more advanced than I was then. You have seen and done things now that are worse than what you'll face here. But here, at least, you'll have the privacy to develop your abilities further. Would you like that?"

We all nod, and she begins stepping back towards us. Her eyes rise to mine in particular.

"I never wanted you to be here, Theo," she says. "But I know now that your path lies before you just like mine did all those years ago. I cannot change that, or stop that, as much as I'd want to. You're braver and more gifted than I ever was. I'm proud of what you've done."

She steps in and hugs me as the girls look on. Then, drawing a strict look back onto her face, she turns to them.

"Do you girls want to avenge your father?" she asks.

Their eyes burn. Their nostrils flare. Neither of them need to answer.

"Good. We all have people who have been taken from us. We all have many others who we're worried will share the same fate. All we can do, now, is fight as best we can. Down here is where it starts."

She moves to the side of the hall, and as she does, her voice calls out to Eve once again.

"Eve, show us this Baron Reinhold, and his Seekers of Knight. Bring them to life…"

My eyes blaze as, ahead of us, figures materialise in the centre of the hall. I see the shape of Baron Reinhold appearing, dressed in his maroon cloak. And there, beside him, to his left and right, four figures take shape, thin lips and grey eyes hidden under black cloaks.

"You want to kill these men," says Cyra, standing by the wall. "Then do it...kill them all."

I look closer at the apparitions, so lifelike and real, and then turn to the girls. They look even more amazed by all of this than I am, hardly able to believe that these people have formed before us. Then, suddenly, the cloaked figures begin moving, stepping forward and leaving the Baron behind. They start at a walk that turns to a jog, quickly closing the space between us.

"Get ready to fight," calls Cyra. "This isn't a game. This is real."

I instinctively move closer to the girls, stepping to my right as they step left. I move in ahead of them, adopting a posture of battle, and my hand drops to my waist, to where my hunting knife or extendable dagger would usually be. Not today.

We have no weaponry, nothing but our fists. But that's never stopped us before.

"Here they come," I growl. "I'll take the two on the left, you two take one each on the right."

I see them nod out of the corners of their eyes as the four cloaked men reach us. Under their cloaks, I see the same face. The faces of Augustus Knight, drawn back by many years and only teenagers like us. They come charging in with their fists raised, swooping quickly towards us.

I focus hard, search the Void, and feel their attacks dawning. In one quick motion, I strike out at the first attacker, my fist rushing through his head as if it's nothing but a cloud of smoke. The body fades into the air as the second attacker comes. I dodge, and strike once more, and dispatch him as well.

As I do, the two attackers on the right fade away as Velia and Vesuvia do the same. Soon, there's no one left but the Baron, still standing in the middle of the hall. A moment later, he dissolves as well.

We turn to Cyra, who steps forward from the wall.

"Those were nothing but ghosts," she says. "But soon, perhaps, you'll be facing the real thing. Down here, the real can by simulated, as you've just seen. But no simulation will match what's really out there."

"Then what's the point?" I ask.

"To face your fear," says Cyra quickly. "And do what you have to in the face of it."

"But I don't fear them," I say defiantly. "I don't fear these Seekers."

Cyra's face darkens, memories flooding her eyes.

"Well…perhaps you should," she declares coldly. "Because, right now, there's nothing in the world worth fearing more. If these Seekers are truly clones of Augustus Knight, then we should all be very afraid."

11
Phase Three

I stand outside a room, looking in through the large window beside a door. Inside, Ellie and Ajax sit, one on either side of a medical bed. On it, the sizeable figure of Link lies, hooked up to all manner of machines that work constantly at the double task of monitoring his health, and bringing him back to full strength.

A doctor stands before Ellie and Ajax, updating them on Link's current state of health. Once he's done, he steps from the room and tells me I can go inside. Tentatively, I enter, and see my best friend's eyes turn up to me.

"Hey, AJ," I say softly. "How's it going?"

I try to keep my tone light, planting a smile on my face. He returns it weakly, his eyes hardly able to stay open, exhausted and drained as he is from the previous few days of constant worry.

"I'm…good," he says as Ellie stands up and heads towards the door.

"I'll give you two a few minutes alone," she says. "Thank you for coming, Theo."

She smiles at me, her own visage broken down by

lack of sleep, and steps out of the room. I take her vacated seat beside Link, his body still covered in multiple bandages and dressings that will add to the tapestry of scars that mark the rest of him.

"What did the doctor say?" I ask.

Ajax takes a breath. "Not much. He's steady, and they're pretty sure he'll be OK. They just don't know when he'll wake up."

"And his powers?" I ask.

Ajax's response is immediate. "I don't care about that," he says quickly. "I just want my dad back."

I nod and go silent for a moment.

"Sorry…" he says. "I'm just really tired."

"You should rest," I tell him. "You're not doing anyone any good sitting here all day. I've started training again, with the girls. Mum's got us working down at the Grid and…"

"Theo, I can't think about that right now."

"Why not? Your dad wouldn't want you wasting away by his bedside. We're at war here."

"War? Wars are fought between armies. This isn't war. I don't even know what this is…"

"Well, whatever you wanna call it, we need to do our part. Both of us. Did Cyra tell you about my vision?"

He nods silently.

"And what do you think about that? A city is going to be attacked, maybe tomorrow, maybe next week, who knows. We need to be prepared to help, AJ."

"Help? And what help will we be exactly?" His eyes gesture to his father. "Look what they did to him. And Drake…we don't even know about what happened to him yet. What hope do we have? I'll tell you…we have none."

I shake my head as I look at him, but choose my words carefully. I know how hopeless he must be feeling right now, and this is no time for an argument. He's not himself, and I know it.

So I take a breath, and compose myself. And when I speak again, I do so with calmer words.

"Maybe you're right," I say. "But that's not the point. Our fathers have always taught us the same thing: whatever the odds, we have to do what we can. That's what they faced all those years ago. And now it's our turn."

I stand, and begin moving towards the door.

"Your father will wake up soon," I say. "And when he does, he'll want to know that you've been training hard, preparing to fight…not sitting here by his bed, when there's nothing you can do to help."

I take a grip of the door handle and pull it open.

"We're going to be training everyday," I say. "Get some rest, AJ. Join us when you're ready…"

I leave with those words hanging in the air, not giving him a chance to respond. I know my friend as well as anyone, and I know that he wants to help. All he needs is time. The only problem is, no one knows how much time we have.

The next few days fall into a familiar pattern. One where I wake early each morning and immediately set my mind to the task of developing my powers further. Each morning, I meet with the girls in the kitchen, where my mother awaits us. Without delay, we move through the city before it rises, and head quietly down to Underwater Level 5. We go through the level, down the corridor, and into the Grid, where Cyra sets about determining the day's activities.

She tells us that, when she trained here, their training was split into two phases. The first involved facing and mastering their fears in order to develop their visions. They'd take it in turn each day to go into the Grid alone, where their greatest fears would be manifested. Day by day, they'd suffer the same torment, breaking them down in order to build them back up again. She recalls how one particular trainee, a boy called Amir, turned from his fears and got lost, his mind stretched too far.

"He broke down in front of us, and lost his mind," she tells us. "Not everyone can handle the rigours of the Grid."

The second phase, however, was when they developed their abilities to see into the Void. That was when the more powerful and gifted among them were set apart from the rest, herself and Link included.

"Phase one was merely to create Watchers capable of seeing and searching visions. Their duties would have them stationed around the country, looking for accidents and other dangers in their sleep. Phase two, however, was about creating warriors. Of course, you three would already pass phase two with flying colours."

"So, what do we do?" I ask.

"There's little more you can do than to continue the good work of Athena," says Cyra. "Only, here in the Grid, we can utilise all of the tools that Eve provides. Tell me, Theo, how many armed men do you think you can defeat?"

The question catches me off guard. After being mentored by Athena, having my mother assume the role is quite jarring.

"Erm, I don't know..."

"Ten, no problem," calls Velia.

"Ten?" asks Cyra, turning to me.

I shrug, glancing at Velia who smirks back at me. "I guess...maybe."

"Well then, let's find out. Girls, step back. Eve, simulate a battlefield. Ten soldiers. Theo, take them all out."

I hardly have time to question what's happening as the room morphs before me. Springing from the ground, crumbling buildings and old rusted vehicles appear. Among them, hidden and out of sight, ten soldiers surround me. I see Cyra walking towards me with an automatic weapon. She hands it to me, before retreating behind a clear partition wall with the girls.

Still trying to catch up, I hear my mother call for Eve to begin. And, suddenly, the sound of exploding weapons fills the great hall.

I barely have time to react. As soon as the weapons sound, bullets fizz right at me. Several I see in time, their white lines crisscrossing around me. Others, however, I miss, pinging at my feet and just missing my body.

I have no choice but to focus hard, the world blurring in a familiar fashion as my senses focus only on the threats at hand. Now, suddenly, the white trails of the incoming bullets appear more clearly, the men delivering them shining out like beacons from their various hiding spots.

I raise my weapon as I duck and weave, picking them off one by one. By the time five of them are down, I'm thinking that ten wasn't nearly enough of a challenge. When eight have been dispatched, however, I feel a heavy strike at my back, and realise my overconfidence has cost me. I'm knocked clean off my feet, hitting the ground with a thud. Moments later, the simulation ends, and the hall clears once more.

Cyra comes towards me, the girls just behind.

"You lost your focus, Theo," she says.

I stand to my feet with a grimace, my back stinging.

"The bullets weren't real?" I ask.

"Not deadly, no. They were rubber bullets. They hurt, but nothing more. Had they been real you might be dead."

"I can do better," I say. "Let me try again. Twenty this time."

"Twenty?"

"Sure. I'm rusty, that's all."

"Well, we need to let the girls have a go first. On second thought…Eve, please split the hall into four."

Now, clear walls appear, rising from the floor and cutting up the sprawling room into four equal parts. "Four? But there are only three of us," I say.

Cyra frowns. "No, Theo, there are four..."

She walks towards one of the quarters, calling out: "Take your positions," as she goes. "Give your commands to Eve, whatever you think you can handle. We'll reconvene in one hour."

I watch as she enters her own space, and calls for Eve to create a battlefield around her. Soon, she's lost amongst it, and moments later, I hear more bullets clattering from weapons.

It's hard to know just how many guns she's facing, but it sounds like a fair few.

For the next hour, we move into our own little zones, and set about working up a sweat. I quickly ask for twenty soldiers to fight, and realise I may have reached my limit. Frankly, I don't see how any Watcher could match twenty men surrounding them. It's not that I don't see the bullets in time, it's simply that there are too many of them around me.

Eventually, they cut me off, giving me nowhere to go. A couple of sharp hits to the stomach and shoulder, with only five or six of them downed, tells me I'm overreaching.

Velia and Vesuvia also end the session clutching various parts of their bodies, perhaps trying to do too much, too quickly, like me. Cyra, meanwhile, appears more calm, sensibly working herself back into the game after so long out of it.

What all this does tell me, however, is that the Grid offers something that Athena could never provide in Petram. There, the most I'd face would be her and Ajax as they fired at me. There was no provision for anything more. Here, my need to focus and search the Void is expanded markedly. When more enemies are shooting at you, you need to be able to look deeper. If you can know where their bullets will be landing earlier, you gain an even greater advantage.

I realise, too, that my mother is a completely different sort of Watcher to Athena. Where Athena is all brutality and ferocity, adopting a no-holds-barred, sink or swim mentality, Cyra chooses instead to explain to us more fully how to search our visions.

To me, that makes a great deal of sense. In a battle to see into the Void, Athena would certainly win. When searching visions, however, and seeing far into time and space, there is no one like Cyra. She teaches us how to set our minds into the correct state for when we sleep, what to look for, and how to stay in the vision for longer, giving us a better chance of identifying when and where it takes place.

In order to expedite this process, and open up our pathways even wider, she sends us into the Grid alone, as she was forced to do all those years ago. With a small waiting room set outside of it, we go in one by one to truly get a picture of what we're facing.

"In there, what you see will seem real," she says. "It will be tough, but it's necessary. We need you to open your minds and hunt down this vision. We need to know where the Seekers will attack us next."

It's not a manifestation of our greatest fears that we face. Instead, we all suffer the same scene when we enter. And despite knowing it isn't real, as soon as the door closes behind me, and the world takes shape ahead, I feel as if it's all happening. And there's nothing I can do to stop it.

Right there, ahead, I see the Baron standing in his maroon cloak. Around him, the Seekers gather, all dressed in black, their faces shrouded in shadow. They all look down to the floor in the ruins of a great city, and lining up at their feet, I see the bodies of those I love and care for.

One by one, my eyes pass over their faces.

My mother. My father. Drake and Ajax and Link and Ellie. Athena and Velia and Vesuvia. Many others lie around them, hundreds, thousands of bodies murdered at their hands. And framing the entire picture is the sight of flames, rising high from burning buildings, the sky blackened and filled with a poisonous fume.

I return from the Grid, my mind filled with the image of death, and my mother comes to me quickly.

"What you saw is what will happen if we cannot stop this threat," she says. "Let the thought consume you, Theo. Let it engulf you. And when you fall asleep, think of it again. Let it come alive in your mind."

She tells the same to the girls as they go in, and return with stark eyes glistening with tears. When they both emerge, they immediately look to their sister, before engulfing them in a hug. When Velia comes out, I see her eyes drift to me as she finally lets Vesuvia go. She walks towards me, eyes dripping tears, and pulls me into a soft embrace.

"I thought you were dead," she says. "I thought you were all dead."

From the side of the room, Cyra looks upon us, now so different to the mother I've known all my life. She stands taller, her eyes firmer, her words strong and assertive and unyielding.

"Search your visions," she says. "Don't let what you've seen become reality."

And then, with a nod to us all, she steps into the Grid herself. Returning once more to the place she hates the most.

12
Suspicions Rising

I barely see Ajax for several days as he continues to be consumed by his own self-doubt. He comes to dinner each evening but barely says a word, not even opening up to Vesuvia as she attempts to bring him out of his stupor.

He doesn't sleep in the room with me, clearly taking whatever rest he can over in the hospital with his dad. One morning, I wake to find him resting on a sofa in one of the large sitting rooms, his eyes flickering as he sleeps. I wonder if, with everything going on in his head, he's seen anything more of the vision I discovered the other night.

My attention, however, cannot be on Ajax right now. I spend my waking hours training, and my sleeping hours attempting to do what my mother has been teaching me. Each time I drop off, my body exhausted from the day's exertions, I think of the deaths of those I care about, of the burning city and the thousands murdered, of the chaos that will ensue if we cannot halt this threat.

And each night, I see more flashes of the attack, the flames and screams and sight of blood becoming clearer in my mind. The girls, too, begin to see flashes of the same, although none of us are able to pinpoint a time or a place, or even see the face of a perpetrator.

Cyra herself appears to be regaining her powers, telling of the same things that we've seen. Soon, we're all able to piece things together, the growing clarity of the attack making it clear that it's growing closer by the day.

"How long do you think?" asks Vesuvia nervously over breakfast one morning.

"Until we know for sure, I can't say," says Cyra. "But it feels close. Weeks. Maybe less…"

As the days pass, I begin to wonder what progress Professor Lane is making with the file. Jackson, who is liaising with her, tells me she's yet to decode anything of note. So far, nothing interesting has come up, something that only serves to heighten my frustration.

We do hear word, however, that the Senate will be voting in a few days time on Drake's successor. Jackson comes to us during dinner, delivering the news.

"Drake has officially been out of contact for over ten days now," he says, his eyes creased into an ever-deepening frown. "The Senate have decided that a new leader needs to be voted in during this time of crisis. The two candidates are as expected: Senator Alber, and Senator Doryen."

Once more, Leeta cannot contain her displeasure at the first name.

"Who's the front-runner?" I ask.

"It's a tight race," says Jackson. "But Alber is looking good from what I hear. Being the head of the Defence Council, it seems appropriate at a time like this that he step up to the top office."

I don't say much else, or even bring my concerns about him to the table. Frankly, over the last few days, the man set to rise to the summit of the city hasn't been on my mind.

The bigger concern for all of us is the fate of Drake. This is just another reminder of his disappearance, and with a new President being sworn in, his absence is once more pushed to the forefront of our minds. The rest of the dinner is a quiet affair, as we all reflect, none of us wishing to put words to our thoughts.

I know how dark they all must be.

When dinner ends, I find my mind returning to Senator Alber once more. As I aid Leeta in clearing the table, I ask her a question that's been lingering in my mind for a little while.

"Leeta," I say, drawing her eyes.

She looks up at me through her plump face. "Yes, young Theo. You have a request of me?"

"Just a question, really. About Senator Alber."

Her ample cheeks draw in as her mouth screws up. "Go ahead," she grunts, the name having a visible impact on her.

"Well, I was just wondering…was he in the Senate years ago, when the Watcher program was abolished?"

She thinks for a moment before answering.

"I believe he was, yes. He will have been fairly young, but as far as I remember, he was quick to establish himself under the new regime."

"Right. And do you know how he voted?"

"I'd have to check for you," she says. "That's something I don't know, Theo."

"OK, well could you find out and let me know?"

"Of course, I'll do so as soon as possible."

Once the kitchen has been cleared and Leeta has departed on her mission, Velia comes to me.

"What was that about? With Leeta," she asks suspiciously.

"Oh, just asking her something."

"What?"

"Just…something about Senator Alber."

"Alber? Are you still on that?"

"Well, there's no harm in being wary of the guy is there? If he's gonna be our next President I wanna know a few things about him."

"OK. And what did you want to know in this case?" she questions.

"Just his stance on us Watchers. I asked Leeta how he voted when the program was shut down."

"And?"

"She didn't know. Says she'll find out for me."

"Surely he'll have voted in favour of keeping it, right? I mean, he's the head of Defence…"

"Exactly," I say. "You'd think he'd want the strongest people possible at his disposal. Although…he wasn't head of Defence back then. But still, his stance shouldn't have changed."

"But you reckon he's voted against it, don't you? I can see how you're thinking, Theo."

"Well, if he did it would be pretty jarring wouldn't it? I mean, I don't know the guy at all, but this all just seems really fishy to me. Let's wait and see what Leeta says."

We don't have to wait too long. By the following morning, as we prepare to depart for our day training in the Grid, she comes bustling up from the main city square. My mother sees her coming.

"Leeta, is everything OK?"

"Oh yes, Cyra my dear. I just have some information for Theo."

My mother frowns and looks at me.

"Right, go ahead then," she says, listening in as Leeta comes to me.

"That thing you asked," she says. "He voted against the program."

I look at Velia, who raises her eyebrows.

"Did he now…" I say.

"Yes, quite an odd one actually," says Leeta. "I looked back at the record and he was quite vocal in speaking out against it. It appears he helped swing the vote away from President Stein and your grandfather."

At this point, my mother steps in, keen to clear up what's going on.

"What exactly is this about?" she asks firmly.

"Oh, nothing particularly exciting, dear," says Leeta. "Theo was just interested to know how Senator Alber voted when they abolished the Watcher program."

"Hmmm, was he," she says, looking at me. "And you say he was actively against the program?"

"Yes. All very odd. But it's typical of the man. He likes to cause a fuss."

"How do you mean?" asks Velia.

"Well, he's always poking around, being a nuisance in the Senate. Aeneas never liked him. Perhaps that's where my own aversion to him comes from. I am rather impressionable, you know…"

I share looks with the girls and my mother as Leeta continues to rattle on for a few moments, heading off on one of her typical tangents. Eventually, it's Cyra who calls an end to her ramblings, telling her we need to get to training, but that we'll see her for dinner later that evening.

"Beef stew tonight," she says. "It's one of my specialities."

"Every one of your dishes is a speciality," says Cyra with a smile. "Have a good day, Leeta."

She does a little bow and waddles off, leaving us to continue on with our day. I see Cyra's eyes dash around, checking that no one was close enough to hear the conversation. I do the same out of instinct, before we head back down towards the Grid.

Only once we're back to the safety of Underwater 5 does my mother bring up the conversation.

She turns to us in the quiet corridor, her eyes dark.

"I don't like what Leeta said up there," she says. "I can see in your eyes…you all have concerns about Senator Alber, don't you?"

The girls look to me. "Theo does," says Vesuvia. "He was going on about it the other night."

"Yeah, I was, and maybe I'm right. Mum, I've just got a bad feeling about this. It's all too convenient. President Stein was killed, and now grandfather's gone missing. This guy's about to be sworn in as our new President, and he's been actively working against Stein for some time…AND he voted against the Watcher program."

She listens intently, her eyes without judgement. Then she speaks, nodding as she does.

"I understand your concerns. You have a naturally inquisitive and suspicious mind, Theo. You get that from me. I can see exactly where your thoughts are taking you, because mine are starting to go in the same direction…"

"You think the same? That Senator Alber is on the Baron's side?"

"It's one possibility, among many," says Cyra

diplomatically. "This could just be a terrible coincidence. He could just be an ambitious politician, as so many of them are. Until we have any sort of proof of affiliation, we are only working with assumptions and speculation. They won't get us anywhere."

"I agree," says Vesuvia. "That's what I told him the other night."

"And you, Velia, what do you think?" asks Cyra.

Velia looks at me with those glossy hazel eyes.

"I guess…something does seem to be a little up. Just a feeling I'm getting. But nothing more."

"OK," says Cyra, her voice turning to a whisper. "All of you, keep your ears open. We need to focus on our training, and in searching this vision for the next attack. But stay vigilant, and if you hear anything suspicious about Senator Alber, come to me immediately. Understand?"

We all nod, before continuing down the corridor. Ready to begin another long day in the Grid.

It's hard to concentrate, though, as Cyra puts us through our paces. At least, at first it is. When I step out and battle a horde of incoming soldiers, I find my mind elsewhere and am quickly overrun. When I'm set against a bunch of mid-level Watchers, manifested by Eve, I'm unable to take them out as well as I should. And it's not because they've been designed to fight harder or swing faster; it's because my focus isn't where it should be.

Cyra, of course, is quick to notice, and reminds me

that losing focus in a real fight might not just mean my own death, but the death of those I care about too.

"Right now," she says, "you're the strongest Watcher in this city. That's a mantle you have to bear on your shoulders, Theo."

"But this is only training," I say. "In a real fight I wouldn't lose focus."

"Treat everything as if it's a real fight," she says firmly. "Isn't that what Athena taught you?"

I nod, unable to deny it.

"Then focus. Forget everything else. Narrow your mind and do what you have to."

I smile at the way she delivers her words.

"What's so funny? Do you think this is a joke?"

I shake my head, but the smile remains.

"No. It's just…you're so different," I say. "You sound like Athena."

The corners of her own mouth rise into a smirk. "Well, perhaps it's Athena who sounds like me," she says. "Remember, I trained her first…"

As it has so often, the thought enters my mind. My mother, in the training cave, teaching Athena to develop her powers all those years ago. In my quieter moments, when I have a chance to think, I'm still amazed by how fast my life has moved along, how quickly I've joined their ranks.

Still staring, Cyra's voice brings me back into the

room. “Now go again, Theo, and this time…focus.”

I nod. “Yes, Commander,” I say, before turning and re-entering the battlefield simulation.

By the end of the day, I’m feeling much better again, my abilities already beginning to flourish in this new training environment. Velia and Vesuvia are also making great strides, this being the first proper training they’ve ever received. It still impresses me how gifted they both are, given the lack of guidance they’ve had. Perhaps, in time, we’ll all end up as powerful as each other.

The thought once more brings Ajax into my mind. I hate the idea that he’s being left behind, that he’s not taking advantage of these new tools we get to play with. If Link is to be permanently crippled by his injuries, it’s down to his son to take his place.

I shake my head, the thought creating a swell of frustration inside me, and just as I do, a noise echoes from the main door. Three times, we hear a knock reverberate around the room, passing from one wall to the next and back again.

We look at each other and frown.

“Who could that be?” asks Vesuvia.

Cyra goes to open the door, but before she even opens it, I feel the frustration fading, and a smile building on my face once more.

I watch as the door slides open, and Ajax’s face appears before us.

“Sorry I’m late,” he says. “I think it’s time I joined the game…”

13
Back in the Game

I hang my arm around Ajax's shoulders, a large grin across my face.

"It's good to have you back, brother," I say. "The place hasn't been the same without your ugly face."

"Hey, you wanna try me," he says. "You've made a few improvements recently, but I'll catch up quick. You know I will…"

"Yeah, sure, but I'll always be one step ahead. You'll never catch me!"

"Sounds like a challenge."

We grin at each other, like little kids back in the woods again, when we'd face each other down and spar right there with only the squirrels and nesting birds for a crowd. In recent times, things have changed. But inside, there's still that love for action. For testing each other. For competition.

It's what's always made us grow.

Truly, though, the reappearance of Ajax has lifted a weight off my shoulders. More and more, I was beginning to feel the burden of all this. With Link out of commission, Drake missing, Athena over on the Deadlands, and my mother still rebuilding her powers after so long in the wilderness, I've been suddenly shunted towards the front of the queue of powerful Watchers.

Having Ajax back is a real pressure reliever for me. And with the girls making swift advancements, I'm already feeling a whole lot better. When we return home to our quarters that night, the growing tension in the air settles for a little while, Leeta's beef stew going down a treat.

Ellie, too, appears to be looking a little brighter, and the reason is another that gives me hope: Link's recovery is starting to speed up.

"They're not waking him yet," Ellie tells us as we eat, "but he'll be up and running again soon. His body is starting to respond to the treatment and fight back."

"Oh that's wonderful news, Ellie," says Leeta. "Link was always a fighter."

"Absolutely," adds Jackson. "I'll be looking forward to speaking with him about what happened. I don't suppose they'd consider bringing him out of his coma a little earlier?"

"I don't think it's worth risking it, not at this stage," says Ellie. "We want Link back, just as he was..."

"Yes, of course," says Jackson.

I can understand his desire to speak to Link as soon as possible. Clearly, any information he could provide would prove useful for Athena and her hunters. I wonder if there's word from her, and it's my dad who I call upon for an answer.

"She's been in contact with Markus," he says. "He told me she's raided a few known troublemakers in the area, looking for clues. By the sounds of it, they're all claiming they know nothing of any of this."

"What troublemakers?" asks Vesuvia.

"Oh, just local snitches and petty criminals that Petram keeps an eye on. A few of the Baron's known associates, however, have upped and vanished."

"Vanished?" I ask.

"Well, gone into hiding might be a better way to put it," says Jackson. "It's unclear as to whether they've done so to avoid questioning, or whether they're currently affiliated with the Baron's plans. Either way, Athena's not having much luck."

"Yeah, well, there's a lot of that going around," says Ellie. "But, let's keep our chins up. Things can only get better."

Her enthusiasm is welcome, and helps to prevent the conversation from becoming too morose. Yet still, I'm not quite sure I agree with her final assertion. As far as I see it, things can get a hell of a lot worse.

In fact, I'm convinced that they will.

When dinner concludes, I speak to my father alone, and once more ask him about any updates to Professor Lane's investigation. He tells me what he told me before, leading me to curse a little too loudly. The others look over as they clear up, before returning to their chores.

"Be patient, Theo. It'll come. But as the Professor said, don't put too much stock on the file. It may turn out to be nothing but a red herring."

"A red herring? We almost died getting that!"

"Yes, I know, and we all agree you four did brilliantly. But the fact remains, you mustn't let yourself get frustrated when things don't go as planned or expected. I've learnt over the years to only focus on the things you can control. You cannot control this, Theo, so don't let yourself get caught up with it."

His words are typically wise, and have the usual impact of pacifying my frustrations. The idea that the file might contain nothing of worth, however, isn't even worth considering. *Surely we didn't go through all of that for nothing?*

However, I take my father's advice and calm myself. Instead, I spend the rest of the evening catching Ajax up on things. And together with the girls we try to teach him what Cyra's been teaching us about searching our visions, putting our minds in the right frame to hunt down where this next attack might occur.

Turns out, Ajax has already seen a few flashes, just like the rest of us.

"Burning buildings," he says. "Bodies everywhere. People screaming. Yeah, I've seen that…"

"How clear?" I ask.

"Fragmented, but pretty clear."

"It's getting close now," whispers Velia. "We have to work harder."

We all agree that that's the only course of action, and return to our rooms that night with a renewed desperation to find some clue that will help us. When morning comes, however, and we gather in the kitchen, our body language makes it clear that no one has seen anything new.

That day, Ajax has his first full day of training since our time with Athena. The first thing that Cyra does is send him into the Grid, alone, to show him what will become of us all should we fail.

He comes out with stark but determined eyes, having seen all of us dead at the feet of the Seekers. For my mother's part, putting him straight into that simulation was a smart ploy. For the rest of the day, he's as focused as I've ever seen him, quickly regaining his strength and taking his powers to the next level. With the help of Eve and the wondrous things she can do, Ajax is going to flourish down here, just like the rest of us.

Over the last few days, our little team has fallen into a pattern of sorts. Now, with Ajax joining us, I see a fresh resolve imbue us all. His strength gives us strength, and over the next couple of days, we begin to make further strides in our training.

Cyra, too, appears to be rediscovering her powers. As we take a break and chat to one side in our little group, I feel Velia tapping me on the arm.

"Hey, check it out," she whispers. "The legend is back…"

I turn my eyes in the direction of hers and see my mother stepping into her own section of the hall in the distance. Amid the carcass of a rubble strewn city, I see a full force of soldiers approach her from all sides. They come forward, rushing close, attacking her in hand to hand combat.

We all stand in silence as we watch her dispatch her attackers, fighting them off with her fists and dodging bullets simultaneously. It's a display of power that I've only ever seen from the likes of Athena or Link or Knight's Terror.

"I guess the meds are wearing off," says Ajax, raising his eyebrows in a rare show of awe.

I smile with pride as I look at my mother, eliminating the final combatants around her. Then, suddenly, the simulation ends and her eyes quickly turn to us.

From across the hall, her voice echoes: "What are you gawping at? Get back to work!"

We all smile at each other, the comparison with Athena undeniable.

"Yes, Commander," we all call, before continuing with our day.

That night, when we all gather once again for dinner, Jackson takes us through the format for the following day. Tomorrow, much of the city will gather in the main city square for the coronation of their new President, sworn into office to take on the mantle during this terrible time.

"The Senate will vote in the morning, in private," he says. "Once the vote has been taken, they will gather on the stage in the main square, which is being erected as we speak. The new President will be sworn in and will make a short speech, outlaying his plan of action. We are all required to be there."

"Great," whispers Ajax beside me. "No training tomorrow then..."

"It's important that you dress well," continues Jackson. "This is an official city event and, afterwards, we'll be attending a private ceremony with the city leaders."

He looks over us all as we share looks and roll our eyes.

"I know it's not what you want to be doing right now, and believe me, I think all of our time can be better spent doing other things. However, certain city traditions must be respected. Any questions?"

I look around and see no one venturing forth with any queries.

"Right then, let's enjoy the rest of this lovely dinner that Leeta has prepared, shall we?"

We dive back into the meal, a sombre atmosphere once more weighing down on us. And in my head, a question forms, although I don't bring it to the table. Instead, I wait to catch my father alone once the evening has concluded.

"I have a question, dad."

“Fire away, son.”

“Well, what if Drake does re-appear? Will he be President again?”

“I’m afraid, once the new President is sworn in, that’s it.”

“But…that makes no sense. Drake is President.”

“He was,” says Jackson softly. “For a brief time, he was. And if he’d been given a proper run at it, he’d have made a wonderful leader of this country. But we have to realistic, Theo…I don’t think your grandfather is coming back.”

He offers a weak smile before turning away. And for the first time, it’s been properly vocalised. He didn’t say it in so many words, but it’s clear what he’s thinking. It’s the same thing that we’re all thinking.

Drake is dead. And we’re in this alone.

14
The Coronation

As has become the custom over the past week or so, we all find ourselves rising in the early morning and gathering in the large, open kitchen of our stately residence. Of course, for most of that time, it was only Cyra, the girls and I, eating a quick breakfast before going to the Grid. Latterly, Ajax has joined that little crew. This morning, however, Jackson and Ellie are also with us, and Leeta too.

We're all well dressed in fine clothing, provided by Leeta the previous day. I can't help but smile at the appearance of Ajax in a suit. Nor can I help myself from staring when I see Velia appear, a simple but alluring white dress hanging over her slender body. The twins emerge looking as identical as always, but I can always tell which one Velia is. Ajax, too, appears to be able to do the same, his eyes tracing Vesuvia's step as she wanders down the corridor.

Jackson doesn't hang around long, his duties as Governor and acting head of security for the city a perpetual drain on his time. Ellie also heads off early to get an update on Link's progress. Leeta, meanwhile, works on preparing a hearty breakfast, which the rest of us happily take advantage of. I'm quick to realise, however, that this morning my appetite isn't up to the task.

It's a sad day. A day where Drake's fate becomes politically sealed. And while we don't yet have confirmation of his whereabouts or condition, this is a clear drawing of the line in the sand that says 'he's gone, and he isn't coming back.'

We spend the morning waiting, with little else to do. Above us, right at the top of this very building, the Senate will be convening to cast their votes. And typical of political process, something that should only take a few minutes is likely to take a lot longer than that.

So, we wait, and talk among ourselves, until we're eventually summoned by Jackson to assemble outside. When we step out of the building, the main square has already grown busy, many of the city residents drawing together to see their new leader take to the stage.

The security is typically tight, and I see the Watchers who accompanied us from Petram stationed here and there under the instructions of my father. Cyra, too, has been liaising with them regularly since they arrived, giving them some of the same advice and training we've been receiving, particularly with regards to searching their visions. It seems that she's leaving no stone unturned in her attempts to hunt down the site of the next attack.

The square, while busy, isn't anywhere nearly as packed as it was during President Stein's funeral. Then, it was positively overflowing with mourners.

Today, there's a similar atmosphere of dread creeping around the place as there was then, the city, while ostensibly safe, still in the grip of fear.

As then, the city leaders take their positions on the front rows ahead of the main stage. Many of those from the regions have gathered, Governors and Mayors and other luminaries awaiting their new President. Up on the stage, however, the seats are as yet unfilled, waiting for the Senators to spill out with the result of their ballot.

We take front row seats, everyone around us just as well dressed as we are. I note the girls shuffling uncomfortably in their attire, alien as it is to them. But as Velia sits down to my left, I can't help but whisper to her: "That dress suits you. You look…nice…"

I turn away fast, feeling immediately embarrassed for having uttered such words. She appears equally abashed, a rare trait for her to display. With a little bit of pink glowing on her cheeks, she turns from my abbreviated gaze, setting her eyes back to the action ahead with a small smile.

On my other side, Ajax sits. He doesn't look overly comfortable in his suit either.

"I can't wait to get out of this thing and back to the Grid," he whispers. "We're wasting time here with this nonsense…"

I don't disagree. We're on the clock here, and every hour counts. Wasting valuable training time on an event like this, at a time like this, is frankly infuriating.

But, as Jackson has told me over and over again, it's no good for me to get frustrated by it. I can't control it, so all I can do is let it happen. That's the philosophy he's trying to ingrain in me. Although it's not one that's settling fast.

Still, Ajax's irritation somehow makes me feel better. It's a perverse thing, really, but I actually find myself relaxing as he stares forward through his scowl. It's as if I'm letting my anger breed vicariously through him, giving me free scope to remain calm.

Soon enough, a rumble flows though the crowd as the doors to the Senate building open. The swarm of men and women come pouring out, strolling casually to the stage and taking their seats. At the back, the two main candidates, Senator Alber and Senator Doryen, are last to sit, taking their positions right in the centre of it all.

I look at the two men, and it doesn't take me long to figure out which is Senator Alber. He stands taller than Doryen, an arrogant smile swamping his face. He's younger, too, perhaps only in his early or mid fifties, a suit tightly fitted to a healthy looking frame. With perfectly coiffed hair and bright white teeth, he carries a smarmy look that makes him instantly dislikeable.

It's clear, too, that the vote has already been announced to the Senators. Doryen, an older and more kindly looking man, holds a more deflated expression, and while he's trying to hide it, it's clear from his eyes that he's been defeated.

As they sit, another of the Senators takes the front of the stage to announce the winner.

"Ladies and gentlemen. After much deliberation, and a final vote, the Senate have chosen your new President. Please welcome to the stage, President Alber…"

There's a muted sound of applause as Alber stands and takes the front of the stage. After a brief ceremony where he repeats a few oaths to uphold the office, and ensure the safety, custody, and future prosperity of the city and nation at large, he stands before us, alone.

His eyes pass over the crowd as he prepares to speak, drifting from the masses to the luminaries sat before him. And all the while, that self-satisfied look stays planted to his face.

"Ladies and gentlemen, boys and girls, I stand here before you to take this office at this sad time," be begins. "In recent months we have lost two great men, President Stein, and Vice President Drayton. It is with regret that I feel the need to take on this challenge, but I will do everything in my power to see it through."

I share a look with Ajax. "He seems pretty convinced that Drake's dead," he whispers. "You think he knows something we don't?"

I don't like the complete assumption, that's for sure. And I don't like how he called him '*Vice* President' either. Sure, that's how he spent most of his political career, but for a brief time he was acting President, and should be honoured as such.

His speech continues, passing quickly from the past to his vision of the future. When he begins to speak about the security of the city and nation, I feel my fists balling up at his words.

"As you all know, this city has been strangled by fear recently. Certain important figures have been killed. But that is in the past, and now we have to look to the future. We cannot continue in this vice of grief and dread. We have had many months without incident. It is time we began to move on with our lives."

I look down the line at my friends, and see them shaking their heads. Cyra stares at the new President angrily. Jackson scratches his chin, looking on pensively. And the more he speaks, the more my suspicions about him begin to grow.

The only thing I can be grateful for is the fact that he doesn't go on too long. Once he steps away from the front of the stage, we're all forced to our feet to applaud. Once more, the clapping is hardly rapturous, a subdued energy among the crowd that was always likely to accompany this affair.

With the crowd beginning to disperse, I gather with my friends and we immediately begin talking about what he said.

"He's going to slacken security," says Velia. "He pretty much said it himself."

"Is he mad or something?" grunts Ajax. "What, so because there hasn't been another attack he's just going to assume everything's OK again? What about my dad and Drake?"

"Exactly. That was only a couple of weeks ago. And we've had these visions too. Does he know about that?" says Vesuvia.

We all shrug, and bring the question to Jackson.

"I have been keeping the Senate filled in on all our goings on, yes," he says. "It seems there's some doubt among many of the Senators as to the importance and validity of these visions. Some of them find it hard to understand these things."

"Right…and I'm guessing our esteemed new President is among them?" I ask sarcastically.

"I'd caution against such words, Theo," says my dad. "As acting head of security, I'll make sure the city remains well guarded. Yes, President Alber has his doubts, but that isn't unusual. Until we have definitive proof that this attack is coming, we have little to go on."

I let out a deep sigh and say a few calming words in my head. Jackson moves off to greet our new leader, while the rest of us begin filing back towards the Senate to be shipped to its summit for a banquet. Frankly, it's the last thing I want to do right now.

We spend the next few hours in the room where President Stein's wake was held. This appears to be a more formal affair, however, with tables set out for a grand dinner, the place decorated for the more joyous occasion. For me, though, this is even more of a wake than Stein's. Because right now, we're here to celebrate the death of reason and logic.

I'm not surprised to find that Ajax, the girls and I

are positioned right at the far end of the room, hidden away from the main action. Jackson, given his position, is afforded a place closer to the top table, while Cyra and Ellie's status also gives them a decent spot. I suspect that both of them would rather be back with us, though, rather than rubbing shoulders with the politicians who have taken over the running of the country.

Still, It gives us all a chance to continue our secret discussions, the four of us now growing ever more convinced that Alber isn't someone we can trust. Any time someone comes over to speak with us, however, we're quick to prise ourselves from our debate and engage with them. Many of them are keen to meet the twins, very few of them aware that Troy had two daughters. The girls, however, don't appear too comfortable with all the attention they're getting, so alien as it is to them.

As the evening progresses, and the formalities break down, I spot the new President coming our way. He glides from group to group, working the room, his eyes linking with mine on occasion as he draws near. Then, with no one left between us, he comes right towards me, leading with his hand.

"Theo Kane, we're yet to meet, young man," he says.

I take his hand and he grips it firmly, does a quick double shake, and then lets go. He performs the same with Ajax and the girls, offering his condolences where necessary regarding Troy, Drake, and Link.

"I hear your father will be OK, though, Ajax?" he asks.

"That's what the doctors say," says Ajax in his own blunt fashion.

"Well, that's good. Let's hope the road to full recovery isn't too long."

He says all the right things, but all in the wrong way. His delivery is off, the tone of his voice sending shivers down my spine. I immediately know what Leeta has been talking about. There's just something very unpalatable about him, an obnoxious and superior air that exudes from his every pore.

"So, how do you like the city?" he asks. It's an open question, designed for all of us.

"It's wonderful, sir," says Vesuvia politely.

"It is, isn't it. I hear you've been exploring quite a lot?"

His eyes narrow a little. The girls exchange a look. This time, Velia answers.

"Um, a bit, yes sir. Leeta was kind enough to show us around when we arrived."

"Hmmm, yes, I know about that. But you've all gone further than that, haven't you?"

His eyes turn from one of us to the next. We fall silent as the rumble of conversation drifts from the other side of the room.

"Let me ask you this, children," he says condescendingly "Do you know what happened when we voted on the fate of the Watcher program many years ago?"

"It was abolished," I say blankly after a short hesitation.

He smiles, and his eyes open up wide. "Ah, exactly. You know your history, Mr Kane. Now, the program remains in the same state as it has since that day. It is still abolished, and illegal. Do you understand what that means?"

None of us answer, unwilling to rise to his patronising tone.

"It means, boys and girls, that Underwater Level 5 is officially off limits. I know that you've been going to the Grid every day. And I know that Mrs Drayton has been training you. That, I'm afraid, is illegal."

I feel my head shaking, my eyes narrowing, and my heart beating wildly. I can't help what I say next, despite who I'm talking to.

"Are you joking," I say, unable to stomach the nonsense he's spouting. "Do you have any idea what we're up against?!"

"Mind your tongue, Mr Kane," he says, his voice lowering. "Training Watchers is an illegal act. Underwater Level 5 has been shut down. On this occasion, I will let you, and your mother, off with a warning. However, should you continue to circumvent my authority, I will have no choice but to expel you all from this city. Do I make myself clear?"

"Yeah…good luck if you do that," snarls Ajax. "You think you can defend yourself against what's coming? We're your only hope."

"Oh, child, how naïve of you to think that. I understand that you are young and ignorant and looking for adventure. But this city is perfectly safe, and there is no great threat out there that we cannot face."

"You're a fool…" I whisper.

His eyes burn, spitting flames. He looks at me with total indignation.

"What did you say to me!"

I look him straight in the eye, refusing to turn from his glare, and merely smile.

"I didn't say anything, Mr President," I say, standing tall. "Congratulations on your new appointment. Now, I think it's time my friends and I were off to bed. It's late and we are just *children* after all…"

I turn away from him, and we move through the crowd. When we get to the door, leading to a corridor filled with lifts, I spare a look back and see his gaze still on me, eyes still burning.

If he has it his way, soon enough this city is going to be burning as well.

What a damn fool…

15
Expelled

We sit around the main table in the kitchen, discussing the day's events. The question that we're trying to answer is: *what the hell do we do now?*

"Keep training, I'd say," announces Ajax, back to his belligerent best. "If he wants to kick us out of the city, let him. We'll see how they do without us."

Velia offers another argument.

"We need to do what he says," she tells us. "Honestly, we have no choice. We don't want to make an enemy of the new President. We have enough of those as it is."

We discuss the two options briefly, but all end up agreeing that Velia's right. Even Ajax, after venting, allows his logic to take charge once more.

As the evening grows a little later, Ellie and Cyra return. We're quick to inform them of our little run-in with President Alber.

"Yes, he told me the same," says Cyra. "I suspected this would happen at some point."

"So, what do we do?" we ask.

"There's nothing we can do but keep searching for the next attack. Maybe then Alber will realise our worth."

That night, further flashes come to me of the city burning. But my mind is too wired, my thoughts all over the place, that nothing settles. I think I see water, splashing on one side, but can't be sure what it means.

It's a loud knock at the door that wakes me. Ajax, too, opens his eyes abruptly at the sound. I say 'come in' in a raspy, early morning croak, and Jackson's face appears.

"Right boys, get your stuff packed up. We're moving out."

"Wh...what?" I say, the fog in my head clearing.

"This residence is reserved for the President. We have a new one now, so we're out. Get your things, and gather in the main hall."

We do as ordered, pulling together our meagre possessions and going to the hall. The twins appear too, looking tired with their hair all over the place and eyes still half closed.

"Did he have to chuck us out so early," yawns Vesuvia.

"It's OK. We're only moving up a few floors," says Jackson. "The place will be smaller, but it'll fit us all just fine."

We're led as a troop down into the main foyer, before getting in the lifts and heading up to the eighth floor. There, down a long corridor, we find that an apartment has been prepared for us. As my father said, it's smaller, but only by comparison to our previous home. When compared to any other place I've stayed, it's still a real palace.

We drop our things in our new rooms and get settled in before taking a look out of the window. There, down at the foot of the building, I see my mother in conversation with a few guards. It looks heated.

Then, my eyes turn to see more soldiers coming in, weapons raised. Behind my mother, I see the six Watchers from Petram standing in a group, taking positions of defence against the incoming soldiers.

"Jeez! Do you see what's going on down there!" says Vesuvia.

"We need to help..." says Velia.

I'm already on it, turning and rushing out of the residence and towards the lifts. The others trail behind me, just jumping inside before the doors close. The metal box quickly drops down to the ground floor, before opening back up and releasing us into the foyer.

I run quickly towards the main doors, and as soon as they open, the sound of voices fills the air, an argument in full force.

"These men and women are here for our protection!" shouts Cyra.

"I'm sorry, Mrs Drayton...but we have our orders."

"What orders?" I ask, rushing forward. Immediately, several soldiers raise their weapons to me, my friends stepping in behind.

“Stay back, Theo,” calls Cyra. “Stay out of this.”

“No! I want to know what’s going on?”

The main soldier looks at me, his eyes nervous. “We have orders to return these men and women to Petram. They are here illegally.”

“Illegally? What the hell does that mean?” asks Ajax.

“They are Watchers,” says the guard, “trained against the wishes of the Senate and the abolition of the Watcher program. The President has ordered that they be expelled from the city and returned to where they came from.”

“But they are here to protect the Senate, for God’s sake,” says Cyra. “Is your new President so stupid as to turn away such guards?”

The man doesn’t answer. In fact, he looks torn, barely knowing what to do or where to look. The other soldiers, now numbering in the dozens as they surround us, appear equally unsure of what to do. Only the Watchers, standing within their cordon, look on with fierce eyes, their expressions unwavering.

“I’m sorry, Mrs Drayton, I have to follow my orders.”

“Where is the President?” asks Cyra firmly. “I need to speak with him.”

Now, another voice enters the fray. From the building, Jackson comes rushing out, calling for calm.

"Everyone, lower your weapons right now," he says, moving right between the circle of soldiers. He turns to them all, his hands raised out ahead of him, gesturing for them to lower their arms.

The soldiers look at each other nervously.

"I am the head of security for the city. Now do as I say."

Slowly, their weapons are lowered. Jackson moves towards Cyra and the guard ahead of her.

"Major…we are all on the same side here. What on earth are you doing?" he asks, his voice a harsh whisper.

"Governor Kane…as I told you wife, I have my orders. They come right from the top."

"President Alber has ordered the Watchers out of the city," says Cyra. "He considers them to be here illegally. It's madness."

Jackson considers things a moment.

"And where is the President?" he asks.

"I'm right here…" comes a loud voice behind us.

We turn, and see President Alber stepping out of the back of a luxurious and armoured hovercar. Ahead and behind, a convoy of security vehicles let loose their occupants, heavily armed guards flanking him as he walks towards us.

"Mr President," says Jackson. "Is this true? You are expelling these men and women from the city?"

"I am," he says dispassionately. "The termination

of the Watcher program is still in place. These people have been illegally trained on Petram, and have no place here in Eden."

"But, sir, they are here to protect us. To protect you..."

"We have no need for such protection, Governor," says Alber. "As you can see, we have more than enough guards and soldiers in the city. These people are to be sent back to Petram where they belong. And they should think themselves lucky. I have half a mind to arrest them, and have Athena arrested for her part in all this as well."

"Arrest Athena!" laughs Ajax. "I'd like to see you try."

Alber's eyes flash on Ajax in anger. Then he turns back to Jackson and Cyra, his voice lowering.

"I suggest you keep these children in check," he growls. "They have also been training illegally. I will give them a pass, because of the things you have done for this country...but know that my patience has its limits."

He takes a breath and plants a smile on his face.

"Now, see to it that these men and women are returned to Petram. And Governor, I trust my residence is ready?"

Jackson nods without speaking.

"Excellent. Now, continue with your duties. And don't question my authority again."

He turns and begins walking towards the Senate

building, not even looking at my friends and me as he passes. And, gradually, the tension in the air begins to clear, and the soldiers around us start to relax.

I see Cyra go over to the Watchers to pacify them as Jackson looks at me, a flame behind his eyes.

"Theo, come here, I need to talk to you."

I move over towards him, and he lowers his voice.

"I've just had a communication from Professor Lane," he whispers.

My heart flares. "She's unlocked the file?!" I ask quickly.

His eyes glance around.

"Quiet," he says. "We need to keep this between us. She didn't tell me exactly what, but she's found something that may be of interest." He leans in even closer, his voice going even quieter. "I'll come for you tonight. We'll be seeing her in secret. Don't tell anyone for now, OK? Not even Ajax."

"OK, dad. I'll keep it quiet. I promise."

"Good. Stay awake, and come to the kitchen at 2 AM. Then we go."

I nod, and he lifts his body up to its full height once more, before moving over towards Cyra and the Watchers to see them on their way back to Petram. I return to my friends.

"What was that about?" asks Ajax.

"Nothing," I say. "He's just not sure about Alber

either," I lie.

"Well, that makes about ten of us then," he says.

I put on a slightly fake laugh, my mind now stuck on a single thought: *the fruits of our labour are about to be realised...*

16
The Cabal

In the darkness of my new bedroom, I check my watch. *1.57 AM.*

As silently as I can, I slip from my bed and put on my clothes. Across the room, Ajax snores quietly, enjoying an untroubled phase of sleep. These days, such things are rare. I'm glad he's stumbled upon one.

Silently, I creep across the room and open the door. Outside, a shard of light spills in from the corridor, illuminating Ajax's face. His eyes scrunch up a little, and he shuffles his position. Quickly, I slide through the crack and shut the door tight.

When I reach the kitchen, I find it empty. I pour myself a glass of water and gulp it down, just as my father emerges from a dark corridor.

"You ready?" he asks.

I nod.

"Good. Let's go."

The city is quiet as we cross it. We pass by soldiers here and there, still maintaining a vigil on the city at night, but they do little to hinder us. Given my dad's position as head of security, seeing him out at this hour isn't completely unusual.

It also allows him access to just about everywhere in the city, save those places that have now been locked down. Among them is the entirety of Underwater 5, making it impossible for us to get to the Grid, even if we wanted to.

We move into the lifts, and drop into the depths of the great city, emerging at Underwater 3. Now, all is dark and quiet, unlike when we first came here. The labs ahead are empty, their daily occupants asleep up on the deck above. We move through the level without seeing a single soul, heading down the long corridor towards the inner wall of the level.

My dad enters his keycard, which for some reason I think won't work. Thankfully, it does, and through the large security door we go, straight into Professor Lane's lab.

It's quiet inside, the hum of activity absent. All of the machines that would usually be whirring away are silent. Only the large screens ahead remain active.

"Good. You came," comes a voice from beneath them.

Emerging from the shadows to one side, the elderly figure of Professor Lane appears. It seems that she's the only one here.

"Come forward," she says. "And let's get to this."

We move towards the screens, empty of data this time but glowing a pale white. Beneath them, the various computers appear to be off. All except one.

"OK, Professor," says Jackson. "What do you have for us?"

She sits in a chair, and begins typing on the computer, speaking as she goes.

"We've been working at decoding this thing for days now," she says. "However, we've only cracked a portion of it. Most of what we've found is as I suspected, just science relating to the creation of the clones. It's quite beautiful work, really, but doesn't help us."

"So, what does?" I ask.

She swivels on her chair and looks at me.

"Names," she says.

"Names?"

She nods, and swivels back.

"We have uncovered and deciphered a portion of the file that discusses the financials of this venture. It seems that Baron Reinhold isn't alone out there…"

She taps a few more times, and up on the screen, a list of names appears. There's got to be a couple dozen of them, all under a single heading: *The Cabal.*

"The Cabal," says Jackson, looking at the screen.

"Yes," says Professor Lane. "It looks like that's what they call themselves, a given name for this particular band of baddies. It seems that many of the rich who were expelled from Eden after the war are on the list. Some I recognise. Others are alien to me, perhaps secret names or aliases. I suspect, in the cases of the latter, that these men are still operating under the nose of Eden and our new regime."

I look at the list, and quickly scour the names. None of them mean anything to me. I turn to my father, who is doing the same. He nods at a few of them, and shakes his head at others.

"I recognise some of these too," he says. "They were loyal to Knight and fled the city, just like the Baron. It appears we have a bunch of very wealthy and powerful men working together on this. It's much worse than I thought..."

"Worse...I didn't think thing could get worse," I say.

"Well they just have. These men have a great deal of combined wealth. Enough to buy soldiers and mercenaries. Beyond these Seekers, we could be facing an army."

OK...it's worse.

I turn again to the list, and scan my eyes down it for a second and third time. Then a fourth, just to be sure.

"Damn...I thought he'd be there. Well, hoped, anyway," I say.

"Who?" asks Professor Lane. "What are you talking about?"

"Our great new President," I say. "I was sure he was working for the Baron."

"Alber?" says Professor Lane. "That's a little far

fetched."

"Hmmmm, not so much," says Jackson. "He does seem adamant that we weaken ourselves at this critical juncture. Only today, he ordered six Watchers from the city, and has actively prevented Theo and his friends from training. It's an odd move at the very least."

"Odd indeed," says Professor Lane, "but not necessarily incriminating. Alber voted against the Watcher program years ago. It only stands to reason that he'd still be against it."

"Yeah, but at a time like this?" I ask. "We need all the help we can get."

"True, but these politicians don't think like that. Some of them will deny it all until their final breath. Alber has always had an unhealthy distrust of Watchers. He's foolish, yes, but on the Baron's side…I'm not so sure. What could he gain from it?"

"The Presidency," I say quickly. The others go quiet and look at me. "All these leaders were killed, to help destabilise us. But maybe the idea is to plant some of Knight's old allies in the top jobs."

"To weaken us," says Jackson, nodding. "And divide us. It would make any coup far easier to achieve."

"Exactly," I say, delighted to hear my father beginning to agree with me.

He looks back at the screen and starts shaking his head.

"I just don't know," he says. "We'll just have to

keep a close eye on Alber, and try to find any links between him and the Baron. And these other names…we need to discover all we can about them. But we have to be discreet. That is absolutely essential."

He turns again to Professor Lane.

"Winifred, do what you can. And keep trying to decode the file. There may be more evidence inside it that we can use."

"Yes, of course."

"But make sure nothing you find leaves this room. Work on this alone if you have to. I want as few people involved as possible. Only use technicians you can completely trust."

She nods again. "I understand."

Then he turns to me.

"The same goes for you, Theo. I don't want you talking to your friends about this…"

"But dad, they can be trusted. And they can help. The girls, they know the Deadlands well. Maybe they can help with these names?"

He considers it a moment.

"They have a right to know," I add. "We got this file, remember. You wouldn't even have it if it wasn't for us."

He looks at me and nods. "Fine. But it goes no further than them, OK?"

I nod. "And mum?"

"I don't see the need to worry her, or Ellie. Not right now. They have enough on their plates, and won't be able to contribute anything that the others can't. Until we have something more concrete, you all need to keep looking for this new attack."

"OK, got it."

We don't stay there much longer, leaving Professor Lane in her lab, and returning to the surface. I go back to my room to find Ajax still sleeping quietly, but struggle to drop off myself. By the time I do, it's already growing early, the first light of dawn arriving outside.

I only get a couple of hours in the end, but wake feeling completely alert. With no training to go to, I gather the twins and Ajax in our room, and fill them in on what happened the previous night. They listen closely, before coming to a similar conclusion to Jackson.

"This is bad," says Velia, her eyes narrowing.

"Real bad," adds Vesuvia, her visage identical.

"Do you have names?" asks Velia.

I draw out a scribbled note from my pocket, on which I'd quickly written down the list of names before we left the lab. Ajax scans it and, like me, appears to recognise none of them. The girls, however, nod at a couple.

"You know one?"

"A few," says Velia. "This one, Lord Kendrik…"

"And that one, Count Lopez," adds Vesuvia,

pointing to another.

"You know them both?" I ask. "Professor Lane and dad didn't recognise them."

"God, why do these people have such stupid titles," mutters Ajax. "Baron this, Count that..."

"Because," says Velia, "they're fake names. These people are criminals like the Baron. But they probably have real identities over in the regions. I don't know, maybe they're legitimate businessmen?"

"There's more," says Vesuvia. "They were at the Watcher Wars."

I think back, and an image rushes into my mind. That of two well dressed men emerging from the Baron's residence with him. I guess it's no surprise that they're part of all of this too.

"Those guys we saw," says Ajax, putting words to my thoughts. "Those two guys with the Baron..."

"Yep, Lord Kendrik and Count Lopez," says Vesuvia. "Maybe the Baron's gone to one of their secret hideaways?"

A thought strikes at me, and my words rush out.

"When we found Link, his car had come from the regions," I say, thinking quickly. "And you say these two men might lead double lives, on the regions and Deadlands?"

"It's possible," says Velia.

"OK...so if that's true, then maybe they do have a secret hideout, like Vesuvia says, some place in the regions where Link had come from. Maybe Drake and Link had tracked them there, and that's when they were attacked?"

The girls nod.

"Makes sense. But that doesn't help us find it."

"Well, if we can find out who these men really are, then maybe we can?" I say. "There's gotta be a database of information that we can look at, old photos and stuff. We know what they look like, right? We saw them at the Watcher Wars. Maybe that'll help us track them down?"

"Yeah…" says Velia, nodding. "I like it. At least it's something, right? A lead to follow."

"Exactly."

The trick, of course, is finding this database and looking through it without alerting anyone as to what we're up to. Naturally, Jackson is my point of call when seeking aid on this matter, so that evening when I next see him, I take him to one side and update him on what the girls have found. I tell him my theory, and watch as he nods along to my words.

"That's a good idea, Theo," he says. "If we can find anything, an old residence or something, then we can have Athena go check it out. All we have to do is find out who these men are, and then work from there."

Once more, my father's security clearance is extremely helpful. That same evening, he takes us all down to the archives on Underwater Level 2, leading us towards rooms of cabinets filled with files and vast networks of information. Sifting through all of that, however, would take weeks, so we quickly find ourselves gathering around a computer and searching the online database.

The question is, where to start.

"Known Knight sympathisers," I suggest.

"The search field is too large. We need to narrow it down," says Jackson. "And, in any case, aren't we looking for men who we think are loyal to this regime?"

"Yeah…you're right," I say. "Can you search by wealth? These men are all rich, aren't they?"

Jackson begins typing away, and soon enough a list of several hundred men and women appear, the richest and most powerful people across the country.

"OK, that'll do. Girls, over to you."

Jackson moves to one side, and the twins step in closer, with Ajax and me on either side. One by one, they click through the pictures, passing dozens of them without stopping. Occasionally, one of us will say 'stop', and we'll peer closer at the man in question, before agreeing that we don't recognise him and move on.

That goes on for quite some time, before we finally pass by a face that has us all saying 'stop' simultaneously. We stare forward at the man and smile.

"That's him," says Velia. "That's Count Lopez."

"Are you certain?" asks Jackson.

Both the girls nod.

We look at the man's real name. Ricardo Alvarez.

"Do you know it, dad?" I ask.

He nods slightly. "It rings a bell. He's a wealthy landowner and industrialist," he says.

We keep on going, searching for the second man, and soon enough we discover him too. Lord Kendrik, otherwise known as Lucius Gray, another man that my father has heard of.

"He's a builder…" says Jackson.

"A builder?" asks Ajax, a little confused. "I thought we were searching for the super rich…"

"Oh, we are. He's not just any builder. He's built towns across the country. He helped us to rebuild much of the areas that were affected by Knight's rule. I don't understand why he'd turn against us?"

"Maybe he was never with us in the first place," I say. "Maybe both these men have been pretending all this time, biding their time just like the Baron. We need to find out where they live. We can send Athena to find them."

"I don't think it'll be that easy, Theo," says Velia. "They'll be off hidden somewhere with the Baron by now. They know we have the file. They must know we'll crack it open eventually. I doubt they're gonna just be waiting for us at home. And anyway, they've probably got a million addresses…"

"I agree with Velia," says Jackson. "We'll record the information we need and send it to Athena. It'll give her something to hunt, at least."

Feeling like we don't want to outstay our welcome, we quickly extract any relevant information and begin making our way back up through the city. As we go, I feel a strange surge of excitement fill me, a sensation that I haven't had in some time. It's a feeling that we're making progress. That, finally, things are starting to come together.

And that, maybe, we'll be able to hunt these people down…

It's quiet and late as we pass back through the central square and into the Senate building. Into the lifts we go, rising up to the eighth floor, and stepping out into the corridor. When we reach our residence, Jackson walks in first. Immediately, Cyra rushes forwards.

"Oh, Jack, there you are!" she says.

He moves in quick and we follow behind.

"What's the matter? What's wrong?" asks Jackson hurriedly.

Her eyes scan us and find Ajax's face.

"No…nothing's wrong," she says, stepping towards my friend. She smiles at him. "It's your father, Ajax," she says. "He's woken up…"

17
A Legend Awakes

"He's awake…" whispers Ajax.

Cyra takes his face in her palms. "Yes, he's awake," she says excitedly. "Your mother is down there now. I've been waiting for you to return."

"Well, what are we still doing here!" says Jackson. "Let's go see the man…"

Leaving Velia and Vesuvia in the residence, we all quickly make our way straight back out of the Senate building and towards the hospital, situated nearby. I can barely believe how the last couple of days have turned out as we rush through the city. From seeing a new president take the oath, to finding out about the Cabal, to this new revelation that Link's awoken, so much has happened in so short a space of time. Truth be told, it's difficult to process it all at once.

Right now, though, all other matters are pushed to one side. For the likes of Ajax and Ellie, the head of their family waking up is of huge emotional significance. And while the rest of us are similarly happy to see him come out of his coma, there are other pressing matters that we need to attend to. Finally, we're going to find out what he knows.

When we reach the hospital, and rush towards Link's room, we look through the window to see Ellie sitting beside his bed, holding his hand.

"You go in alone," says Cyra to Ajax. "We'll give you a moment."

Ajax nods, and from the window we watch as he paces inside and moves to his father's beside. Immediately, Link pulls him into a hug, his mountainous body clearly weak and still in pain. The grimace on his face as Ajax grips too tight makes that clear for all to see.

We stand as a family for a few minutes, watching the reunion, before Ellie waves us in from outside. In we go, Link's dark brown eyes tracing our steps as we enter.

Jackson and Cyra step forward. My mother gives him a kiss on the cheek. My father extends a hand.

"It's good to see you, old friend," he says.

"We've all been so worried," says Cyra.

Meanwhile, I stay quiet at the back, watching things unfold. Waiting impatiently for someone to begin the questioning.

After a few more minutes of small talk, it's not surprising that it's Jackson who dives in first. The change in his tone is noticeable, his body language turning more serious and business-like. He fixes Link with a stare and asks: "What happened out there?"

A silence hits the room. I can almost hear the thumping of my heart in my chest; feel the pulsing of the veins in my neck. I watch closely as Link's eyes go cold and blank, his expression growing more severe. Then, from his lips, his deep voice sounds.

"It's hard to remember," he says. "There are only fragments…as if I've woken from a dream, and I don't know what's real and what isn't."

"Do you remember where you were?" asks Jackson. "When you were attacked."

He shakes his head, racking his memory. "Somewhere…near the Deadlands…close to Knight's Wall."

"What were you doing there?"

"I…I can't remember exactly," he says. "Drake and I were tracking leads in the area. Then, we were attacked." His eyes turn to Jackson, then Cyra. "Drake…is he OK?"

A fresh silence briefly swamps the room.

"We don't know," says Jackson. "We were hoping you might be able to tell us."

"I…I don't know," he says, still struggling to recall what happened. "We were attacked. There was a flash, it seemed to come from nowhere. I don't remember much else."

"We found you near a car," I say, stepping towards the foot of his bed. "It was riddled with bullets, pointing in the direction of Petram and away from the regions."

"Yes," he says, nodding a little. "I remember

getting to the car, driving away. But…I don't remember Drake being there. I wouldn't have left him…"

"It's OK, Link," says Cyra. "We know you'd have done all you could."

"I'm so sorry, Cyra," he says. "I can't remember much else…"

"The doctors said this might happen," adds Ellie. "His body has suffered enormous trauma, and sometimes memory can be badly effected. It may return in time, or it may not. We'll just have to wait and see."

"There's more," I say, desperate to eek out any more details. "When we first brought you to Petram, the doctors brought you out of your coma, just for a few moments. You said one word…Knight. Do you remember that?"

"No. I'm sorry, Theo. Why would I say Knight?"

We all look at each other.

"What's been happening since I've been under?" he asks. "Someone, tell me…"

Where to begin, I think to myself, as Jackson once more takes the lead. With a few additions from the rest of us, my father quickly catches Link up on the main happenings of the last few weeks. The revelation of these Seekers, these clones of Knight, is naturally what hits home the hardest.

"The Watcher who attacked your home in Lignum," he says. "He was a clone of Knight? One of these Seekers?"

"We believe so," says Jackson. "There are four, and there were four attacks. But they're just the tip of the iceberg. The threat is much larger than just them."

"We think you were attacked on the Deadlands by the Seekers," I add. "That's why you said Knight when you woke from the coma. We thought you'd seen a face that looked like him…"

"I guess that makes sense," he says. "But, I don't remember the attack."

"It must have been them," says Ajax. "No one else could have taken you and Drake down."

We all agree on that point. But regardless, Link's testimony so far has proven a little underwhelming. Somehow, I thought that he'd have more to say. Perhaps he'd know where our enemies were hiding out. Something…anything to go on.

In the end, however, we don't learn a great deal beyond what we already know, and end up leaving Link to rest some more. Returning to the residence, I update the girls on what happened. They seem equally disappointed as I am, though we don't show that off to Ajax. For him, having his father wake up is all that matters. And while that's important to me too, it's frustrating that he hasn't been able to offer any useful information.

"So, we still don't know what happened to Drake. And we don't know exactly where he was attacked. And we don't know who actually attacked them. Is that all of it?" asks Velia, summing things up.

"Pretty much," I say, sat in their room. It's just the three of us, no Ajax this time. She probably would have chosen her words more carefully had he been with us. "But…we have a few more dots," I continue. "Think about it, he said he was somewhere near Knight's Wall, and they were following leads. Maybe there is a secret base in the area that they got too near to? Maybe that's why they were attacked?"

The twins both nod. "Yeah…a hideout owned by Lord Kendrik, maybe. He's a builder, right? Maybe he's built a hideaway somewhere for the Baron?"

It all makes sense, but until we find information that might lead us to a possible location, it all just remains as nothing but speculation.

That night, my mind is too unfocused to pursue the vision of the attack. As I now know, when your mind is too busy and when your thoughts tumble all over the place, you're unlikely to hunt down any specific details within a vision. The following morning, I discover that the same has happened with the girls and Ajax, the latter's thoughts too focused on his father's recovery to effectively search the future.

Only Cyra, experienced as she is in such things, is able to offer anything new. She looks a little more haunted that morning, dark patches around her eyes suggesting she had a rough night.

"It's growing near," she tells us. "Very near now. I fear we're unprepared to do anything to stop it…"

She retreats into her own thoughts again and

returns to her room.

"She was tossing and turning all night," says Jackson. "She's beginning to struggle again, having these visions night after night. They're growing stronger…"

"But that's good," I say. "We need her strength, her foresight."

"But at what cost?" he asks. "Her mind has suffered so much. There's only so much it can take."

"We have no choice, dad. None of us do. You know that."

He nods and smiles at me. "You're growing wise, Theo," he says. "You'll make a great leader one day."

"Thanks, dad," I say. "That's assuming I live long enough."

A frown settles over his eyes and he takes my shoulders in his hands. "You'll live long enough," he says firmly. "You'll love long and happy once this is all over. We all will."

I can only hope that's true.

That day, with no ability to train or do anything much of use, we find ourselves lingering around the apartment. Jackson, busy as always, heads off, while Ellie and Ajax spend much of the day with Link. The twins and I, however, stay at home, unable to do much but continue to speculate and wait for something to happen.

Cyra mostly hovers around in the residence too. She advises that we utilise our time trying to fill our minds with the torment we've been seeing in our sleep. It's an unpleasant thing to do, but it needs to be done. She knows all about that.

When evening dawns, Jackson brings up fresh news from the Deadlands.

"I've spoken with Athena about what we found. She has already identified a few locations owned by Lord Kendrik and Count Lopez, or Alvarez and Gray…whatever you want to call them. Hopefully she'll have some success."

"Where are these locations?" I ask. "Anything near Knight's Wall where we found Link?"

"I don't believe so," he says. "But it's early days. Perhaps she'll catch a break and find a better lead."

Staying in that apartment, I begin to get cabin fever. With everything building up, bubbling to the surface, I begin to feel useless being locked up on the eighth floor of the Senate building, just waiting for things to happen. The following day, I accompany Ajax on his visit to Link in a bid to find out if he knows anything else.

I ask a few more questions of him, and he seems even more frustrated than I am that his memory is so hazy. For such a great warrior, who's dedicated his life to helping people, simply sitting and recovering in that hospital bed is tantamount to torture. Unlike when I saw him the other night, there's a palpable frustration inside him that's clear to see. No longer does he look tired and weak. His face has morphed back into that of the relentless warrior I know, his body quickly regaining its strength.

As we sit there with him, he looks to the corridor outside.

"OK boys, I need to stretch my legs…"

For the first time in weeks, he plants his feet to the floor and slips from his bed. Gingerly at first, we help him out into the corridor. When a nurse sees him, she quickly attempts to guide him back to the room. He waves her away and continues, his posture gradually rising and growing stronger with every step.

When we step out onto the streets, he takes in a long breath of fresh air and looks up to the large domed roof above us, the sky shining bright and blue beyond.

"It's odd, seeing this place after so many years away," he says, looking around. "I never liked it much."

"Well, hopefully you'll be back out there soon," I say, delighted to see him on his feet again. Then I broach a topic that I know hasn't been mentioned to him yet, a sensitive subject to say the least. "Do you think…your powers will all come back?" I ask.

His eyes slowly slide down to mine. His jaw sets, and that alone tells me his thoughts on the matter. Still, he offers a few words as well.

"Theo…my powers *will* come back," he says firmly. "I'm not going to let a few bullet holes rob me of them."

I look at Ajax, and we smile at each other.

"It's good to have you back, pops," he says.

Link smiles a rare smile, and looks around at the world that was so nearly taken from him. "It's good to be back, son."

Seeing Link literally back on his feet helps to lift our spirits that night. It's one thing seeing him lying in his bed. It's another entirely watching him walk out into the street, his expression growing with resolve with each passing moment. I know that he'll be back in fighting shape soon. The question is, will it be soon enough?

My mother doesn't think so, convinced as she is that the attack is imminent. And that night, when I find myself in the silence of my room, the evening late, I realise that's she's right.

With my mind once more cleared and primed for the task, I drop into an uneasy sleep that brings images of fire and death and destruction to me once more. This time, there's nothing blurred and indistinct about it. It's real, so real I can reach out and touch it, like one of the manifestations in the Grid.

Around me, fire rages, consuming buildings as they burst and crumble. People rush about, screaming, shot down by bullets. I see soldiers now, enemy soldiers, all dressed the same. But not soldiers of Eden. Different soldiers. Mercenaries. Bought by the Cabal. Sent to destroy.

But they're not alone. Among them, I see a

familiar cloaked figure. Dark eyes peer from under a black hood. Skin as pale as snow shines out, stark against the dark outfit. He stands amid the carnage, completely relaxed, not reacting at all to the destruction around him.

And then, as the world falls to chaos, the vision fades out.

And my mind jumps wide awake.

18
Time Grows Short

"Any day now…it's happening," I say rapidly. "And it's not just a few people either. It's a small army…and they've got a Seeker with them."

I stand in the kitchen with my parents alone. It's still late, the dawn a way off, and the city below continues to sleep. But not us. As soon as I saw what I did, I had to tell them.

"Right. But you still don't know where?" asks Jackson.

I scrunch my face up. "If I'd travelled a bit more, maybe I would. If it was one of you, maybe you would," I say. "But no, I have no idea. All the buildings were engulfed in fire and were being destroyed. It was carnage, dad…chaos."

"OK, but we know it's a major city, right? The streets around you suggest that? And the number of people?"

I nod, and so does Cyra. "It's definitely a major city," she says. "And most likely near enough to us for it to be clear. One of the coastal cities, perhaps, or another sea city…"

"Or here?" I ask. "What about here?"

Jackson quickly shakes his head. "No. We're too well guarded here. No one can get in."

"Are you sure about that? Didn't you manage to infiltrate the place back during the war with just a few people?" I say, looking at my mum.

Cyra nods. "That's true…"

"But the city has changed a lot since then," says Jackson. "There are no weak entry points, certainly not enough for an army to infiltrate. In any case, you'd both recognise it if it were Eden. The place has a unique structure, and the people dress in a unique way. By the sounds of it, these people in your visions were dressed in less formal attire?"

Again, both my mother and I agree on that point.

"Fine. Then we need to send out warnings to all the major urban areas along the coast and out to sea. We'll redirect soldiers to them as protection and to offer us some forewarning of any attack. Until we know exactly where the strike will occur, that's the best we can do. I'll speak with President Alber immediately."

Jackson doesn't like to wait around. Within minutes, he's dialling Alber's secure line. I hear the urgency in his voice down the phone as he speaks with the President's new Chief Secretary who we all know well.

"Leeta, I need you to wake him immediately. Tell him I'll be down in five minutes."

He slams the phone down, apparently not giving Leeta a chance to respond, and sets about getting himself dressed.

"Can we come?" I ask as he prepares to leave.

"No, stay here," he says. "This is a matter of security and it'll be easier with just me. We know how Alber feels about you both right now."

Begrudgingly, we watch him leave without being able to contribute.

"He's right you know," says Cyra. "We're walking a fine line with Alber. It's best we stay out of his way."

"I guess. Do you know what happened to the Watchers in the end? The ones sent back to Petram?"

"I spoke to Markus. He didn't exactly like what was happening here, but sounded happy to have his people back. I suppose they'll be useful for Athena if she wants to use them, or just in protecting Petram. Honestly, I've half a mind to go and join them. I'm getting a bad feeling about being here..."

"Me too, mum. Maybe we should, now that Link's on the mend? You hate it here anyway. And you know, I'm kinda starting to feel suffocated here as well. Have you mentioned this to dad?"

She shakes her head. "He's head of security now. And he's committed to keeping a stable government in place."

"I don't see why. Now that Alber's taken charge I'd say we just leave them to it. We'll have a better chance linking up with Athena and her Watchers. I don't like how we're divided like this. It weakens us."

"You're right," she says, nodding. "Perhaps that was Baron Reinhold's design all along. Maybe that's just what Knight wanted. Divide and conquer. He tried exactly the same thing during the war. Luckily, it didn't pay off. He was too blinded by his arrogance to see his death coming."

"And now…he's living again," I say. "Through these clones."

"They have his strength, perhaps…but they can't have his mind. That was twisted over many years. These clones, they're just kids really."

"Yeah, kids bred to be just as twisted, mum. You didn't see what I saw over there. The Baron had a shrine to Knight. He worshipped him. Those clones would have been fed nothing but hate for years, living down in that dungeon. They won't know anything else but to do what they've been taught."

"To create chaos…" she whispers.

I nod. "To bring this world to its knees. It starts with this attack."

As we talk, we hear footsteps coming back down the hall, storming forward. Jackson comes through the door, his face thunderous.

"What happened?" asks Cyra, rushing up to him.

"He wouldn't listen," growls Jackson. "He's a belligerent fool, and he's going to get a lot of people killed."

"He won't beef up security?" I ask.

"No…he doesn't believe in your visions. He said he doesn't want to cause any further fear among the people. The man's blind. He's tying my hands behind my back here. There's nothing I can do."

"Then maybe we *should* leave," I say, looking at Cyra.

"Leave?" asks Jackson.

"Yeah, why not!" I say. "We're getting nothing done here. We're just hiding. Let's gather our strength in Petram…and hunt these people down."

"Your son might be right, Jack," says Cyra calmly. "What good are we doing here? Link is safe to travel. I think it's time we moved on."

"But this attack? We cannot leave the people to suffer…"

"Oh, we won't," says Cyra. "We'll always defend them. When the attack comes, we'll go and help however we can. And then…we won't come back to this city. There's a shadow coming back to these streets. It's time we stepped back into the light."

Outside, the faintest glow begins to shine through the window, the sun bringing the world to life. Jackson walks towards the glass and looks out at the streets, yet to fully wake. He must know by now that he's done everything he can here. That the threat is out there, and we have to face it head on.

As he stands there, I watch him closely, and gradually see his head begin to nod.

"OK," he says after a period of deliberation. "I've had it up to here with this place." He turns around, and looks at his wife. “Cyra, we’ll do it your way.”

As morning continues to dawn, we inform the others of our decision. Each of them appear immediately sold on the plan.

“I’ll speak with Link,” says Ellie. “He’ll be happy to see the back of this place too.”

“Good,” says Jackson. “Girls?”

He turns to Velia and Vesuvia, who share a look as they always seem to, utilising their special telepathic powers. Both nod at the same time, and turn back to him.

“This place is boring now,” says Vesuvia.

“Yeah, without the Grid, what’s the point in being here?” adds Velia.

“So you’re on board?” I ask with a smirk.

“And you, Ajax? Anything to add?” asks Cyra.

“I think we’ve had enough talking. Now it’s time for action,” he says.

“I guess that about sums it up,” laughs Jackson.

We quickly consider if there’s anyone else we should take with us on departure, and one name immediately springs to mind.

“Leeta,” I say. “She’d rather do anything than have to work for President Alber.”

“I agree,” says Cyra. “I’ll mention it to her, and see what she says.”

“OK, but be discreet about it,” warns Jackson.

"With her proximity to the President, it's dangerous. I don't want him hearing about any of this. When the attack comes, we'll ship out to do what we can. And then...we won't be coming back. Now come on, let's get to work."

For the rest of the day, we set about preparing ourselves to make a hasty retreat when the time comes. Ellie and Ajax go to the hospital. Jackson continues his duties in order to keep up appearances. Cyra sets about informing Leeta of our plan. Only the twins and me are left in the residence, little for us to do but wait.

I go over the vision I had the previous night again in my head several times, sitting alone in my room. It's so close I can almost touch it now. At any moment, it might be happening, the fighting suddenly breaking out under our noses.

I know that most of these visions are impossible to identify. The number of times I've seen someone killed as I sleep, unable to do anything about it, has blunted my mind to such things. What once was a horrifying experience has now become the norm, my reaction rarely more than a feeling of cold impassiveness as I try to determine where and when the offence is taking place.

And with this vision, one that has plagued us all for days, the same risk applies. If none of us can find out where it's going to happen, and when, then we might just wake one morning to find that a city not far away has already been obliterated.

Only this time, it won't be a single person being

killed by a thief, or a family burning in a house fire. This time, it will be an entire city that suffers the consequences of our failure.

We cannot allow that to happen.

So all that day, I sit alone, and I search my mind for more clues. Sitting in complete silence, I enter a state of total concentration, searching the future, dedicating every ounce of my mental capacity to the task. But as the hours go by, all I see is the same thing as before. The same destruction. The same carnage. Just memories embedded inside me of a vision that's yet to take place.

Eventually, I'm broken from the spell by a knock at the door. My father walks in and shuts it quietly.

"Professor Lane has asked to see us again, Theo. We cannot wait this time. Come on."

I'm quickly off my bed.

"What's this about?"

"She didn't say. Now come."

This time, we don't wait until the hour is late and the streets are clear. There is no need for such subterfuge now, the pieces all moving fast and furiously. With a speed to our step, we quickly descend back down towards her lab, motoring along the closer we get.

When we enter, the place is once more alive, a number of technicians busily working away as early evening advances. Once again, the Professor waves us straight over to her computer, where she sits in her swivel chair.

"Ah, that was very quick," she says. "I thought you might be coming down later."

Jackson looks around and lowers his voice so that no one else can hear.

"There's no time, Professor. Things have become urgent."

"Urgent? What's the rush?"

"I'll tell you in a moment. Now what do you have?"

Her face crinkles into a smile. She gently dabs her glasses a little further up her nose.

"Well, I hear you're looking for a secret base," she says. "And I think I might have found it."

19

The Secret Base

I look at the large screen positioned above Professor Lane, just as I did several days ago. Then, it was covered with a list of names. Now, I see a vague schematic that makes absolutely no sense to me at all.

"We uncovered this inside the file," she says. "From the layout and design, I can determine that it is a subterranean facility, and quite a large one at that. I have a suspicion that Baron Reinhold is basing his operation from this site."

"And what makes you say that?" asks Jackson.

"I say it because it has been built by one of the names you gave me, Jackson. Lord Kendrik, or to give him his real name, Lucius Gray. He appears to be the Baron's right hand man, and this facility is his."

"OK…so where exactly is it?" I ask excitedly.

"Its location isn't exact, but we've found clues that it's situated somewhere along Knight's Wall. Are you aware of Lucius Gray's main role within our current government?" she asks.

I certainly don't know. My father doesn't appear to either.

"Well, as you *are* well aware, Lucius has been instrumental in helping to rebuild some of the infrastructure of the regions, in particular. Mainly, his role has been in creating towns and other settlements after the war."

"Yes, I know that. What's the link?" asks my father.

"Well, it appears that much of the brick and mortar used for the construction of these towns and settlements have come from the skeleton of Knight's Wall. Obviously, there was a lot of raw material there going completely unused..."

"Oh yeah!" I say, breaking the conversation. "I remember Drake telling me about that...when we came here for the first time, dad, from Petram after Troy's funeral. Drake told me that Knight's Wall was basically being recycled."

"Yes, absolutely, that's a good way of putting it," continues the Professor, my interruption not causing her to lose her stride. "Lucius's primary function has been taking the wall down, and then using it to build up some more functional structures that we can actually use. And, in doing so, he's had free reign over huge swathes of Knight's Wall, without so much as a single government official actually monitoring his activity."

"And...you believe he's taken that opportunity to build this facility somewhere along it?" asks Jackson.

"Precisely. But not just anywhere. From what we can decipher, this facility looks to be suspiciously close to where Link was discovered. I'm not saying for certain that the Baron is there…but somewhere along that stretch, you'll find this base."

As she talks, her words fade, and my mind turns back a few weeks.

"Oh my God…" I whisper.

It's loud enough for the others to hear. Their eyes lift to mine as I stare forward at the schematic.

"What is it, Theo?" asks Jackson keenly.

"I…I think I know where it is," I stammer.

"Well…don't keep us in suspense, dear boy," says Professor Lane sharply. "What do you know?"

"I saw it…well, I think I saw it," I say, my mind jumping ahead. "When we left Petram with Link in the medical plane a few weeks ago, Athena gave me a pair of telescopic goggles. I was just playing around with them, you know, looking down on the lands and stuff as we flew. I remember…when we passed over the skeleton of Knight's Wall, there was a section still being dismantled. At least, that's what it appeared like…"

"But the wall *is* still being taken down in places," says Jackson.

"I know…but this was near where we found Link. And, I remember seeing the glint of a weapon. Someone down there was carrying a gun. I didn't think anything of it then, but now it makes so much sense. Without those goggles, I never would have seen it. It's as if Athena knew…"

"Do you remember where it was?" asks Jackson. "I mean, exactly where it was. It's hard to determine from that height..."

"Oh...I think I remember," I say, smiling.

They both look at me quizzically.

"It was at the base of The Titan's Hand."

It's a place that needs no explanation. Immediately, both of them begin to nod, the pieces quickly coming together.

"Yes...yes that must be it," says Professor Lane. "Trust these men to build a base beneath such a striking monument..."

"And it's smart, too," adds Jackson quickly. "That rock formation is never visited. The people still have some strange superstitions about it, and it's extremely remote, and yet still fairly centrally located within the country. From that point, you could quickly strike out at the regions or the Deadlands, whatever takes your fancy."

"Well done, young man," says Professor Lane. "And trust Athena to have given you those goggles. She's got wonderful foresight, that one."

"Just like Drake," I say. "He knew things were going down at the Watcher Wars. That's how we found the file in the first place. And it's where we sighted the Baron, and Lord Kendrik too."

"Well, if your grandfather is alive, that's where he'll be," says Professor Lane, pointing a crinkly old finger at the schematic. "How will you proceed?" she asks Jackson.

"With caution," he says. "I don't want this going any further than the three of us for now."

"But what about Athena?" I ask. "She could be there in no time. If Drake's alive we need…"

"No, son," he says, cutting me off. "If this place is really ground zero for these people, then Athena and her Watchers will not be enough. We'll need to gather our full strength to stand any chance at all, and form a watertight plan to make our assault. That takes time. If Athena finds out, she'll go straight in. She's powerful, yes, but she isn't a strategist, and she's got a reckless streak that refuses to die. This must stay between us, understand?"

"Yes, sir," I say.

"Of course," says Professor Lane. "Who would I have to tell anyway?" she adds with a smile.

"Well, it might just slip out," says Jackson. "Now, back to what I was saying before, Winifred." He leans in closer. "We're planning on leaving soon. There's something not right about this place, and we're doing no good here twiddling our thumbs. We need to get out there and take action…and I suggest you come with us."

"Yes, I thought that might be the case. I'm not surprised, really. But I consider my place to be here. I've become part of the furniture in this lab. It's all I know, really…"

"Ah, that isn't true, Professor," says Jackson. "You lived on the Deadlands for quite some time. Have you never thought about returning?"

"On occasion. I do miss the high valleys sometimes, and the mountain air of Petram," she says wistfully. "It can get terribly stuffy down here."

"Then come with us," says Jackson again. "And continue your good work elsewhere."

"I suppose I could. Nothing would stop me from returning, if that's what I wanted. I'll think about it, dear boy. There may yet be more secrets to uncover in the file."

"That's all we can ask," says Jackson with a smile. "But I urge you to think quickly. I get the feeling that things are about to move fast."

Before we leave, my father gives the old Professor a hug. It's a reminder for me just how much she's helped him over the years. Not just now, with this file, but with his bionic arm, and with my mother's medication. She's done some wonderful things, and continues to be of great use.

"Be safe, Winifred," he says to her, kissing her gently on her wrinkled cheek. "I'll see you again soon."

"It's you, Jackson, who needs to be safe out there," comes her retort. "I know what you're facing. Please, don't put yourself in any unnecessary danger."

"Me? I wouldn't dream of it," he says with a rare, impish grin. "Now get packing," he says as he guides me towards the door. "We'll take a walk up in the mountains when all this is over..."

With that, we walk through the security door and

out of the lab, back into the long, quiet corridor towards the lifts. It's growing late now, most of the other labs closing down for the night.

"It's funny," I say, "how life seems to go on, even under all this shadow."

"What else can we do?" he asks. "We can't let fear change us, son. We have no choice but to go on."

"I guess. Was it the same during the war?"

"There are similarities, for sure. But back then it was very widespread. It all started small, like pebbles that start an avalanche. Soon enough, though, all the regions were sucked into it. When that happened, life stopped for almost everyone. The country stopped functioning."

"Maybe the same thing will happen again," I say, thinking once more of the enemy soldiers, of the burning city. "The only difference now is that we're the ones occupying Eden. We're the ones in power. I guess that can easily change…"

"I'm afraid that's the nature of the world. Empires rise and fall. Kings and rulers lay waste to the lands, only to rebuild them for themselves and their subjects. Humankind is constantly fighting over territory and power. This is just the latest chapter in that endless book. And I'm sure there will be many more."

"That's actually a kinda comforting way of looking at it," I say, shrugging. "It makes you think that you're not that important. That your entire life will just be a blip and nothing more…"

"In the grand scheme of things, yes," says my father, stopping me as we walk. "But your life means everything to me. And it means everything to your mother. And your friends, and everyone who cares about you. It's the same for us all. And that's why we fight. It doesn't matter if no one remembers us in a hundred years time. What matters is now. This is our time, and we are going to make the most of it."

He holds me firm for a second, his hands on my arms, before turning me back towards the lifts. On we walk, strolling casually despite everything, talking of the wider world and our place within it.

"It's strange to think," I say, "how my whole life has been so quiet, just living in those woods. And now, here I am, right in the middle of all this. I think, sometimes, that I brought this on us. I wished for this, dad, for something big to happen. For some crazy adventure. But this is real life. I feel like I was a kid back then…I know it sounds weird, because that was only months ago, but I feel like I've changed."

"You have changed," he says immediately. "I see it daily, you growing into more of a man, and Ajax too. And you can't blame yourself for wanting adventure. All young men do. It's a rite of passage and only natural. All of this would have happened anyway, always remember that. Think of it like this: maybe it's fate that the two of you fought to unleash your powers. It might just save us all…"

We reach the lifts, and step inside, the metal box swiftly shooting up towards the deck. When we step out, the streets beyond the perimeter wall are starting to clear. Here and there, people continue to return home from work, some looking exhausted, others with more of a spring in their step. But across all the faces I see, there's a growing calmness and relaxation. Clearly, President Alber has done well to soothe their concerns, loosening up the grip of fear that's bound this city for so many weeks.

I wonder how many of them know what's really coming. Maybe none truly do. Here, on this seemingly impenetrable fortress in the ocean, the people are burying their heads deep in the sand once more, their collective ignorance rebuilding.

They think this place is safe? They really have no idea.

But, in the end, maybe that's best. Because there's a limit to how much fear people can take and still go on. If they really knew the threat that was out there, this place would shut down, and the people would do nothing but hide in the homes, waiting for the heroes to rise.

And as we walk, my eyes lift up, and I see one of those heroes, standing in the middle of the street. Her blonde hair flows from side to side as she looks in all directions. Her blue eyes are wide and wild, searching for something. Searching for us.

When we she sees us, she immediately comes running, pacing as fast as her legs can take her. My heart bolts from my chest at the sight, her words tumbling from her mouth as she runs.

"New Atlantis," she shouts, breathing hard.

She grinds to a stop in front of us, and takes a moment to catch her breath. Then she fixes her eyes on her husband, and says again.

"New Atlantis…they're about to attack New Atlantis!"

20
Battle Begins

My mother's eyes are manic, bright blue and shining in the fading light of the city. She stares at my father, and repeats her words again.

"They're about to attack New Atlantis!"

"Are you sure?" he asks quickly.

"Jack, I'm certain. I just saw it now…I recognised an old building. It's coming at any moment. We have to act!"

"Right…come on, follow me!"

My parents turn and begin running straight through the streets as I follow in behind. Ahead, the Senate building looms, in the distance beyond the main city square. People watch us as we dash past them, eating at little restaurants or strolling casually through the open courtyard. Soon they'll know that the world isn't yet safe. Once more, fear is going to grip tight at this place.

We take no notice of their stares and whispers, our eyes set on the building ahead. Outside, the many soldiers that guard it allow us quick passage through the archway, Jackson shouting for them to open the doors and let us through. They do so without hesitation.

Inside, my parents continue straight up towards the stairs ahead. Reaching the top, my father's hand begins banging loudly on the large double doors to the residence we have recently vacated. A few moments later, the door opens, and Leeta's face appears.

"Jackson…Cyra…what's going on?"

"We need to speak with President Alber urgently," says my father.

"I believe he's eating his dinner…" says Leeta.

Jackson steps right past her, his eyes turning towards the rear of the house where the main dining room is situated. Unlike our time here, where we chose to dine in the kitchen, President Alber is sure to use one of the more stately rooms of the house. Jackson knows that all too well.

"Jackson…you can't," says Leeta as we pass. Getting no reaction, she turns to my mother. "Cyra…what's happening?!"

My mother has the same tunnel vision as my father, following him right in. Only I stop to briefly inform Leeta as to what's going on.

"Mum knows where the attack's coming from," I say quickly.

"Where?!" she asks, eyes widening with worry.

"New Atlantis. We need to warn the people and get troops there immediately…"

I continue on, leaving Leeta behind, and rush to

catch up with my parents. Through the palatial residence we go, down long corridors and through large halls until we reach the back. Without knocking, Jackson storms through a door and into a grand dining room. Sat alone at a solid wooden table is President Alber, his eyes rising in confusion at the sudden interruption.

"Governor Kane," he says, a glass of wine clasped between his fingers. "What is the meaning of this?!"

"Sir, we have confirmation that an attack is about to take place in New Atlantis. I urge you to send troops there immediately."

He plants the wine glass to the table.

"What confirmation do you have?" he asks. "I have heard nothing…"

Cyra steps forward.

"I have confirmed the location in a vision, President Alber," she says, trying to stay as respectful as possible. "We've been searching for details for weeks, but now I am sure – New Atlantis is the target."

The President lifts his wine back to his lips and shakes his head.

"Mrs Drayton, I've heard enough about these visions that you and your group seen to have. I will not go sending troops to New Atlantis, and risk causing a panic on a hunch…"

"Sir, I can assure you this is more than just a hunch. You must be aware of the abilities we Watchers possess?" says Cyra calmly.

He doesn't appear to have an answer. I watch him, my anger brewing, as he sits back and considers things a moment.

"And how do you know that this so-called vision of yours is real? It could very well be a dream and nothing more. I'm afraid I cannot act until I have definitive proof..."

"Mr President, once you have definitive proof it will already be too late," says Jackson. "We have to act now, or many lives will be lost. Please, I urge you to see reason."

"Governor, I appreciate that you support your wife on this matter. But this country isn't run on visions and hocus pocus. That is not how my office is going to operate. Now, please...let me enjoy my dinner in peace."

Standing behind my parents, I see them looking at each other, a fury raging behind both of their eyes. But neither of them act upon it, both of them maintaining their composure. In the end, they don't need to.

Because from behind, a fresh set of footsteps comes clattering down the corridor. We all turn to see Leeta catching up with us. In her hand, she holds a small communicator.

"Sir, you have an urgent call..." she says, rushing in, her eyes haunted.

Alber lets out a noise of exasperation and takes the device. He lifts it to his ear, and on the other end we can hear the scratchy voice of a man shouting.

"Hello…" says the President. "Who is this?"

"Sir…they're coming…" comes the tinny voice down the line.

Alber's eyes raise to ours briefly.

"Confirm. Who is this? Where are you?!"

"Major Benson…sir…they're coming…"

More static crackles, the sounds of screaming and rushing people filtering down the line. And then, two final words come from the end of the radio.

"….New Atlantis…"

The communicator shuts off, the room falling silent.

Then, in the quiet, Jackson's voice growls.

"How's that for confirmation," he says.

Alber lifts his eyes to us again.

"Go…" he says quietly. "Defend the city."

Without so much as a word or nod, Jackson spins around and storms quickly out of the room, the rest of us running behind him.

"Cyra, go to the main hangers immediately. Prepare the jets for take off," he orders, talking as we go. "Theo, go up to the apartment and get Ajax and the girls. Meet me outside as soon as you can."

"And what about you?" I ask.

"I'm going to gather my strike force. We have no time to wait… now go."

We split immediately, shooting off in separate

directions and leaving Leeta behind, calling for us all to be careful.

I quickly go to the lifts and click the button for the eighth floor. Seconds later, I'm bursting through the door to find Ajax and the twins sat in the kitchen.

They look at me, panting and wide-eyed.

"Theo…what's going on?" asks Velia.

"The attack…it's happening."

"WHERE!" she shouts.

"New Atlantis. We're leaving, right now. Get your things."

They rush to their rooms, returning moments later with their bags. Meanwhile, I fetch the bags prepared by my parents, as well as my own. After this, we don't intend to be coming back to this city unless we have no other choice.

Within only a minute or two, we're rushing back out of the apartment and towards the lifts, frantically talking as we go.

"How do we know?" asks Vesuvia. "Did you see it?"

"It was my mother," I say. "She recognised a specific building in the city…it's happening right now."

"What about my mum?" asks Ajax.

"Where is she?" I ask.

"In the hospital with dad," he says.

"Good. They'll join us when it's over. We're going to stick to the plan. My father is gathering his strike force right now..."

We reach the ground floor and discover that Jackson has been quick to work. Outside the Senate building, a number of soldiers have gathered, with a convoy of military cars awaiting us. Jackson barks orders as they step inside. His eyes turn to us.

"Good, you got the bags. Now get in the cars."

We pile in as he takes the wheel, snaking through the city at great speed. The streets are gratefully clear, only a few stragglers still out and about. They watch us pass with wailing sirens, knowing that something big must be happening.

Soon enough, we're exiting the tall skyscrapers and are rushing across the wide open expanse outside of the aircraft hangers. Several of them sit open, figures rushing in and out of them. I peer forward and see Cyra issuing commands, making things ready for a speedy departure.

We come to a quick halt and spill out, the gathering of soldiers quickly sent towards one military jet or another. I count at least a hundred of them, perhaps more, all heavily armed and ready to rock. Taking our things, we move into the central hanger and climb aboard one of the aircraft. It's bigger and more bulky than any others I've been in, a thick shell of armour surrounding it, heavy duty guns and turrets fixed to its flanks.

Inside is a large space, mostly open, with benches running down each side of the plane. A number of highly trained soldiers have already boarded, sitting in a line and getting themselves mentally prepared for battle. Jackson moves in to speak with them as Cyra takes us off to one side.

She opens up a large trunk, inside of which are specialist outfits.

"These are for you. They will expand to your size and fit well. Professor Lane has been working on them specially for us."

She picks one out, a black bodysuit that looks like it offers full body protection.

"The material is bulletproof, and will deflect just about anything unless it comes from point blank range. It's infused with a special absorption technology that will take the brunt of any round that hits you, so you won't be knocked back unless by a very heavy duty weapon or explosive round. The only weak points are at the joints. Be aware, however, that high powered guns from close range can still do serious damage. These are a failsafe, and nothing more. They are not a free pass to be reckless. Understand?"

We nod as she passes them around, Professor Lane having once more proven her considerable worth. The twins and Cyra move off into a private area to strip down to their undergarments, before dressing and reappearing, dressed in pure black. Soon, we're all clothed in the fabric, lightweight and surprisingly comfortable as it hugs the body tight. Jackson, too, gets a set, needing it far more than we do, while the rest of the soldiers make do with their more traditional body armour.

I forget, sometimes, that my father has no such ability to see into the Void or dodge bullets. He merely relies on his superior weaponry skills and military experience, leading his strike force right into the fray. Of everyone, it's he who I should be worried about most, more vulnerable as he is. And yet, there's something in his eyes that calms me.

It's a look that says: don't worry, I've done this a hundred times before.

As the plane begins rumbling its way out of the city, accompanied by several others, we sit down on the benches as Jackson hands us all our weapons. They're highly advanced, with the ability to fire various types of rounds, from regular high velocity bullets, to incendiaries and explosive rounds. Thankfully, we've all had ample opportunity to train with them in the Grid, so need no further instruction.

We sit together in a line, shooting through the sky at a tremendous speed. Outside, the world is dark and covered in black cloud, the stars and moon hidden from view. Down the plane, Jackson stands ahead of his soldiers, issuing a rousing speech designed to psyche them up for battle.

Ahead of us, Cyra stands, clothed in black and carrying her gun, blonde hair tied back and blue eyes half hidden behind a tight glare. She's worlds away from the quiet woman from Lignum. Before us stands the warrior from the stories of the past.

"I don't want any of you doing anything stupid out

there," she says. "You have all trained well, and are all supremely gifted. But you won't have faced anything like this before. Danger can come from anywhere at any time. We will move together as a team, and take down whatever threats we face. We are the tip of the sword. These people are relying on us."

We all nod and set our jaws.

"We'll do whatever it takes," says Ajax.

"Good," says Cyra. "And if we should come across one of these Seekers, we fight together. That will be our only chance."

The plane rumbles, shaking as it passes through a thick band of cloud. Outside, rain begins falling, the heavens crying down as bloodshed once more spreads through the world below.

His speech over, Jackson moves towards the cockpit at the front of the plane, Cyra joining him. I look over at the soldiers, all of them older than the four of us, and consider how brave they must be. Out there, they won't see danger as we do. They won't be able to avoid a stray bullet, or a shard of shrapnel. If an explosion rips apart the ground at their feet, they'll be dead before they know it. They won't have a chance to change that fate, to run and duck and dodge from the perils that bombard them on the battlefield.

And as I look at them, I know that I will do everything I can to save as many as possible. Not just these brave soldiers, but the innocent people down in the streets. Men and women have been sent here to kill and maim and slaughter. To cause the sort of carnage and chaos that Knight's legacy promises.

And our job is to break that legacy down. To stop it before it even gets started.

From the front, a call comes out: "Three minutes to contact."

Faces firm up even more. Eyes grow more intense. Grips tighten around guns, fingers lingering on triggers. I look through the small window behind me and see nothing but black, the odd strike of lightning now storming from above and giving momentary shape to the clouds.

Another call comes: "Two minutes to contact."

I feel my heart surging inside me, but my breathing remains calm. I look over to Ajax, staring straight ahead in complete focus. My eyes swing to the twins, their youthful, pretty faces in start contrast to where they're going, what they're about to do. Anyone else would think they don't belong. But they do. They were born for this like Athena was.

"One minute to contact."

I turn and look towards the front of the plane, and stand to my feet. Through the open door to the cockpit, I see my parents looking out ahead. Still, there's nothing to see but black clouds beyond the windows.

I find myself walking towards them, needing to get a closer look. And soon, among the black, the hues of red and dark orange begin to glow.

And when we emerge from the clouds, I see the reason.

The city of New Atlantis is already burning.

21
Face to Face

"Right, get ready!" shouts Jackson, marching back into the belly of the plane. "We're landing right in the action. Helmets on!"

I see the soldiers place protective helmets over their heads. Quickly, Cyra passes out some of our own, lightweight like our bodysuits and fitted with radios so we can communicate.

"Follow me, straight out," she says. "On your feet."

We rise and turn to face the rear door to the aircraft as it swings into position, hovering over the landing pads in the docking area of the city. Below, flames glow outside of the windows, the sound of gunfire and explosions already audible above the roar of the storm.

We descend fast, hitting the ground with a thud. To our left and right, other transports land, turrets firing as we go, clearing a path for us to safely get down to the ground.

A second after we settle, the rear door opens and extends down, creating a ramp into the carnage. Immediately, a view of the city in the distance is revealed, the high towers of New Atlantis wreathed in flame and belching smoke into the black sky.

"Go, go, go," calls Jackson from the front, stepping off the plane first with his strike force following behind. At the back, Cyra leads our own team of Watchers, her eyes narrow and focused as we exit the plane. On the ground, the other soldiers move in tight formation, quickly taking up covering positions as their commanders converge on Jackson. We move in too, hidden behind the blockade of the external city wall amid the docks, the city beyond being ravaged by an unknown number of assailants.

"We move in our units," shouts Jackson, giving orders to the officers. "Left and right, we sweep through the city and eliminate all threats."

"We're leading," I hear my mother say. "We're going straight down the middle."

Jackson looks as if he wants to deny her. Prevent his wife and son from going headfirst into battle. But he can't. Together, we're worth more than all these soldiers put together.

Instead, he merely nods.

"Clear a path," he says. "I trust you."

Their eyes meet for a second longer, before Cyra turns to us: "We're moving in. Follow me. Search the Void and watch each other's backs."

Leaving the other soldiers hidden behind the barricades, we pass through the main gate and begin moving towards the city. The clattering sound of gunfire rattles from all parts of it, left and right and way into the distance, the soldiers and guards stationed here doing their best to fight off the attackers.

Around us, the tall towers, known as seascrapers, rise high and plunge low. Some reach so high into the heavens they tickle the clouds, and dive right down to the depths of the ocean floor. It's a city I've always wanted to see.

But not like this.

I look over the side of the roads and streets as we go, and see the shadows of the towers extending deep into the ocean. Above us, other platforms connect the buildings on various levels, possible danger coming from on high as well as ahead of us. Looking forward, I see the flashes of barrels bursting with bullets, some at street level, others glowing across platforms, cutting down people as they escape from the chaos.

We move deeper, heading for the thick of the action, but quickly realise that it's widely dispersed. This city was never considered to be under great threat, and with so few soldiers stationed here to protect it, the attackers have had free reign to spread their havoc throughout without much resistance.

Until now.

As we move in towards the sound of gunfire, I turn back to see our own troops now spreading out from the docks, sweeping through the city to make it safe. Soon enough, their weapons join the chorus, making the world ever more deafening.

We push straight on, hunting down the highest

concentration of vermin we can find, following our ears as we pass over bodies of innocent people littering the path. Every one of them sends a shard of anger through me, causing us to gallop that little bit faster.

Soon, we're in sight of our first targets. Ahead, I see a group of a dozen mercenaries, garbed in the same dress that I saw in my visions. Soldiers of the Baron. Soldiers of Knight. Here to carry out his legacy.

Over the radio in my helmet, I hear my mum growl: "Show no mercy. Kill them all."

They're words I never expected to hear from her. From the stories of the past, I know she always found it hard to kill when fighting her enemies in the war. Back then, though, the people were deceived by Knight, and all of them were innocent. Not so now. These men deserve everything that's coming to them, and she knows it.

They turn to see us charge towards them, confused perhaps that we're not taking cover. Hidden within our black bodysuits and masks, they can't possibly see the face of The Golden Girl coming at them. They can't possibly know what they're about to face.

They find out too late.

Sending a hail of bullets at us, they hit nothing but air. Hundreds of rounds fill the air, but few hinder our step. Realising what we are, they quickly disband, rushing for cover as we return fire. But we're too quick on the draw, and all twelve soon join the corpses that litter the earth.

I stand over a couple of them, cut down by my own hand, and see the grizzled faces of these guns for hire. And on their uniforms, I see a badge, an insignia to show their allegiance: a flaming shield, with a mask in its centre, and the fiery handles of four swords sprouting from its corners. The mask must signify Knight; the four swords his Seekers; and the flames, the chaos they're set to bring to this world.

I have little time to stand and analyse the badge, though. Ahead, Cyra calls us on, another grouping of mercenaries appearing from a side street. They move in formation, guns raised, taking cover as they advance. Above us, on the platforms, we see others doing the same. All appear to see us at once, the air once more filling with the white trails of deadly bullets.

Again, we take advantage of these soldiers' temporary ignorance, not knowing who we are or what we can do. Blasting high and low, we decimate them in no time, utilising all the tricks our guns provide.

When a soldier steps into the open, a quick shot to any exposed areas between their armour is enough to take them down. When they take cover behind the carcasses of cars or behind walls, we flick to explosive rounds and clear whatever object they're hiding behind out of our way. We march through the street, exterminating these vermin, each downed enemy marking revenge for the many innocents caught up in the bloodshed.

Occasionally, when we find an enemy or two alone, we flick our weapons to non-lethal rounds in a bid to disable them. If we can take one alive, and make him talk, we might just discover more of the Baron's plan, and get confirmation of the location of his new base of operations.

Each time we manage to subdue an enemy, however, they turn to their failsafe, sucking down a poison capsule safely hidden within their mouth. Before we can extract any information at all, they're foaming at the lips and joining the rest of their fallen comrades in the dirt.

Around us, the buildings continue to burn bright, and the inhabitants of the city continue to rush here and there, seeking cover or searching for missing loved ones. Some come up to us, begging for help, and we're forced to escort them to safety before another mercenary troop stumbles upon us.

Our focus remains total, though, any sign of danger seen by one of us or another. Mostly, we all see the main threats coming, some a little earlier than others. We form an impenetrable circle as we advance, no enemy able to catch us off guard. When they try, they invariable fail, the sting of our weapons bringing them down.

Deep in the city now, we move down a narrow side street, the larger central platform in the city's centre ahead. I can see the glow of the flames that populate it at the end of the alley, smell the burning smoke and hear the screaming of women and children. We rush on, desperate to offer aid to anyone who needs it, Cyra leading us at the front.

Suddenly, she pulls to a stop, and raises her hand. And just as she does so, I see it too, the narrow streets around us turning white, flames about to fill the space and cremate us where we stand.

"Inside!" shouts Cyra. "Anywhere!"

The others see it now, our leader giving us just enough warning. Immediately, Ajax kicks open a door and pours in, Velia and Vesuvia following. A little further down the street, Cyra does the same, disappearing inside another building. On the other side of the road, I send my full weight at a large glass window, shattering it and spilling into a dusty room. I see people cowering in corners, hiding in shadow, finding refuge behind any solid objects and furniture they can find.

"GET DOWN!" I shout.

Immediately, I hit the deck, and as I do the air appears to boil and rush around me. Just outside, fire spreads down the alleyway, its tendrils sneaking into any spare space it can find. Above me, it bursts through the window I've just smashed, shattering others with the force of its charge. I coil my body into a protective position as the fire darts inside the building, hungrily chasing people down.

What Cyra forgot to tell us, however, is that our suits are flame resistant. The fire attempts to catch light around me, but my suit won't allow it. For a few moments I feel the burning heat, before suddenly the fiery fingers retreat once more outside. I look to the far end of the room to see that the people are safe, hidden away from the flames.

Immediately, I'm back to my feet and rushing into the alley, now cleared once more but carrying a heavy shroud of smoke. I look to the doors that were broken in by my companions, and shout out their names.

I hear responses coming from within, their voices coughing as they set about offering aid to those caught in the sudden blaze.

I make a move to go inside and help, but something catches my eye. To my right, down at the end of the alley in the city square, I see the shape of a dark figure standing amid the mist of swirling smoke. The hues of orange and red flame glow around him, buildings crumbling as they break down and burst. But he just stands there, looking down the alley in my direction.

I turn to him, and see that there's a young woman at his feet, cowering beneath the heavy blanket of smog. From his cloak, a hand extends holding a gun, pointing it straight at the girl's head. And beneath his black hood, I see the pale face I've seen so many times in my visions, shining out from the shadow.

Rooted in place, I watch as his thin lips curl into a smile. And a split second later, a single shot fills the air.

"NO!" I shout, watching as the bullet cuts through the innocent woman's head. Her cowering body slumps into the dust, her life stolen. And in that moment, my body swells with a furious dose of anger, and without thinking, I begin running straight down the alley.

Charging for the open space ahead, I set my eyes on the cloaked man who I know to be a Seeker. I don't think, I just act, drawn in by the callous murder of an innocent girl. The clone stands there calmly as debris falls from above, some of the buildings crumbling as they burn. Here and there, large clumps of stone and brick come clattering down, some behind me, some ahead. But nothing fazes the man in my sight, nothing causes him to stir.

Soon I'm bursting out of the narrow street and into the open square, surrounded by flame and covered in smoke. But the shadow of the Seeker is clearly visible, standing and waiting for me, drawing me in. I move straight towards him, raising my weapon to my shoulder and letting loose with a ferocious barrage of fire. Finally he moves, gliding left and right, flowing like the wind as he avoids the bullets with ease.

I continue to shoot as I get closer and closer, but nothing has an impact on him. With a grace and fluidity, he dances around the attack, refusing to return fire as he goes. Soon, my gun is chattering loudly, empty now of rounds. I drop it to the floor and reach to my belt, pulling out my extendable knife. With a quick click it slices into the smoky air, my grip tight as I reach my quarry.

I slash and roar, panting hard, desperately trying to inflict some damage. The smoke churns around his cloak as he avoids my attacks, his face still hidden under his hood. Frantic now, my movements grow more erratic, less focused, not a single blow threatening to get close to its mark.

I feel my lungs burning, coughing as the fumes pour up my nose and into my mouth. He has no such problem, his mouth locked tight and nose hidden in shadow, blending in with the black smog as it continues to spread from the burning buildings.

Behind me, the faint sounds of voices rush on the air.

"Theo…Theo…"

The voices of my allies filter down from the alley, getting a little clearer as they hurry towards me, drawing ever nearer. I briefly turn to see them coming through the fog, dodging falling rubble as they advance.

Then, in a sudden flash, my enemy lashes out as I turn back. His hands move so fast, so abruptly, that I don't see them coming. From the billowing fog a fist connects with my jaw, sending my neck twisting hard and my brain rattling in my skull.

I stagger back and see another strike zeroing in on me, flashing just before it hits. I have no chance to avoid it or move. In two quick motions, the Seeker has me staggering back, my vision blurring and eyes watering. I trip on a block of detritus, falling backwards to the floor. And there, above me, my enemy looms.

I look under his hood, and see a smile. Teeth of pure white shine out from thin, pallid lips. His hands appear from his cloak, bringing a pistol with them once more. He lifts it to me, and his smile broadens, and under his hood I see those grey eyes piercing me.

But they're not quite the same as I've seen. Not like the other boys, the dead clones. Not exactly like Knight. Within them, there's a hint of another colour, lighter, obscured by the shroud of smoke. And on his face, I see something I recognise, something I haven't seen before.

And then, from his thin mouth, a voice comes; clear amid the roaring of the battle that continues around us.

"No…not this time," he whispers, hissing like a snake. "I'm not going to kill you yet, Theo." His smile flattens out, and his eyes darken and disappear once more into shadow. "First, I want you to see your world burn."

He steps back, still staring at me, the shouting voices of my friends continuing to roar behind. His eyes flash up at them, and then back down to me.

"Then," he continues, "I'll kill you all…"

With that, he turns swiftly, his cloak flowing behind him, and begins moving away, his body quickly engulfed by the fog.

22
The World Burns

"Theo…Theo…"

Once more, the voices of my friends reach my ears. I sit there, my vision still slightly blurred, my eyes stinging from the relentless smoke. Just staring into the distance as the Seeker fades before me.

"Are you OK?! What happened?!"

It's Ajax who reaches me first, his strong arms lifting me to my feet. He holds me firm and stares into my watering eyes as the rest join us.

"What happened, Theo?!" he asks again.

"It was…a Seeker," I whisper, staring back at the fog. "He got away…"

"What did I say about fighting them together," comes my mother's voice, panting slightly. "What the hell were you thinking? You could have gotten yourself killed."

"He killed a girl," I say. "Right there at his feet. He murdered her. I just…lost it."

"You have to be smarter than that," she says. "Don't get emotionally attached. Now where did he go?"

I gesture towards the far end of the square, where the Seeker disappeared into the mist.

"He's gone, mum," I say. "We won't find him now."

Around us, the rattling of gunfire appears to have lessened, the fighting beginning to ease up. From a couple of streets, some of our soldiers come, lifting their weapons to us as they advance. It takes a moment for them to recognise us amid the smoke, lowering their arms as soon as they do.

Immediately, they begin moving off again, disappearing down side streets to continue the fight. After a moment's delay, we do the same, following our ears towards any remaining focal points of the battle.

As we go, we spy a couple of jets, escaping the city walls and disappearing quickly into the night sky. Our men shoot after them but they're too quick, the final remaining mercenaries and soldiers in the Baron's army retreating from the battle.

Yet the damage has been done, the city devastated. Everywhere, bodies of the innocent lie amid those of the city guards and the paltry number of soldiers who were stationed here. Dozens, maybe hundreds, of mercenaries lie too, all wearing the same uniforms, all fitted with the same badge.

Immediately, we get to work on dousing the flames and saving what we can, the city residents emerging from their bunkers to help. The pumps are quickly turned on, spreading the water from the surrounding ocean to where it's most needed. And slowly but surely, the raging inferno is quelled.

As we help where we can, the voice of my father sounds over our communicators. My mother and I share a look of great relief.

"Jack, are you OK?" she asks.

"I'm fine," his voice crackles urgently. "And you?"

"We're all fine," she says.

"Good. I need you to return to the jets immediately. I've given the order to all soldiers to gather at the docks."

"What's going on?" she asks, reacting to the grave tone of his voice.

"It's not over, Cyra," he says. "Come…now."

His voice clicks off, and we turn our sights back on the other end of the city. As we go, we see the rest of the soldiers getting the same message, all of them quickly gathering and converging back at the jets, leaving behind the city dwellers to do what they can to halt the fires and identify the dead.

The numbers of our own soldiers appears to have lessened significantly. As soon as the docks come into view, it's obvious that nearly half of our brave men and women have either lost their lives or been wounded. Outside of the jets I see Jackson and the other officers gathering, my father issuing further orders. We gallop towards him as quickly as possible, his eyes rising to us as we approach.

"Jack…what's going on?" asks Cyra.

Between my father and the officers, a map has been spread out on a small container box from the docks. On it, several major urban areas have been marked. As soon as I see it, I know exactly what's happening.

"The fighting isn't over," says Jackson. "Word is coming in from the coast that other cities are being attacked. This is a coordinated assault, just like before with the assassinations. We have to go and help immediately."

He turns to the officers and begins issuing orders for them to board the jets with their troops.

"Gather your men," he says. "Make sure they're evenly dispersed. The attacks are coming in at three major settlements." He points down to the map at two coastal cities and one a little further inland. "Wait aboard the planes for further orders."

The officers immediately rush off, filtering the news to their troops and arranging them into new strike teams. They board the three jets as Jackson turns his attention to us.

"We need to split up and do what we can. Cyra, you will accompany me and my strike force. Ajax and Vesuvia, I want you going with Captain Price. Theo and Velia, you will go with Captain Botica."

The girls look at each other. It's obvious that they don't want to be drawn apart, and yet they offer no complaint. Vesuvia will be safer with Ajax than she will with her sister, and the same goes for Velia and me. The look that Ajax gives Velia makes it clear that he'll do everything he can to protect her twin if it comes to it.

"We don't yet know how many troops are attacking each city. Do what you can to drive them out. We have soldiers being mobilised at bases down the coast and across the regions to offer aid."

"But if you should encounter another Seeker, don't engage them," adds Cyra, looking at me. "Without our full force we won't be able to defeat them, so don't do anything foolish…"

"*Another* Seeker?" asks Jackson hastily.

"There was one in the city," says Cyra. "He got away. If there are three other attacks happening, it makes sense that each will be led by one of these clones."

Jackson nods. "Indeed. Now come on, we have no time to lose. Go to the planes, and pass on my orders to the officers to leave. Good luck."

Without any time to think or engage in any further debate, we go our separate ways, Velia and I rushing towards the plane containing Captain Botica and his men. When we board, I notice that the force of soldiers has been significantly depleted, many of them bloodied and carrying minor injuries, but with steel in their eyes that suggests they're still up for the fight.

I go straight towards Captain Botica and pass on my father's orders, and immediately the pilot begins lifting the jet back into the air and setting our course for the coast.

The storm continues to brew, growing more

forceful as we cover the brief expanse of water between New Atlantis and the coastline. Outside, the dark clouds continue to spit their rain, but we maintain a low altitude to keep our vision clear ahead beneath the clouds.

As we go, Captain Botica gives orders to his men, leaving Velia and me alone. We sit side by side in our black, bulletproof bodysuits, preparing to take the lead in dismantling the assault on the city of Piscator, traditionally a fishing city right on the Eastern coast.

I can see the worry in Velia's eyes as we sit and wait, knowing it's for her sister.

"She'll be fine," I tell her. "Ajax won't let anything happen to her."

She does a quick nod but her eyes remain hooded. Because now, rather than five Watchers, we're down to two, and they're down to two, and my mother is going to be out there fighting alone. And with time to think as we travel, it's fear for her and my father that begin to consume me.

However, that time isn't long. With the jet cutting through the rainy skies, we quickly cross the narrow sea, the coastline soon appearing as a black silhouette against the sky. And along it, the glow of fire appears once more, cities and settlements blazing all along it.

The world is burning...

I look to Velia, the frown and concern in her eyes now turned to shock. I reach down and take her hand in mine, bringing her eyes back up to me.

"We'll be OK, Velia," I say. "I promise you, we'll all be OK."

The words are designed to comfort her, not that she's the sort of girl who needs comforting. Her jaw stiffens a bit and she nods, her hazel eyes glinting beneath her helmet. And then we both turn back, and look through the main cockpit window, as the fiery coastline continues to rush up towards us.

Once again, we go through the same routine as we did only an hour or two ago. This time, however, it's not my father, but Captain Botica who stands before his men, giving them courage. And this time, there's no Cyra to lead us, my mother the sole Watcher in the jet drifting further South to defend another major town.

Instead, I take the lead, trying to form some sort of plan for Velia and I to see through.

"When we land, we'll do what we did in New Atlantis," I say. "We'll bust a hole for these men…we'll save as many people as possible."

She nods in agreement, and I relay the message to Captain Botica.

"We're glad to have you two with us," he says earnestly. "We'll be following right behind and helping as much as we can."

"Thank you, Captain," I say, just as the jet begins to slow, sweeping down low as it nears the edge of the city.

I stand and look out upon it, fire raging at various

points across the warehouses and the sprawling area of docklands where much of the trade passes from the regions towards the sea cities. The little flashes of gunfire are also visible in the darkness, the battle raging between the city guards and the Baron's mercenary army. And beyond, a little further down the coast, the sight of an approaching convoy can be seen, a range of hovertrucks delivering fresh forces to the battlefield from one of the military bases further South.

"Looks like we have more men incoming," says Captain Botica with a determined smile. "Now let's drive out this scum..."

The jet swoops lower, dropping fast and once more coming in to land in the open areas around the docks. The area is largely clear, most of the fighting happening deeper into the city, allowing us to land without any opposition. The ramp opens up and our soldiers are quickly off once more, Velia and I following them out.

Taking cover behind some large containers, I glance out of the merchant sector and towards the large industrial warehouses used for fish packing. Many are lit up and pouring smoke to the dark clouds, the incessant dribble of rain having no discernable impact upon the blaze.

I turn to Velia, and make sure her helmet is properly fixed to her head.

"Are you ready?" I ask her.

A tiny smile lifts at the corners of her mouth. "I was born ready," she answers.

I don't doubt her for a second.

And, for a second time, we rush head first into battle.

23
Mercator

Our defence of the city comes from several angles. In the heart of it, those already stationed here for that task continue to fight off the Baron's mercenary forces. From the South, the convoy of military trucks rumble on, still a mile or so out. From the coast and moving inland, Velia and I, with Captain Botica and his men behind, move straight in for the kill.

We move together, side by side, guns raised to our shoulders. The chattering of gunfire gets louder as we approach the first section of fighting, the city here so very different from New Atlantis. There, the many platforms and paths linking the seascrapers made the fighting vertical, their soldiers and ours all passing by at various levels from the ground up. Here, however, the world is all flat and populated by larger and wider structures, warehouses and long barracks used for accommodation for those who work here.

Within those wider streets and inside those expansive structures, the battle is fought, the dark skies and slashing rain making it difficult to make out whose side any attacking force is on from a distance. As we approach, however, the now familiar uniforms of the mercenaries take shape, little groups collecting together and taking cover as they continue to cause as much destruction and chaos as possible.

I watch on as high velocity weapons are targeted at groups of our own men and the buildings they fire from, or the old beaten up cars they hide behind. Missiles fly from launchers, ripping into buildings and sending hails of debris in all directions. Grenades are tosses from all angles, causing the same havoc. Incendiary devices quickly consume areas of the city in flame, the shock and awe tactics of the mercenaries having the desired effect upon the residents of the city.

With Velia beside me, we take few precautions for our own safety as we charge straight in to disable the most perilous threats we can find. Incensed by the wanton brutality of what we're seeing, we prime ourselves for the fight like we never have before, sliding between attacking bullets and achieving a level of accuracy in our own attacks that neither of us have previously attained.

Behind us, Captain Botica and his men do what they can to provide covering fire, sniping from points of safely and skilfully taking out men as we make our open advance. We don't bother with taking cover. We don't need to. Right into the heart of the fighting we go, bullets and explosions spraying around us, everywhere a fresh threat appearing from the growing mist.

We begin to trust in the durability of the suits we're wearing. Some shots we don't even bother avoiding, letting them graze our bodysuits and fling off in another direction. When sprays of shrapnel come right at us, filling the air, we cover our faces with our arms and let the little bits of stone and brick crack against us, having no impact at all.

It's not that we can't avoid such things, it's simply that we don't need to. Very quickly we come to learn just how impenetrable our armour is to certain attacks, allowing us to advance more swiftly than we otherwise would.

Yet we know, too, that our suits won't stop everything. Any straight shot from a high velocity weapon is quickly avoided. Any explosive device, too, is passed by before it can consume us. We go about our work right on the edge of the line, the needs of the people of this city requiring that we take a few chances.

Once again, however, the devastation of the surprise attack has had the effect that the Baron wants. It's obvious that the people were caught off guard; many innocents caught amongst the fighting. Many have lost their lives, and many others remain hidden where they can, praying that we're able to drive out the assailants before they, too, join their fallen comrades.

If the simultaneous assassinations of the great leaders of the country was phase one, then this is most certainly phase two. Only now, individual people aren't being targeted. Now, it's places, huge urban areas where the collective losses of the people are far more all consuming than before.

As we go, it becomes evidently clear that this is a plan that's been brewing for many years. A long gestating operation to first disable the upper echelons of the nation's leadership, and then obliterate its most influential towns and cities.

Who knows how much wealth the Cabal have accrued. Who knows how many men they've been able to buy. Who knows how many secret hideouts and locations they have dotted around the country. Not in our wildest dreams did we see this coming.

Not, at least, until it was too late.

Because over the last few weeks, we have all seen flashes of this. We saw the burning buildings, and heard the screaming people, and knew that a great attack was about to strike. Yet we were all drawn into the same misjudgement: that it was only a single attack, on a single town, that we had to worry about.

Yet really, we must have been seeing several attacks. The little flashes we all saw in our visions weren't just of New Atlantis. They were of Piscator too, and the other towns currently being besieged by the Baron's forces.

We were blind to such an invasion. We underestimated just how much power the Baron, and the Cabal, had accumulated. And now, it's the innocent people, the hard working people, from all over the country, that are paying for our miscalculation.

In the midst of the fight, I hardly have time to consider the repercussions of the all of this. I merely use it as fuel to do what I need to, rampaging through the city like a whirlwind, ruthlessly dispatching any enemy who comes into my sights.

I take absolutely no prisoners. Even the thought of trying to capture an enemy soldier alive abandons me. Instead, my fury rises with each passing minute, with each innocent person I see lying lifeless in the dirty, bloodied streets. And as the storm continues to thunder, and the world continues to burn, I have no idea how many lives I take. I enter a state of total and utter focus, surging from kill to kill without remorse, without guilt.

Because now, this truly is a war. And in war, there's no space for such emotion.

Velia isn't any different. Whether from a distance using her rifle, or up close using her knife, she takes enemies out like she's ritually slaughtering lambs for a feast. We leave so little for Captain Botica and his men that they eventually begin moving off in another direction, seeking revenge of their own.

And soon, with our support forces moving through the city from the South, the enemy begin to retreat. And just as they did in New Atlantis, they escape to their jets and disappear into the dark skies, their job well and truly done.

We don't encounter a Seeker this time. However, by the stories we hear from some of the people creeping from their hiding places, one was certainly here.

"A cloaked man," one woman tells us. "He led the forces into the city. He killed so many…"

She proceeded to break down in tears, Velia moving to comfort her. And despite such a vague description, it's obvious who she was talking about.

With the fighting now complete, and the remains of the city made safe, my thoughts once more turn towards the others. Velia, too, appears to suddenly remember that her sister is out there as well, going through what we have just been through.

We quickly attempt to contact them using our helmets, but it doesn't take long to realise that their range is too narrow. So, back to the jet we go, rushing towards the docks. When we reach it we find the pilot still aboard, and ask him to contact my father, and Captain Price, to get us updates on the other attacks.

He's quick to tell us that Jackson has already been in contact.

"Governor Kane is safe, as is your mother," he tells me. "They quelled the attack quickly, and are now on their way here."

"And my sister?" asks Velia quickly.

"Captain Price," I add. "Have you spoken with him?"

"Not yet. I can try to get through."

"Please..."

He sets about dialling in to the young captain, but doesn't get a response. After several efforts, all yielding the same result, he looks at us with a little shake of the head.

"No luck I'm afraid. It's likely that they're still fighting..."

"Keep trying," I say, as I lead Velia into the belly of the plane to take a seat.

"I'm sure Vesuvia is fine," I say, just as I did before.

My thoughts, meanwhile, are now locked to the fate of Ajax. And despite what I tell Velia about her sister, I can't help but be concerned that something has happened to my best friend.

We sit for a little while, reflecting on the battle, our thoughts on our loved ones. Soon, however, the pilot is calling us from the front once more.

"Governor Kane's jet is incoming," he says.

I'm quickly up and out of the plane, my eyes to the dark skies. The rain continues to fall, causing me to blink as I look up and see the clouds lighting up, and an aircraft come bursting out of them. The plane lands and the doors quickly open, and out onto the docks rush my parents.

My mother draws me into an abbreviated hug.

"Is Velia OK?" she asks, seeing that I'm alone.

"She's on the plane," I say. "Have you heard from the others?"

My father shakes his head. "I've tried Captain Price several times but haven't been able to get through. It's possible he's been killed."

He says it very matter of factly, but he's probably right.

We return to Velia as my father's men move into the city to aid with the clean-up. Quickly, I brief him and my mother on what happened.

"Did you encounter a Seeker?" she asks.

"Not personally, no," I say. "But there was one here. Did you?"

She shakes her head. "He may have already gone by the time we arrived."

As we talk, Jackson continues to try to make contact with Captain Price, whilst the pilot does the same. Eventually, after several long minutes, we hear a crackling sound on the pilot's radio.

"Sir…we have contact," he calls from ahead.

We all move into the cockpit and gather around.

"Captain Price, do your read," says Jackson. "This is Governor Kane…"

"Sir, Captain Price has been killed, sir…"

We share concerned looks.

"Who am I speaking with?" asks my dad.

"This is corporal Milner, sir. We suffered extreme casualties…"

His voice crackles over the static, fading away.

"Corporal, do you copy…corporal…"

"Yes…sir…the enemy forces…just left…"

"What is the state of our men?" asks Jackson quickly. "Are the Watchers OK?"

"The boy…yes sir…"

"And the girl?"

I look at Velia, unmoving as she stares at the radio.

"Injured…sir…"

She takes a sharp intake of breath and I move over and wrap my arm around her. I see her want to speak herself, but she can't seem to. Jackson does the necessary talking.

"But is she alive?" his voice rushes.

"Yes…alive, sir…"

The static continues to worsen, until suddenly the radio goes blank.

"OK," says Jackson, "we're going up the coast. Let's go," he tells the pilot.

The pilot doesn't delay, quickly bringing the jet to life and lifting it into the air. Jackson, meanwhile, is straight onto his radio speaking with his own strike force and Captain Botica, ordering them to stay in the city and ensure its safety.

"Where exactly did the other jet go?" I ask my mum.

"A city called Mercator," she says. "It's a major trading post up the coast."

"How far?" asks Velia, clearly desperate to get there as soon as possible.

"It won't take long. Only thirty or so miles to the North," she says.

For the duration of the journey, Velia disappears

into her own thoughts, while the rest of us consider the implications of what's going on.

"There might be more attacks coming," says Jackson. "All of the regions are now on high alert, and the entire military is being mobilised."

"But the military is weak now, isn't it?" I ask. "Hasn't it been shrunk down over the years?"

He nods. "Unfortunately, yes. Peace will do that sometimes. It can make a country weak and vulnerable."

"But no one ever saw this coming," says Cyra. "We can't have known the Baron would have such a force under his command..."

My father and I share a look. With everything that's happened, we haven't had a chance to properly discuss what we saw only hours ago down in Professor Lane's lab. In fact, my mother hasn't even been clued in yet as to the existence of the Cabal, and the many powerful foes we're dealing with.

Her intuition is enough to convince her that something is wrong.

"What are you hiding?" she asks, peering at us.

"It's not just the Baron," Jackson says. "There's a group of them known as the Cabal. They have enough cumulative wealth to match us militarily."

A heavy frown covers the tops of her eyes.

"How long have you know about this?" she demands.

“Not long,” says Jackson.

From the front, the pilot calls out that we’re coming into Mercator.

“We can discuss this later, Cy,” says Jackson. “I’ll explain everything once we’re all back together.”

She begrudgingly agrees as we land in yet another city, our whistle-stop tour of the coastline continuing. It’s not exactly how I envisaged seeing this part of the country for the first time.

As we step into the trading city of Mercator, it’s clear that the fighting has also concluded. No guns are being fired, no explosions are heard. And yet, the place burns as the others did, and howls of pain and the screams of grieving women and men continue to sound around the city.

We find a grouping of soldiers near to where we land, in an area of the market being used as a mobile command centre and field hospital. Inside, many of the wounded from the city, both its inhabitants and soldiers tasked with defending it, lie in various states of health. Some suffer from superficial wounds. Others are in a more critical condition. And beyond, in another section, the bodies of the dead have been accumulated, their surviving loved ones crying rivers of tears as they kneel around them.

As Jackson quickly moves in to speak with the soldiers and find out the state of affairs in the city, the rest of us set our sights on the wounded and injured, searching for Ajax and Vesuvia.

We move in, hunting them down amid the masses,

people reaching out for help as we go. I find it hard to move past them, my own medical knowledge insufficient to offer any sort of aid. Cyra, meanwhile, finds herself stopping and helping where she can, the sight before her one she's experienced before.

But not me. And not Velia. Together, we continue on, until we finally catch sight of Ajax and Vesuvia amid the throng. She rushes from my side to her sister, lying flat on the ground with a bloodied bandage wrapped around her leg. I follow behind, and Ajax stands to greet me with a quick embrace, his own body clean of his own wounds but covered in the blood of others.

While the sisters reunite beneath us, I ask my friend what happened.

"An explosion," he says. "I saw it in time and we ran…but a bit of debris tripped her up and her leg got caught by some shrapnel from the blast."

"But she's OK?"

He nods. "She's got some serious gashes on the leg, and the bone is probably fractured. But she'll live."

"Thank God," I say. "How are you, though…"

My eyes scan the blood all over him.

"I'm fine. I killed a lot of people, Theo…"

It's not a boast. It's far from it. Such a thing as taking lives is never something to be proud of, no matter who it is. Only such terrible circumstances as these would necessitate such a thing.

"I know," I say. "It needed to be done."

He nods, and we turn our eyes down to the girls, wrapped up in each other's arms on the ground.

"Her part in this is over," I say, looking at Vesuvia's leg. "But not ours."

Ajax looks at me, the exhaustion so clear in his eyes.

"I wonder…what's next?" he asks wearily.

"Next," I say, "we'll be going straight for the lion's den."

24
Defence to Attack

The evening is late when we gather once more in our group, finding a quiet place to sit and rest away from the field hospital. We sit around a table inside an office used by traders right on the waterfront, the flames of the city now put out and the storm having passed on.

Outside, the sky has grown clear, the stars and moon visible. Already, it's late into the evening, dawn casually approaching on another day as if nothing has happened. And yet, when the sun rises, the full extent of the destruction of the coastline, and New Atlantis, will be revealed.

Down the coast, and a little further back into the regions, more news has come in of smaller attacks. Some have involved small forces of men, ransacking little towns and settlements that aren't able to defend themselves. Others have seen bombs and explosive devices go off, hidden in buildings and town squares and primed to explode all at once.

Across the country, the threat of terror has spread, the entire world waking early to news that war has sprung up suddenly, and ubiquitously. And all over, soldiers have been quickly mobilised and sent far and wide, many of the military bases that still operate emptied out in an effort to protect those who have yet to be hit.

Immediately after the battle, our thoughts turned to our loved ones spread across the country. My aunts and uncles and cousins. My grandparents on my father's side. Jackson's family, in particular, is a large one, all of them still living in the old region of Agricola where he grew up. The others, too, have people they're worried about, all of us quickly trying to track down information as to whether the settlements they live in have been hit. Thankfully, the news is good on that front, all of them confirmed as safe and sound.

In the office, my father stands before us, hands planted on the table, body wearily hunched over as he stands.

"I've just spoken with President Alber," he says. "Eden's doors have been locked tight, and no one is getting in or out. Most of the regional leaders, and city leaders from across the county, are still there after his coronation. They're safe for now, but we cannot know for how long."

Around the table, the rest of us sit, including Vesuvia who took it upon herself to discharge herself from the field hospital, announcing that there were others more in need of medical treatment and care. Her leg is heavily strapped, and the constant grimace on her face shows that she's in a lot of pain. And yet she's here, proving her courage once more.

The news from Eden brings Ajax's voice into the conversation.

"What about my parents?" he asks. "They're locked in there now? We were meant to be leaving after this and going to Petram…"

"I'm afraid our plans have changed, Ajax," says Jackson. "We could never have anticipated such an overwhelming assault. "It may be better for Ellie and Link to stay on Eden for now."

"Then what is this new plan?" asks Cyra. "You clearly know something that we don't, Jack."

My father looks to me, then around at the others.

"Earlier tonight, just before we learned of the attack on New Atlantis, Theo and I visited Professor Lane. As you all know, she's been working hard to decipher the encrypted file, and so far has uncovered some useful information such as the names of those in the group known as the Cabal. Tonight, we learned something new…"

"What?" asks Cyra.

"We think we know where the Baron's stronghold is. We can't be sure, but it's the best information we've got. And right now, it's time we turned the tables on him…and attacked."

He draws out a map of the regions and Deadlands, with the skeleton of Knight's Wall cutting a path between them, and places it down on the table. His finger traces a path from Petram, across the empty wasteland, and past Knight's wall towards the regions. It stops at a certain point, where a natural formation of rocks and peaks link with the wall.

"We believe that Lucius Gray, otherwise known as

Lord Kendrik, has been building a secret facility right here, beneath the remnants of the wall."

"But that's…that's where The Titan's Hand is," says Cyra, peering closely at the location of Jackson's finger.

"Exactly. Lucius Gray has been helping with the dismantling of the wall over the years, using the raw materials to build up towns and settlements," says my father. "However, that's just been a front. Behind it all, he's been a member of the Cabal as Lord Kendrik, and has been developing a secret base of operations somewhere along this stretch. We believe that he's developed it right here, at the base of the thumb of The Titan's Hand."

"Why there?"

"I'll let Theo answer that. Theo…"

I quickly tell them all the same story I told my father and Professor Lane earlier that evening, about my sighting of the men stationed at The Titan's Hand when we flew from Petram to Eden several weeks ago.

"And you're sure of this?" asks Cyra. "We know that the wall is still being dismantled. That's all it could have been."

"I'm fairly sure, mum," I say. "I definitely saw a gun. And, well, it just seems to fit perfectly."

"And if it's not there," adds Jackson. "There's definitely a base in the area. Now, we can't be sure that the Baron will be there, but right now we have no other usable intel. We have no choice but to swap lanes and attack, and try to put our enemy on the back foot. Right now, they'll expect us to be licking our wounds and consolidating. They won't see this move coming."

"OK..." says Cyra, now starting to pace and think. "So what's the plan? Attack it head on?"

"More or less. But we need to be smart. We'll scout the place out from a distance and then infiltrate under cover of night."

"And if the Seekers are there?" asks Ajax. "Why don't we just bomb the opening and bury whoever's in there? They'll be trapped underground with nowhere to go and a million tons of rock on top of them..."

"No," I say, my voice cutting in. "Drake might be in there. And even if he's not, we need to find out what they've got down there. If we bury it, and they're not in there, it'll be a complete waste."

"Theo's right," says Jackson. "We have to do this the smart way. We'll gather our full force and take the fight to them."

"So...you mean it's time to call Athena?" I ask, half smiling.

He nods. "It's time," he says.

Naturally, however, Vesuvia won't be able to join us, yet another of our more gifted Watchers having to sit this one out. Velia, too, says she doesn't want to leave her sister.

"What if they attack again?" she asks. "Someone needs to protect the people..."

"I doubt they will," says Jackson. "The pattern so far has been clear. They coordinated the assassinations, and then regrouped. Now they've done the same, only on a far grander scale. I don't even want to think about what they have lined up next. For now, though, we're back into the calm before the next storm. And we need to take advantage of that."

"He's right, Velia," says Vesuvia. "You'll do much more good out there."

"But I don't want to leave you."

"I know," she says, her thumb wiping a growing tear from her sister's eye. "But you have to. Get out there and kill the Baron for what he's done to our people, to our father…to everyone."

Velia begins nodding. "OK," she says softly. "Just be safe, OK?"

Vesuvia smiles, and they hug again. "Always."

For the next few hours, we rest and try to regain our energy. Outside, the world still moves around at a hectic pace as the dawn begins to rise, a red glow joining the blood that covers the streets. All across the country, the scene will be the same, the world alive to the threat that can seemingly come from anywhere and at any time.

I find it difficult to catch any sleep at all, and I know that it will be the same for everyone from now on. How can you rest, even dare to shut your eyes for a moment, when you know that at any time a bomb might tear through your building, or a horde of mercenaries might pour into your town, mowing people down for no reason at all?

How can you take your children to school when you have to walk through a river of blood to get there? How can you go to work, knowing that your wife or husband or son or daughter now lie dead in the dirt? How can you go on when you fear that your own life, and the lives of those you love, can be stripped away so easily, and by an enemy you never even knew existed?

Soon, though, the spectre of Augustus Knight will begin to rise before the people once more. They'll learn that all of this violence has been conducted in his name, led by a fanatic who sees him as a God, seen through by young men who carry his very genes. And those who recall the War of the Regions two decades ago, who lived through that terror, will now have to suffer the same fate again.

As we rest, however, the comforting sight of military forces will be appearing across the regions. Major towns and cities will have their defences erected. Regular people will picks up arms and prepare to defend themselves. The capitals of Eden and Petram will close their doors and display impenetrable armaments that no force can breach. Everywhere, fear will prime the senses, and bring forth the brave. The country has had its nose bloodied by a cheap shot. Now, though, its gloves are coming up.

My father remains busy for those hours of rest. He continues to coordinate with the various leaders of the nation and, more importantly, the military commanders from the major bases, primarily Fort Warden. Cyra, too, refuses to sit inside and do nothing. She spends her time out in the field hospital patching up minor wounds and using the limited medical knowledge she possesses to do what she can.

When Ajax and I ask to help, however, we're told that we'd be much better served regaining our strength. Velia, too, is ordered to stay inside, remaining by her sister's side as she sleeps. Only when dawn has fully come and gone and the world is bright and sunny outside does my father return and cast his eyes upon us.

"Have you spoken with Athena?" I ask hurriedly, sitting up.

"I have," he says. "I have ordered her to gather whatever Watchers she can and meet us South of Knight's Wall, twenty miles from The Titan's Hand. I have arranged for some vehicles to be ready for when we land. We'll be journeying the final stretch on the ground in order to remain undetected."

He looks at us, his eyes still alert despite being up all night.

"How are you all feeling?" he asks. "Have you slept?"

He sees a round of shaking heads.

"OK, I understand that it's hard right now. But we all need to get some sleep before tonight..."

"You included, dad," I say.

"Yes, I will try to find an hour or two later on.

However, I'm used to not sleeping, Theo, and know I can function regardless. We need you all sharp, OK. Now we leave in a couple of hours. I'll make sure you're not disturbed. Please…get some sleep, all of you."

He leaves the room, shutting out the sound from outside again. But still, it filters in from the distance, creating an endless jumble of different noises as the city continues to patch itself up. We do as he says, though, and try to get comfortable, blocking our ears off and calming our minds. Whether it works for the others, I can't tell.

It doesn't work for me.

Those two hours drag on, my mind and body feeling heavy and tired, but seemingly unwilling to shut down. Perhaps I'll be able to unwind when we're in the jet again, the low hum of the engines and soft sight of clouds a better tonic to help one drift off to sleep.

But right here, in this tortured city, with the scent of pain and blood everywhere, I know I'll get no rest. So against my father's orders, I stand and creep outside, leaving the others there, their eyes now shut and bodies at rest. I walk into the bright sunlight and see the devastation before me in full view for the first time.

Still, even now, buildings smoke and embers burn and people continue to cry and wail as they sift through the rubble, searching the dead for those they love. The scale of it is staggering, the Baron's forces doing such damage in such a short burst of time.

And it's not just here. In New Atlantis and Piscator and all down the coast and through the regions, dozens of other places will be suffering to a greater or lesser degree.

I wander back towards the field hospital, and the smell of decay quickly reaches my nose. Within the rabble, I spy my mother, blood soaked up to her elbows and sprayed across her black bodysuit, flecks of red dotting her cheeks and blonde hair. She won't stop working until she has to, until she's depleted the aid she can provide or is dragged away on an even more important task.

But I can tell that her presence is uplifting for the people. Any time someone lays eyes on her for the first time, they stare for a moment in wonder, amazed to see Cyra Drayton among them, helping them, drawn out of retirement once again.

They look at her and think: *she did it before, and she can do it again.*

As long as she's around, and other heroes remain, they will always have hope. And though they don't yet know me, or Ajax, or the twins as they do my parents and Ajax's parents and Athena, I know that soon they will.

Because together our generations will unite.

And together, we will destroy Knight's legacy.

25
Preparations

Before morning has turned to afternoon, we find ourselves gathering once more on a military jet, ready to be shipped out of the city and towards the westernmost edge of the regions.

To my great relief, we don't climb aboard the same aircraft that brought us out here, with the basic interior lined with benches. Instead, Jackson has sensibly opted for a more comfortable and less conspicuous jet, more like those we have been travelling in up until now on our trips to Petram and Eden.

We climb in and I move straight for the rear with Ajax and Velia, all three of us finding pairs of chairs to ourselves against the windows. Despite the fact that I haven't slept and they have, they appear even drowsier that I am, having just been woken from an all too brief slumber. Immediately, they settle into their respective seats and begin to drop off again.

My mind, meanwhile, is still fairly active. Ahead, my parents talk with the pilot, giving him his instructions. And on the plane, too, are about a dozen of my father's most potent soldiers, men drawn from his strike force and tasked with offering us support. Before we boarded, they'd set about filling the storage compartments of the plane with various weapons and armaments. As far as I know it, they're going to create a cordon around the entrance to the base and make sure that no one is able to escape.

Athena, meanwhile, has reported in, telling us that she's currently en route and will be there waiting for us when we arrive. I haven't yet heard how many Watchers she'll have with her, but I can only assume that she'll have all that Petram can spare.

The thought excites me as we lift off, making it even harder for my mind to shut down and let me sleep. I just wish that we had Link and Drake with us too. I can only imagine what it would be like to witness the two of them, plus my mother and Athena, do battle with the four Seekers.

Of course, we don't have Link and Drake, but we do have Ajax and Velia and me, as well as those that Athena has trained. Whether that will be enough is anyone's guess. At the moment, none of us truly know how strong these Seekers are.

So far, the evidence is limited. We've seen one do battle with Link in the woods, and while the exchange was brief, they looked fairly even. Then again, from that distance, most Watchers would be able to avoid the incoming bullets they were sending at each other. I didn't know it then, but now I do; it wasn't a good indicator of strength.

We've heard Knight's Terror speak of these boys as if they're truly something special, especially one. Coming from a man who, for the most part, happily dealt with all four of us down in that training room, that's quite the compliment.

And now, I've seen up close just how fast these clones are. Only last night, I faced off with one and came up short, unable to inflict even the mildest of damage on him. Had the others not come running, he might have ended me right and there.

I hate the thought. Hate the idea that this boy has been bred for this very purpose and dealt with me so easily. I know I lost focus when he killed that girl, and I know I attacked in a manic and uncontrolled fashion, but still…it aggrieves me that I was so impotent against him.

I drift away into the recesses of my mind and stew on that thought for a while. Soon enough, my thoughts are tumbling elsewhere, sending me down a spiral as my eyes close and my brain begins to finally shut down. I blink and stare out at the fluffy white clouds, and let the hum of the engine vibrate through me, drifting off with a thought that I was quite right about this particular tonic.

So busy is my mind behind my closed eyes, however, that I keep waking at various intervals, before drifting off again. Each time I wake, I look to the side and see that Ajax, and Velia sitting ahead of him, remain in the same position. My parents, on the other hand, appear to be spending most of their time discussing their plans, sometimes alone, sometimes with the soldiers, and occasionally I wake to find them up in the cockpit, speaking on the radio. I don't know who they're talking to, but imagine it's probably Athena.

A couple of hours pass by in that fashion, my sleep broken so frequently that I hardly feel I get a stretch of more than five minutes without interruption. And before I know it, Jackson is addressing the entire group as the sun continues to slip across the sky, indicating that the afternoon is getting into full swing.

"We'll be landing in about 30 minutes," he tells us, his voice loud enough to bring Ajax and Velia out of their slumber. "If any of you are still tired, we will have an opportunity to rest once we hit the ground. Should we locate the base at the expected location, we will spend time scouting it first, and will not consider making a move until nightfall."

Nightfall, I know, won't be for at least another five or six hours, and even then I assume that Jackson will want to wait a little longer before making his move. The news is welcome, given my current state of mental alertness. Strangely, I felt a lot better before I dropped of at all. After teasing my body with the odd bout of stolen sleep, it's grown hungry a whole lot more.

Once more, I find my mind shutting down after my father's announcement, only waking when the shift of the plane is noticeable enough to toss me from my dreams. I open my eyes and see that the ground is much closer now, the stretch of earth known as *no man's land* spread out before us. And there, waiting on the outskirts of an old abandoned town, I see the sight of two cars and a large truck parked in the dirt. And around it, stand at least a dozen figures.

We drop fast now, performing the standard vertical landing, anyone still sleeping thrust straight back to the land of the living by the sudden jolt as we hit the earth. When the doors open, the humid air flows in, bringing with it a swirl of dust. I achingly stand to my feet and move to the exit, and there, standing right outside the plane, see my mentor.

"I hear those telescopic goggles came in handy," she says with a knowing smile.

I step off and give her a brief hug, as my parents descend and do the same. Behind us, Ajax and Velia come out rubbing their eyes and blinking at the sudden bright light.

Athena scans our rabble, clearly noting the weariness in our eyes.

"Are you sure you're all ready for this?" she asks.

"We'll be ready," says Jackson firmly. "How many Watchers do you have?"

"There are thirteen," she says. "The same six chucked out of Eden, and another seven who I've been working with."

I look behind, and see them all standing around by the trucks and cars, far enough away for our words to be out of reach.

"How strong are they?" asks Cyra.

"They're all good soldiers," says Athena. "A couple are more gifted than the others, but all will do a job, and all are loyal."

"Good," says Jackson. "Now let's get moving."

His own strike force step off the plane, and immediately begin unpacking their weaponry and transferring it over to the truck. It's clear that these guys are incredibly well equipped, loaded with the most high tech weaponry Eden currently has going. Thankfully, they've brought plenty for everyone, and Athena's Watchers are quickly provided with the most powerful automatic rifles available, as well as some stronger and more durable body armour than they're currently wearing.

Once the truck has been loaded with weapons and people, the little convoy begins grinding along an old broken road leading away from the ruins of the town. In the truck, my father's strike force gets an opportunity to bond with the Watchers. The jeeps, meanwhile, are populated with the rest of us from the plane, as well as Athena. I sit in the front car with Jackson and Velia. Behind, Athena drives with Cyra and Ajax.

I watch the world pass by as we go, these lands once more different to what I've experienced so far. They're dusty and plain, and yet not as stark as the Deadlands. Here and there, old relics of towns and cities dot the horizon, remnants of a world from many decades ago when the rebels and the regions fought for supremacy. Ever since, these lands have been known as no man's land, unsettled by anyone, and with the more flourishing regions to the East, and the Deadlands to the West.

Knight's Wall, of course, was the dividing line, once visible from many miles away as one approached it from either side. Now, however, the vast majority of it has been dismantled, leaving an open run for anyone wishing to travel from one side of the country to the other. Only the natural barriers of the earth now create a need for anyone to deviate their path, craggy peaks and ranges of mountains and impassable hills appearing in the distance as we go.

One such formation, however, is quick to catch the eye. As we roll through a valley, peppered with old trees and withered shrubbery, the sight of five colossal peaks come into view ahead, the thumb and four fingers of The Titan's Hand reaching out from the earth, hundreds of metres into the sky. I give a sleeping Velia a nudge, lifting her from her dreams, and draw her eyes to the peaks. She spends the next few moments as I do, staring at them in wonder.

Soon, however, we're slowing once again, my dad guiding the convoy into an area of rocks that tower above us on all sides. Hidden from the sun, we move in and come to a halt, still half a mile or more from the base of the thumb.

Outside of the cars, we all gather in the shade of the peaks above us, the air close in this little canyon. Jackson addresses us, going over the brief once more. His directives are primarily aimed at his own strike force, trained as they are in scouting and gathering intel. The rest of us are trained for another purpose, and will get to do our part later on.

Right now, however, Ajax, Velia and I are issued with the order to stay in the canyon and get some more rest. None of us have much argument about that. We search for a quiet spot beneath some overhanging rocks, the constant shade making the air cool enough to be comfortable. We take up our positions and set about getting some more sleep as the others go to work.

I watch for a little while as my father and his strike force prepare themselves for a recce, before silently moving off in formation towards The Titan's Hand. The rest are, like us, tasked with doing little but waiting, giving Cyra a chance to recover from the gruelling exertions of the last twenty four hours.

And in that quiet space, I slowly drift off to sleep once more.

Unlike on the flight, however, this time I don't wake for an extended period, my ears pricking up to the sound of my father and his team returning several hours later. With a flutter of the eyelids, I look upon them and notice that their numbers are now depleted, several of them having not returned.

My initial thought is that they must have been caught in a firefight. I stand, my head feeling less heavy and body refreshed, and rush over to them.

"What happened?" I ask, looking around. "Where are the others?"

"We left a few of them out there at lookout points," says Jackson, unwrapping himself from his body armour. He lays his bionic hand on my shoulder and smiles. "You were right, son. There are armed men there. It looks like the place..."

My eyes light up. "Are you sure?!"

"It's a base of some kind, that's for certain. However, we don't know who's down there. Our thermal imaging equipment could only penetrate so deep, and picked up several bodies around the entrance and on the upper level. We did, however, see the same insignia as the mercenaries were wearing on their uniforms above the entrance. The Baron is hardly being subtle."

"You mean the flaming shield and mask and all that?"

"Exactly. My men are in constant contact with me and have their eyes on the entrance. If anyone we know shows their face, they'll call it in immediately."

"So what's the next step?"

He takes a breath, and I see the wrinkles around his eyes deepen.

"Now, I need to get a couple of hours sleep. We'll move out when the night has fully settled in."

As he goes off to find a quiet place to rest, Athena takes his place. We talk for a little while in private, catching each other up on what's been happening since I left Petram. By the sounds of it, her hunt to this point hasn't been a resounding success. Similarly, our attempts to track the source of the recent attacks didn't exactly go well. Now, perhaps, we both have an opportunity to right a few wrongs.

Mostly, however, she's keen to learn how our training progressed.

"It went well," I tell her, "until the President cut us

off, that is."

"Yes, I heard what happened from the Watchers I assigned to you. I hear Alber wanted to come and arrest me," she says with a wry smile.

"I doubt he'd have ever seen that through," I say. "The man's like a petulant child. Everyone over there is so blind to what we're facing…"

"*Was* so blind," she corrects me. "I think the last day or two has opened up a few eyes. Now tell me about this Seeker you faced in New Atlantis…"

I go about describing the young man and our encounter. She listens intently, perhaps figuring out how she might match up.

"By the sounds of it, you let emotion interfere, Theo," she says.

"That's what mum said."

"And she's right. That's what she taught me, all those years ago. Remember to stay calm in any such encounter. It's noble to want to help people, and to get upset when you see them wronged, but it won't aid you in battle. I've faced Watchers before who were too emotionally charged, and in such a state it's easy to lose focus. Think of the most gifted Watchers…"

My mind brings up a few names. Herself. Link. Knight's Terror. All portray a cold detachment when they fight that's essential to reaching their potential.

She adds another name to the list.

"Augustus Knight, while I never fought or met him, was famously callous, as you well know. It doesn't mean that you need to be cold-hearted in other facets of your life. It merely means that, during combat, you refuse to let anything impact your judgement. I can only assume that the Seeker killed the girl to draw you in and scatter your mind. And it worked well."

"I guess there's too much of my mum in me," I say. "Is that what held her back from being as strong as you or Link?"

"Partially," she says. "Your mother always had so much strength and passion, and occasionally she'd channel it in the right way. When she did, she was as strong as anyone. If she'd been building her powers like Link or myself these last twenty years, you can bet she'd be right there at the top alongside us. You, Theo, have that same potential, and so does Ajax. It's just a matter of focus and control. Always remember that."

She leaves me with that lesson pervading my thoughts as I return to my friends under the overhanding rocks. Beyond the canyon, the warm light of the sunset has begun to arrange itself over the lands, the sky darkening with each passing minute. To my side, Velia and Ajax remain at rest, still gathering their strength for the fight. I look at them and wonder whether we're ready for this, whether we're even going to find anyone down there.

Will we find what we're looking for down there? Will more of this riddle be untangled? Or are we just walking into a trap, the Baron still one step ahead?

I guess, soon enough, those questions will be answered.

26
Attack on Titan

Dressed in my black bodysuit, with my slim-line helmet and night-vision goggles, I feel like a fully-fledged member of my father's special forces unit. Velia, Ajax, and Cyra are dressed as I am, while Athena remains in her traditional desert battle dress along with her squad of Watchers.

My father and his actual strike force are also heavily armoured and weaponized, all set for action and ready to lead us out of the canyon and towards the base. The most recent reports from the scouts are that the entrance has remained guarded, but no one has gone in or out. And now, with the skies black and a convenient set of clouds swamping the moonlight, we're about to make our move.

Like a well-drilled military unit, we scurry across the ground, keeping close to the rock formation as it grows and builds ahead of us. In the distance, the silhouettes of the giant fingers remain visible in the darkness, drawing us in and growing larger as we get closer.

We cover the earth quickly, not needing to stop or slow for any reason. With the eyes of our scouts covering us, we know we have an unimpeded path towards the entrance at the base of the thumb, quickly reaching the towering rock on the Eastern side. A little way down, the old remains of this section of Knight's Wall still stand, nothing but a front for what's lurking beneath.

Stopping, Jackson whispers his orders to his strike team, their task to surround and cover the entrance, setting up their canons and other heavy duty weapons to make sure no one but us escape. As they move off and get ready to take their positions, Jackson turns to the rest of us, now the only one remaining without any Watcher powers.

"Athena and Cyra will lead," he says. "The rest follow behind. I will remain at the rear and provide support when we come under fire. I understand that I cannot see into the Void, but I wouldn't miss this for the world."

I see the Watchers look at my father with respect. He's been through numerous operations before, and knows just how to handle himself.

"OK, we all have our orders," he continues. "My men will snipe the perimeter guards. When they're down, we go straight in, silently, and take out anyone we see. Once we've covered the upper floor, we'll regroup. Now, turn your weapons to silent. We do this without a sound."

We move into position, creeping along the rocks and towards the rare remaining section of Knight's Wall. Having seen it all from above, I can picture exactly where we are, the men just around the other side where the entrance is.

All eyes turn to Jackson as he whispers into his

radio: “OK, on three, take them down,” issuing the command to his men, hidden off in the darkness. “One…two…three,” he hisses.

A second later, he gets confirmation. Then he turns to us and nods. “Go,” he says.

Immediately, Athena begins moving around the broken down wall, with Cyra right next to her. Behind, two Watchers follow, the most gifted of Athena’s troop. Then, Ajax, and myself make up the next row, with Velia and the other Watchers a step or two behind.

We pass around the wall, and immediately the sight of several dead men appears, little red holes the size of acorns in the centre of their foreheads. They lie in the dirt, expertly dispatched by the snipers, their guns dropped to their sides.

In the face of the wall, I see a narrow entranceway, with the insignia of the Baron’s army, of Knight’s legacy, emblazoned above it. Immediately, we filter through into the darkness, moving now in single file, as our night-vision goggles light up the path ahead.

There’s a set of steps cut into the stone, leading straight down. Silently, Athena moves to the bottom, her knowledge of the place bolstered by the schematic provided by Professor Lane. When she moves down the steps and around the corner, I see her gun quickly lift and fire, a bullet punching out of it. A second later, I hear a body hit the floor.

She continues on as the rest of us go around the corner, looking ahead to a large room that offers passage to the lower levels from various points. A couple more guards linger inside, their eyes barely having a chance to register shock at our arrival before they're closed for good. With a few hand gestures from Athena, we spread out through the level, moving down metal passageways as our feet lightly clank, taking down any remaining sentries we encounter.

Once the floor has been cleared, we gather again near the entrance, where the stairs to the lower levels reside.

I hear my parents and Athena in whispering conversation.

"I don't like this," says Athena sharply. "Why are there so few people here?"

Jackson looks equally perturbed. "The numbers match up to what our heat scanners registered. Move to the next floor, Athena, and clear it out."

She does as ordered, taking a smaller crew down to the lower level. I'm included in it, along with Ajax, my mother, and her two favoured Watchers, leaving the others above for support. Whispering on comms to keep the rest in the loop, we move down the set of metal stairs and reach another level. Ahead of us, large rooms are linked by wide archways built into the rock, the place lit by hanging lights fixed to the ceiling. A deep silence pervades the entire space ahead as we search forward with our eyes, our goggles now unneeded and lifted to the tops of our helmets.

We move inward, creeping from one room to the

next, all of us constantly focused and searching the Void and coming up with nothing. The rooms are spacious and filled with different things: weapons storage and living quarters and spaces for dining. It looks like the sort of place you'd house and build a secret army. An army, perhaps, that has now been deployed.

The entire floor is clear of people, deserted. It looks like they've already shipped out.

The facility runs deep, however, with several more floors to check. With a little bit more pace, we continue down, the Void throwing up no hidden surprises. I keep a close eye on Athena as we go, she being the one most likely to see any sudden assault before anyone else. But the deeper we go, and the more we search, the more relaxed her eyes become.

Soon, it becomes evident that the place has been abandoned, temporarily at least. As the Watchers are tasked with searching any nook and cranny, the main party congregate together on the bottom floor and discuss our next steps.

"We could lay a trap," says Ajax. "This place is obviously used for housing an army. Most of them are probably dead after last night. We can kill the rest when they return."

"But this doesn't make sense," I say. "I mean, surely the mercenaries who escaped the cities would have returned by now?"

"Unless they're planning a new assault," says Velia.

"My question," says Cyra, "is why are they protecting the entrance and top floor if they're no longer using the facility? If not the Baron and the rest of the Cabal, there has to be something here worth defending."

It doesn't take long for us to get a few answers. From various passages, Watchers come running, delivering further news of any discoveries they've made. One says he's found an enormous room of files. In them could be a great deal of information regarding the Baron's operation and plans.

Another comes running in, reporting on an expansive science facility on the level above. "It looks like they're cooking something up there, Commander," she tells Athena. "Bombs and other devices. Most likely what they've been using in the attacks."

"Good work. I need to check this out," says Athena.

"I'm coming too," adds Jackson, the both of them rushing off as the rest of us wait for any more reports.

Others return with less interesting information, before moving off elsewhere to continue the search. Then, a third piece of critical intel is delivered, one of the Watchers assigned to Eden rushing straight for Cyra.

"Mrs Drayton," his voice gallops between breaths, "I've found someone."

"Who?" asks Cyra with narrowing eyes.

The man takes a breath. “Your father…I think I’ve found your father.”

Her eyes shoot wide open, and so do mine, and with a sudden turn of speed we begin chasing the man down through the tunnels and into the growing darkness. Far from the central room of the bottommost floor of the base, the Watcher guides us towards a locked room, bolted shut by firm fixings. He gestures for my mother to look through the narrow slit at eye-level in the door, and she leans in.

Seconds later, she’s leaning away again and telling us to get back. From her pocket she pulls a little device that she fixes to the locks. We disappear around the corner as the thing starts flashing red. Just as we get out of harm’s reach, it explodes loudly, causing dust to scatter from above and a booming echo to surge down the tunnel.

We reappear round the side to find the locks blasted open, the door now hanging free. As I follow my mother inside, I look upon the interior and see the shape of a figure up against the back wall, hidden in shadow, his arms raised above him and fixed by chains to the ceiling.

Cyra speeds towards him.

“Dad…dad…” she says.

Behind us, Velia scuttles around, searching for a light. She finds one on the wall and clicks the switch, and a nasty bright glow bursts to life on the ceiling. I blink for a second, my eyes adjusting. And when they do, the beaten face of my grandfather materialises from the yellow shroud.

He hangs there by the wall, his wrists locked tight by metal restraints above his head, his chin drooped to his chest. His upper body is bare, red slices and black burns painted all over his torso and arms and chest. Blood oozes from various wounds, his trousers soaked and stained red.

For all the world, he looks to be dead.

"Dad…" my mother repeats, looking up to him and lifting his chin. "Dad…can you hear me?"

The raw emotion in her voice is palpable. My insides strain as I watch, barely able to look as her fingers lift to his neck and feel for a pulse. Those few seconds seem to last an age. Her sullen eyes steadily narrow. And then, suddenly, they burst open.

"He's alive…he's alive!" she shouts. "Someone help me get him down."

In one quick motion I move straight in, drawing out my extendable dagger and bringing forth the blade with a click. I slide it straight through the metal of Drake's restraints and catch him as his weight falls. Velia and the other Watcher clear a table covered in torture utensils, sweeping them to the floor as they assault our ears with a clattering chorus. Together we gently lay Drake down, before my mother's eyes sharply lift to the Watcher.

"Go get the medic," she says. "Run!"

The man turns on his heels and is off, charging away to find the Watcher medic that Athena smartly brought along for the ride. As he goes, Cyra turns her attention back to her father, guiding her eyes carefully over his wounds.

To my untrained eye, most appear to be superficial, inflicted via torture in a bid, perhaps, to extract information. Their sheer volume, however, suggests that he's lost a lot of blood, a fact given merit by the scarlet colour of the trousers and the pallor in his cheeks.

"Is he going to die?" I ask softly, looking on.

"His pulse is weak," says Cyra. "He needs proper attention. We need to get him to Petram immediately."

We work with what we have, wrapping up a few of his smaller wounds with the meagre medical supplies we have to hand, and doing our best to stop the bleeding on his deeper cuts. As we do, he begins to stir, his eyes flickering behind their lids. Then, a slit opens, and he stops.

"Cyra…" he croaks. "Is that you..."

My mother grabs his hand, a tear slipping from her eye. "It's me, dad. We've come to save you."

"No," he says weakly. "No…you shouldn't have come."

"Why not?"

His eyes flicker again. "Theo…where's Theo?"

I step forward. "I'm here, grandfather, I'm right here."

He lets out a breath. It sounds like relief.

“Dad…why shouldn’t we have come?” asks Cyra intently.

“Eden,” whispers Drake. “They’re going to take Eden…”

As he speaks the words, my mind flashes once more with scenes of fire and death. Before me, I watch as the buildings burn and the fog of black smoke fills the sky. I listen as the people scream and the fire crackles. I breathe in and smell the scent of blood, of searing flesh and melting metal. I feel the panic of the people, locked in the city like fish in a barrel with nowhere to run, nowhere to hide.

And when the world clears ahead of me again, I know that everything that’s happened up until now has been a decoy. That all the attacks were designed to confuse and divide us.

That all along, the real target was the capital city of Eden. The city where, right now, just about every luminary from across the country is hiding.

They’ve lured us out so we can’t protect them.

They’re going to exterminate them all.

27
Decoy

"We need to get back to Eden immediately! We have no time to waste."

Jackson's voice cuts through the clamour of activity around us as we stand outside in the tunnel. Inside the room, the medic works to secure Drake's wounds, ably helped by several other Watchers. However, they can only offer temporary care with the supplies we have. He needs to get to Petram quick.

"Did he say anything else?" asks Jackson. "Before he passed out?"

"No," says Cyra. "Just that they're going to take Eden. What did you find in the science facility?"

"It's more like a factory for weapons," grunts Athena. "They were buildings bombs and other explosive devices. We have gathered some data that my Watchers are looking into."

"You think they're going to use these devices on Eden?" I ask.

We all glare and glower but no one says anything. Given Drake's testimony, that's a safe assumption to make.

From down the tunnel, another Watcher comes running.

"Commander," he says, addressing Athena. "We've found a new area. It's filled with transports. It looks like there's another tunnel that leads out of the base."

"What sort of transports?" comes Jackson's voice. "Are there any aircraft?"

"Yes, sir," says the man. "A few planes and some ground-based armoured vehicles. There are tracks leading from the tunnel. It looks like most were used during the attacks."

"Good, well done soldier," says Jackson. "Go back and make sure the planes are operational. Where is it?"

"Two floors up, sir, right on the North end of the base."

As the Watcher rushes off, my father's eyes swing to the torture room, where Drake still lies on the table being worked on by the medic. He steps inside, speaking hurriedly.

"We have a plane that can take him to Petram," he says. "Is he OK to be moved?"

"Sir, he *needs* to be moved," says the medic. "He needs a blood transfusion and surgery on his more serious wounds."

My mother and I wince at the words, but set about helping them load Drake onto a foldout stretcher and carry him through the level. We rush along to the central, spiralling chamber, before moving up two levels and heading North.

As we go, Jackson orders for his strike force to be fetched from above and to meet us down in the vehicle hanger. We continue on, navigating our way through the sprawling base, until the sound of engines begins to filter down a tunnel ahead. Soon, we emerge through an archway into a grand garage, capable of housing dozens upon dozens of vehicles. Only a few remain, however, parked against the walls.

At the end of the room, a large tunnel works its way up, presumably extending through the mountain and exiting at a secret location. And to the right, where the remaining jets are parked, is another tunnel, rising directly up above them.

It's over by the jets that we catch sight of several of the Watchers. There are three planes, two of which are currently active, their engines glowing blue. The other, however, sits dormant, several panels on its underside open and hanging with mechanical wires and other electronics.

"This one isn't working, sir," says a Watcher as we walk over. "It's clearly got some sort of fault that they were working to fix."

"And the other two?" asks Jackson.

"Ready to go, sir."

"Good. Let's get Drake on board."

We move my grandfather up onto one of the planes, just as my father's strike force begin coming down the tunnel into the hanger. One of them is assigned to fly Drake's jet, with the medic climbing aboard to escort the patient to Petram.

Without any time to delay, we step back and watch as the jet rises into the air, lighting up the black tunnel above as it moves up through the mountain. It gradually disappears from view as the tunnel curves away, and doesn't return.

Now, our attention turns to our own escape. Through the tunnel, the final few stragglers come running, all of us now gathered. We're ordered up onto the jet, a military one just like those we used to travel to New Atlantis, with two banks of benches up against each wall for us all to sit on. Ahead, one of Jackson's men takes the wheel, with Athena acting co-pilot. My parents remain up ahead in the cockpit as the jet lifts off, rising into the darkness.

We all look out of the little windows as we rise, curving around as the other jet did, until the faint sight of the cave's exit comes into view, the stars visible beyond. When we punch out into the night, squeezing carefully through the narrowing tunnel, I look down to see that we've secretly exited right out of one of the enormous, craggy fingers of The Titan's Hand.

Setting our course to Eden, Jackson and Cyra march back into the belly of the plane. All eyes are drawn up to my father as he steps before us.

"Listen in, everyone," he starts, eyes flowing from one of us to the next. "As all of you have heard by now, Eden is the target. As we speak, almost every regional and city leader from across the country is camped within the city walls. They think they're safe, but they're anything but. Baron Reinhold has set this up from the start. He's going to eliminate them all. It is up to us to stop him."

"You think they're going to try to take the city?" asks one of the soldiers.

"That is the assumption we're working with," nods Jackson. "They have already destabilised the coastline and regions, and have weakened us overnight. If they take Eden, and kill our leaders, then they will take control of the country."

"But how will they get into the city?" asks Velia. "Isn't it in lockdown?"

"Yes," says Jackson. "But we don't know what tricks the Baron's got up his sleeves. We need to warn them, and we need to defend them."

He returns to the cockpit, as Cyra comes and sits down next to us. At the back of the plane, several Watchers begin sifting through files and data taken from the base, searching through documents found in the weapons facility.

As Cyra moves in beside us, Velia turns to her. "Have you spoken with my sister?" she asks.

Cyra shakes her head. "Not specifically, no, but Mercator is currently safely under our occupation. We have been relaying the message to all of the military commander across the country…"

"But not Eden," I cut in. "You haven't been able to contact Eden?"

She shakes her head. "Not yet. We're still trying,

and are a long way away. There may be interference at this range."

"Or the communications may have been cut already," says Ajax. "They might already be in the city."

"But how will they get in?" asks Velia, once more bringing up the topic. "Isn't the city meant to be impenetrable?"

"Yeah, unless they have someone on the inside," I say. "Someone with all the necessary power to open up the hanger doors and call off the air defences…"

"You mean…President Alber?"

I nod. "Think about it. All the leaders from across the country came to the city for *his* coronation. Now, he's locked them in because of these attacks. It's all been coordinated between him and the Baron…"

"You might be right," says Cyra. "The first wave of attacks took out the top leaders…Aeneas, Troy, General Richter. They knew Drake would go on the hunt, and they captured him, and tried to kill Link, but he got away. After that, it was only a matter of time before a new President was installed. Alber was always going to get the nod, everyone was always going to come together for his coronation…and now, the Baron has them all right where he wants them."

"And he lured us out using the other attacks as decoys," I add. "He lured us away, and Eden locked everyone out. But you can be pretty sure that

Alber's going to open up the doors when the Baron arrives."

"And use his Seekers to cut everyone down," says Velia.

"But he can't know what we know," says Ajax. "If we really think that this is all true, we need to be careful with what we tell Eden. If they know it's us, they won't let us back in."

"So what do we do?" asks Velia.

"We lie," I say. Everyone looks at me. "We're in one of the Baron's jets, right? We pretend we're part of his crew, and then just hope we can get inside."

"But that'll only work is they're already in the city," says Velia.

I begin nodding. "Something tells me…they already are."

My mother stands from our huddle, the sudden movement breaking the discussion. "I'll relay this to Jackson," she says. "If you're right…we need to tread carefully."

She turns and moves off towards the cockpit, leaving the three of us alone.

"You really think they're already there?" asks Velia.

I see Ajax nodding as I do. "They're there," he growls. "This is just one big setup."

The world is still dark outside as we cut through the sky, the clouds now dispersed and the moon glowing bright. Inside the plane, the Watchers and soldiers sit in feverish discussion, many of them coming up with wild theories of their own as they work their way through the many documents brought on board.

Gradually, the scale of the Baron's operation is brought to light. Thousands of people have been involved in it over the years, not only the rich members of the Cabal at the top, and the many mercenaries under their command, but the various other men and women in between. Researchers, scientists, weapons developers and engineers, politicians and even military officials currently operating in the Eden army are named inside one document or another.

The tendrils of this go even deeper than we thought, right back to the end of the War of the Regions two decades ago. Ever since, a growing army of people, dissatisfied with the way things turned out, have been working in tandem, under the direction of Baron Reinhold, to see out this plan. A plan created in the twisted mind of Augustus Knight all those years ago, and fleshed out by the man who reveres and admires him so much.

And now, their plan is coming to fruition, years of collaboration and conspiracy building to this point. They're going to eliminate all those who oppose them, and take back the country. And in their wake, the doctrine of Knight will be restored.

And we're the only ones that can stop it.

I continue to send my eyes to the windows as voices rush around me, searching the grounds below for some sight of where we are. Occasionally, Jackson or Cyra or Athena come back from the cockpit with updates and to hear the latest news dredged up from the document search. When they do, they provide details of where we are, and how long it will be until we reach our new target.

Each time they do, I look out and try to wonder where we are. In the darkness, it's impossible to make anything out. When we reach the coast, however, that all changes.

Because down along the shoreline, little fires still burn here and there, lingering remnants of the devastation of the previous night. When we move out to sea, the shape of New Atlantis comes into view, embers continuing to glow up and down the high towers, lights sparkling on the surface of the water surrounding it.

As we pass, Jackson comes to the front, our plan now firmly in place and passed around from soldier to soldier, Watcher to Watcher.

"The sun will be rising soon," he announces to us all. "By the time it does, Eden will be in our sights. We're going to communicate with the hanger control centre using our plane's identification number, and hope they fall for it..."

"So you think the city has already been infiltrated, sir?" asks a soldier.

My father begins nodding. "I'm afraid so. And now...now it's our turn."

He returns to the cockpit for the final run. I look

ahead out of the window and see that the sky is changing colour, brightening to signal a new day. And today will be one of reckoning.

Today, all of the pieces are finally coming together.

28
Showdown

"OK, no one speak," says Jackson. "Keep completely silent. I will do the talking."

Ahead, the city of Eden looms, the grand platform rising high out of the ocean, tall and wide and seemingly impenetrable. From the outside, it all looks normal, the ocean quiet and calm, the sunrise bringing a healthy glow to the morning air.

Inside, however, it will be anything but. Overnight, the Baron and his forces will have made their way in, welcomed with open arms by President Alber. They will have done so without opposition, the city's forces called off, the snake allowed to slither right into the fox's den without so much as a shot being fired.

As coups go, I have to hand it to them. It's all been masterfully played, each move building to the next, deepening the crisis that we're facing. But now, all they have to do is see to the mass murder of those who oppose Knight's vision, reflected through the Baron's words and actions. And in one fell swoop, this nation will see the old order restored.

I stand on the outskirts of the cockpit, listening intently as my father dials into the city's security centre. As the leader of the city's defences over the last few months, Jackson has developed an intimate knowledge of its security protocols. As part of that, he's gotten to know well the few men tasked with running the city's defensive systems, including the external guns and the hanger gates.

Now, his ear for voices is going to be put to the test.

The line crackles for a moment as we approach, all of us silently holding our breath. Then, through the static, a voice appears.

"Eden control tower, identify yourself."

I watch my father's face carefully as he tries to identify the voice. He looks to us and shakes his head, his eyes narrowing. He doesn't recognise it.

"Morning control, ID number KN243."

We wait nervously for a response. It seems to take an age.

"What is your purpose?"

"Special cargo," says Jackson. "We've gathered some more leaders from the regions to join the others, under orders from Baron Reinhold."

Again, there's a brief delay, as we wait with bated breath.

Our subterfuge has to hold...

Then, the voice comes on the radio once more.

"OK, KN243. Hanger bay 4 is opening for entry. We'll have a troop waiting to escort the subjects to the central square."

We look to each other as Jackson says thank you and clicks off the line.

"The central square," I say as soon as it's safe. "That's where they're gathering everyone?"

"Sounds like it," says Jackson. "Good job, all of you. The ruse has worked for now, but it won't last as soon as those soldiers see us. We'll have to take them out quick, and get to the tower before anyone can call in for help."

"No problem," says Athena. "I'll take care of it."

"Good. We have to be quick, no mistakes. Don't let anyone speak when we get off the plane. I'll relay to the troops."

Jackson moves into the belly of the plane to pass on his orders. Everyone appears buoyed by the fact that our plan has so far succeeded, the plane now a Trojan horse about to deliver us right into the heart of this coup.

"A day ago, when we left the city, it was ours," says Jackson. "Now, it's down to us to take it right back from under the noses of these usurpers. We're counting on all of you. A single missed shot can mean failure. Get yourselves ready."

As we swoop lower towards the outer walls of the city, everyone prepares themselves for another fight, checking their armour and weapons and getting ready for combat. Ahead, the door for hanger 4 begins to open, the main control tower a little way down the city's perimeter.

I look upon the large gun placements on the external walls, ready to strike at any incoming enemy. Part of me expects them to suddenly let loose a barrage of fire that not even we could do anything about, for me to look into the Void and see the plane explode around me. But they merely remain in place, statically looking out to sea as we pass by and move closer to the open passageway into the city.

Ahead, through the main window, I see soldiers moving into the hanger, their weapons raised. From this distance, it's clear to see which uniforms they're wearing, the Baron's mercenary army now having taken control of the city. I wonder, with Alber on board, whether the city guards and soldiers will join up too, happy to go with the flow as the new regime takes charge. Most have little in the way of loyalty one way or another, and with some of the military commanders now known to be loyal to the Baron, it's possible that it might just be us against the world in here.

I have no time to take such a concern to Jackson, the plane now moving into the shadow of the hanger. Cleverly, the pilot turns it as we enter, making sure that when the door slides open, we have clear shots right out into the pack of soldiers awaiting us.

We take our positions, some of us kneeling, others standing behind, and all of us with our guns set to silence. I stare down the barrel of my rifle at the door, my breath calm, my heart beating steadily, and wait for the door to rise.

The jet stops with a bump. Outside, I hear voices. Then, suddenly, a heavy hiss of air sounds and the door escapes upwards, opening up to reveal the troop of soldiers standing before us. They barely have time to react as our guns snap together, two dozen of them all firing at once.

The entire greeting party is immediately gunned down, some taking single bullets to the head, others blasted with many to the chest. They drop, almost as one, into a heap of flesh on the floor, all of them incapacitated in a flash.

"OK, go go go…" says Jackson.

We move down into the hanger as quickly as possible, the door at the other end open and brightly lit as the sun shines down outside through the domed roof of the city. We grab bodies and move them quickly to the side, hiding them wherever we can as Athena moves forward with her two favoured Watchers. They quickly disappear from the hanger, checking the coast is clear before moving right and preparing to infiltrate the command centre.

It doesn't take them long to reappear, their mission seen through without a hitch. As soon as they re-enter the hanger, we shut the door, blocking us out from anyone who might see in from outside.

"They won't be telling anyone we're here," says Athena, marching towards us with blood splashed across her suit.

"Did you get any information out of them?" asks Jackson.

"Didn't have time," she says. "All we know is what he said on the radio. We need to get to the central square immediately."

"But that'll put everyone in danger," says Velia. "They'll just open fire…"

"What choice do we have?" asks Ajax. "They're going to murder anyone important anyway. We can't just stand here forever."

"But what about the visions we've had," adds in Cyra. "Some of them were clearly of here. We know the city is going to burn. If we go in, all guns blazing, maybe that's what triggers it?"

"Maybe," says Athena. "Or maybe not. Maybe they're going to start burning all those people right there in the square at any moment. Maybe that's what you've seen. Our job is to make the city safe, and that means taking out the Baron and his Seekers. They are the priority."

"And if innocent people get caught in the crossfire?" asks Cyra.

"Then so be it," says Athena. "We know what war is like, Cyra. If the few have to die to save the many, then that's just how it is. We need to do our job, no matter what."

Her worlds are cold and callous but necessary and true. Death is just a part of war that is unavoidable. It doesn't matter what we do, we won't be able to prevent everyone from dying.

"OK," says Jackson, surveying the action and compiling a plan. "Athena is right. We need to act, and we need to do it now. We will move into the city, and split up, coming at the square from various angles. If we can get a few of the enemy's top brass in our sights, we take them down. It will cause panic, and hopefully they won't see it coming. We'll try to usher as many people to safety as possible in the chaos."

He waits for us to nod before moving off to pass the orders to the other soldiers and Watchers. As he does, a strange feeling of dread begins to build up inside me. My heart starts to race. My breathing grows shorter and more abbreviated. My eyes narrow, imbued with a fresh intensity.

To my side, Velia slips closer to me, noticing.

"Theo…are you all right?" she asks.

I barely hear her. Instead, I lift my eyes to Athena, who's own façade has darkened. Ajax, too, has gone quiet, suddenly introspective, blinking as his gaze swings over to the hanger door.

"What's going on?" asks Velia again, yet to be swamped by the same sensation. Then, suddenly, her eyes pull down, and her pupils dilate, and a whisper falls from her lips. "We're not alone…"

Walking slowly, methodically, Cyra passes me, moving towards the hanger door. I watch as she inches closer to the small window that looks out at the wide open space beyond, and the tall towers of the city in the distance.

For a few moments, she stares out, before turning.

Suddenly, the entire hanger is completely silent as

she speaks.

“They’re here,” she says. “They must have seen us coming…”

29
Battle Royale

Towards the door, my father marches, speaking as he goes. "Who's here?" he asks.

No one speaks as he reaches the window and answers his own question.

"Oh my God," I hear him say quietly.

From the back, one of the soldiers calls out: "What is it, sir? What's going on?"

Jackson turns, his knuckles white as he grips hard at his weapon. "The Seekers," he says. "They're all outside."

A wave of fear spreads across the troop of our soldiers. It doesn't land with the rest of us. We all look to one another, our eyes turning as hard as oak, every fibre of our bodies tensing and ready for action.

Then I see a smile grind up Athena's face.

"Good," she says. "Now we get to face them head on." Her gaze sweeps to her Watchers. "To the front," she whispers harshly.

Jackson, meanwhile, takes a step away from the door, ordering his men to find cover from which to snipe from. "We offer support," he says. "Lay down fire. Be careful with you aim."

The hanger becomes a rush as everyone speeds to their positions. I look to Cyra and Ajax and Velia, and we pass nods down the line.

Then, from the control panel to the door, Athena turns to us all.

"Focus," she says. "Search the Void and cover each other's backs. We outnumber them four Watchers to one. Those are good odds for me."

I see some gritty smiles spread around the Watchers, but can only think that most of them will offer no threat all. Athena must know it too.

Still, she'd never say such a thing, and I feel guilty for even thinking it. With her hand on the button, she counts down from three to one, my heart galloping faster and faster as each second passes.

Then, with a loud click, the hanger door begins to rise up, once more grinding towards the ceiling and retreating before our eyes. Bright light spills in from outside, and beyond, standing about twenty metres from the hanger door, the four Seekers await us, standing in a line, all wrapped in their black cloaks with their faces hidden under the shadow of their hoods.

A short lull ensues. As the door reaches its end, no one acts. Then, from nowhere, I hear my father's voice roar from the back.

"OPEN FIRE!"

Immediately, the deafening sound of exploding bullets fills the morning air. From behind, my father's strike force fire from their positions. From the front, the rest of us kneel and steady our weapons to our shoulders, spreading a wall of bullets at the four boys ahead of us. The flashing is so wild and blinding that I can barely see what's in front of me, barely see it as the boys glide away, sliding left and right, up and down, gradually moving backwards from the ferocious attack.

After thirty seconds of endless fire, my father calls a halt to the barrage. The dust begins to settle, and we look again to see the boys standing as they were, only a few short paces back.

They're luring us into the open...

A second attack is ordered. This time, we vary the threat, some pouring out regular bullets, others sending explosive rounds at the boy's feet, and a few scattering the earth with fire as incendiaries burst to life.

The carnage ahead blinds us, however, making it impossible to see where they've gone. Naively expecting to finish the job there, I hear a couple of soldiers and Watchers let out a cheer as the firing stops, and the world ahead cracks and burns. Moments later, a breeze sweeps in, dragging away the flames and dust, and leaving behind only the sight of four identical figures, now even further back than they were.

"This isn't going to work," calls Athena. "We need to fight them up close. Blades out," she shouts.

From their armour, the Watchers draw swords and knives from various slots. Velia and Cyra do the same, while Ajax and I take our retractable weapons in hand. And together, walking in a line, we begin moving out of the hanger, and into the morning sunshine.

I look out to the left and right, at the many hangers lined up along the edge of the city. I look ahead, at the buildings in the distance that signal the start of the residential part of the city. I look across the grand open space around us, and see no sign of any enemy support. No soldiers. No mercenaries. No one here for us except these clones of Augustus Knight.

Is it hubris that they're here all alone? Or is it merely confidence? It won't take long to find out...

We fan out, spreading ourselves around them, twenty of so sets of eyes all watching each other, all searching for the first attack. Soon enough, we have them enclosed between us, and yet they haven't even moved, haven't changed their formation. Still, they just stand in a line, hidden in black.

Their reaction seems like it's delayed, but it's anything but. Slowly but surely, with total ease, they begin turning to face us, four sides of a square looking out. I look around our group, and see that we're well dispersed.

Athena stands ahead of me, flanked by two of her Watchers. To the right is Ajax, with one of the more powerful of Athena's warriors for company. Cyra is to my left with the other. And alongside me, Velia primes herself for action, with the rest of Athena's troop littered here and there.

Step by step, we close in on them, swords and daggers and spears glinting bright under the sun. Then, from their belts, I see all four of them simultaneously reach into their cloaks and draw out long knives of their own. They do so without looking at each other, the telepathic link between them seemingly allowing them to act as one, like a single organism with eight arms and eight eyes, able to view us from any angle, defend from any strike.

Several metres from them, we all stop, their heads still slightly ducked low, only the bottom halves of their faces emerging from the shadow. I look over to Athena, whose eyes quickly sweep across to all of us. And then, suddenly, she makes her move.

She reacts like lightning, flashing forward towards the Seeker ahead of her. To her sides, three other Watchers pounce in behind as she slices across at her enemy. He brings his knife up to defend himself just as the rest of us join the fight.

Left and right, the corners of my eyes catch sight of my mother, and my best friend, meeting their foes with clashing swords and spears. And as they move, so do I, and do does Velia next to me. With an additional two Watchers supporting us, we dive straight in, four blades cutting straight down on the hooded clone, calmly standing before us.

His movement is so fast and so late. Just as our swords are about to hit, he twists and turns between them, flashing with his own dagger to deflect the swipes he can't avoid. I can only imagine how they must look to any spectator, the four of them moving almost as one, dancing together as over a dozen blades attempt to cut them down.

It seems, for a moment, that they're feeling us out, and luring us in. Then, in a sudden move, they all strike forward at exactly the same time, identifying the weakest among us. Their blades all find the flesh of four of Athena's Watchers, cutting through them with fatal strokes, driving straight through their armour like it's nothing. Blood sprays and spurts from four chests, four hearts pierced and quickly giving out. Immediately, our numbers are reduced by a quarter, four bodies now lying on the sleek floor, seeping crimson around our feet.

It all happened so fast that I barely saw it, and with such cohesion that it truly feels as if we're fighting a single foe. Not once did they look to each other, or utter a word. There was no sign that they'd agreed when and whom to strike. It just happened, their knives cutting off lives and then quickly retreating, standing again as a four as they look out at us.

We take a breath, and in the brief lull a roar suddenly pours from Athena's mouth. I look into her eyes and see a burning river of fire flowing down her face as she once more charges in and resumes the battle.

We all do the same, my focus complete and total. All around goes blurred, just the Seeker ahead of me clear. He floats and glides as if walking on air, moving like I've never seen anyone move. It seems as if he has no trouble at all, a small smile of joy laughing on his thin lips as he finally gets to engage in battle, finally gets to do what he was born to do, bred to do.

I hate the look. It's a look that tells me this is nothing but a game to him. That says we're no challenge at all, and if he wanted he could just strike out, along with the others, and end another four lives.

The thought angers me, but I don't allow my emotions to rise. I do as Athena told me, taught me. I focus deeper, narrow my attention to him alone, and forget about the others. Hard as it is, I allow concerns for my mother and friends to slip from my mind. I calm my breathing and steady the beating of my heart, and enter a state of complete relaxation.

And in that state, I act.

Moving forward, I begin to see his own display more clearly. I can sense where he's coming from, where he's moving to. The shape of his limbs as they glide, the direction of his torso as it twists; I see it all, and feel it all, and begin to determine where his body will end up next.

And soon, a little smile joins my own lips as I begin to flow like he is, fight like he is, our blades missing and clashing in equal measure. I look to his face and see that the smile is beginning to fall, that under his hood, within the shadow, his eyes are starting to narrow.

Velia continues to join the fight with me, her own attacks beginning to grow more acute and accurate. The Seeker's movement grow a little more erratic and less graceful, and I see that the others are doing the same. Athena stands tall, her slim and lithe physique gliding as they are, matching her foe with every step he takes. Cyra and Ajax, too, stand toe to toe and don't give anything away, all of us now tightening our grip, closing in once more.

Soon, the Seekers begin to break up, and so does the fighting. They burst free, moving away, drawing us into separate groups as they give themselves more space and freedom to move. Now, suddenly, there's no symbiosis between them, each of them becoming his own entity.

In our little groups, we appear to spar evenly now, the clones surprised, perhaps, by our abilities. Never before will they have encountered someone like Athena, hardened by two decades of hunting and searching the Void. Maybe, after being trained by Knight's Terror, they considered him the pinnacle of what they'd face.

Oh, how wrong they are.

Nor, would they expect to find such fight in me, or Ajax, or Velia. Even Cyra, known to have turned from her powers, may have been underestimated. Our time training in the Grid, adding layers to our abilities, has clearly paid off.

Maybe we do have a chance…

I feel a growing surge of hope as the battle goes on. In my extreme focus, however, I don't notice a couple more bodies fall, two more Watchers feeling the sting of one of the Seekers' blades. In a flash, I notice the blood seeping across the ground, and see that our numbers are being further reduced.

And then, one of them shows his true colours.

It's the one fighting with Athena who appears to change. I flash my eyes on him and see that he's taken out those fighting alongside her. He cuts them down in one, and then advances on her, slicing his dagger across her body and cutting into her arm. She staggers back as Cyra dashes over to help, and in that moment, my own focus begins to wane.

It just takes a moment like that, and suddenly I'm on the back foot. From nowhere, my own foe sees his chance, rattling the butt of his knife across my face, sending me staggering back. Velia, looking at me, is also quickly dispatched. I hit the floor hard, blinking through my blurring eyes, and see that only Ajax and Cyra fight on unharmed, the others nursing injuries or sprawled on the floor.

I try to get to my feet, but feel the force of another blow. It's not a cutting knife, however, that meets my flesh, but a fist designed to knock me down but not end me.

The others get the same treatment, forced back by the sudden ferociousness of one Seeker in particular. I see my mum hit the dirt, and then Ajax too. One by one, we're incapacitated, knocked down but not killed.

And then, with us all on the floor, a flood of soldiers suddenly come running from all angles, enclosing us. They come forward and bind our wrists as I look at the carnage, at the many Watchers lying in pools of blood.

But not us. Not my friends and family. We've

been spared…for now.

My eyes then turn to the hanger, searching for my father. But I see no sign of him or his men. Soldiers go rushing in as one of the Seekers approaches me again. And on his face, I see that the smile has returned.

They were always going to win.

30
Lambs to Slaughter

We're chucked unceremoniously into the back of a truck. I look across my allies to see that they're all OK, groggy from the fight but nothing more. Only Athena's body spills much blood, crimson dripping from her upper right arm where the Seeker found a space between her armour. Using her shackled hands, my mother quickly tears off a piece of fabric from Athena's outer shirt and wraps it tight, cutting off the flow of blood.

Other than our little band, only a couple of Watchers remain, the rest of Athena's troop having been easily dispatched. It's no surprise to me that both are the ones most prized by their mentor, the only ones capable of defending themselves against such foes.

I dread to think what would have happened were we not adorned in such armour as we are. Our bodies carry signs of many near misses, little slices appearing on our black bodysuits. And yet, when it came to it, we weren't killed. They had us at their mercy, and yet they didn't act.

Why…

It doesn't take long for my query to be answered. As we glide through the city in the hovertruck, I notice that we're heading straight for the centre, gathered together and herded like the rest. When the truck stops, and the doors open, the light that spills in briefly blinds me. We're ushered out by the soldiers and the scene before me clears. Ahead, right where the President held his coronation, flocks of luminaries stand in huddles, tightly locked together into a pen.

We're pushed towards them, our hands bound in front of us, and sent in to join the rest. These men and women, who so recently were sat in the same space, proudly watching a new man ascend to the summit of the city, are now here as captives. Their own arms are bound, some of them sporting signs of a fight on their faces. The faces of many others shine with tears, all of them with cowering and fearful eyes as men with guns surround them.

We're pushed into the bunch, and my eyes spot Leeta there, her plump cheeks pinker than ever and her usually well manicured hair dishevelled and out of place. It looks like many were taken during the night, few dressed as they usually would be in their full regalia, unceremoniously dragged from their beds like lambs to slaughter.

Because that's why they're here, and they know it all too well. Around us, dozens of soldiers stand with their machine guns pointing straight at us. When the order it given, they'll open fire. Most will drop dead in seconds, suffering no pain. We who can see into the Void, however, will watch our deaths coming from afar, unable to do anything about it.

Now, as I look ahead, I see the reason our lives

were spared. Moving before us, stepping up into a little stage, Baron Reinhold saunters with an air of victory pulsing from his body. With him I see other men I recognise: Lord Kendrik and Count Lopez, other members of the Cabal whose pictures I've seen. And right to his left, the smug face of President Alber appears, not a glint of guilt in his eyes.

"TRAITOR!" comes a sudden shout from the crowd.

Others join in, calling the man out, losing their own sense of dignity as they spit in his direction and curse his name.

I see him look in shock at the reaction he's getting, before his face thunders and he stamps his feet like a petulant child. The crowd only shout louder, some of them trying to break free of the cordon, scampering to the stage.

A sudden flurry of bullets fills the air. I watch as two men and a women are gunned down near the President's feet. The people hush and go quiet, their cries of hatred and anger turning to those of fear. Alber himself looks down at the bodies with stark eyes, Senators and Mayors and other leaders he might once have called friends.

Then, the Baron's voice reaches over the throng.

"Now now, soldier, let's not get premature," he says, raising his arm to calm the killer's itchy trigger finger.

The man nods obediently and swings the gun back

to the crowd, who duck from its path and shut their eyes. Their looks of fear bring a smile to his hateful face. I make a note in my head to kill him first should I somehow get out of this.

The Baron's voice rises again in the sudden silence, echoing a little around the city square.

"You know why you are all here," he says. "You were all given the chance to swear allegiance to your one true ruler, Augustus Knight. You chose not to do so. For that, you are sentenced to death."

"I'll never swear allegiance to him!" shouts a brave man, elderly and unbowed by fear. "Knight is dead…and good riddance."

The Baron's eyes sharpen as he stares at the man. He looks to his left, where one of the Seekers is standing guard, and then to his right at another. His eyes find the final two, before a smile rises on his face. At once, they all slowly peel back their hoods revealing their faces to the crowd. The people look in shock, seeing the young spectres of evil rising up once more.

"As you can see, ladies and gentlemen," says the Baron. "Augustus Knight is far from dead…"

I look from one Seeker to the next, seeing their faces clearly for the first time. They all look identical, older versions of the boys we saw in the tubes down in the cloning facility. One, however, carries a lighter tone to his hair, his eyes flashing with a dash of blue amid the grey. I recognise him immediately as the one I sparred with in New Atlantis. The one, perhaps, that Knight's Terror said was 'truly special'.

But not to me. I stare at him with a deepening scowl as his eyes swing to mine, locking for a few long seconds. I don't deviate, unwilling to turn away before he does. But he, too, continues to stare right into me, a strange look to him that is both familiar and yet unnerving.

"Ah…Theo," comes the Baron's voice. My staring contest is broken as I'm drawn to his face. "I'm so glad you could make it…and is that Ajax and Velia I see. Oh, and your mother, too. We're yet to meet, Mrs Drayton. It's a real pleasure."

"Save your words, Reinhold. I don't care for them," cuts Cyra's voice. "You try to come off sounding like Augustus, but really you're just a second rate imitator."

"Oh…I have no desire to sound like or emulate Augustus," he retorts. "There will never be another man like him. His mind was a work of art, a thing of beauty. The things he did for this country will never be forgotten by those who truly understand him. All of you here…you're nothing but a blip in *his* history. And his history will go on…"

"It won't go on," shouts Cyra. "You have your clones, but they're just low quality copies of the man. Augustus Knight is long dead, and he will never be coming back."

Again, my mother's words don't cause the reaction I'd expect. The Baron merely smiles gently.

"Cyra…the Golden Girl," he says, sighing. "A

simple hero of the people…who truly knows nothing. You think his death was the end? You think he didn't foresee it all? You think he didn't put plans in place for when it came? None of you here know the full depths of him or what he was capable of. And none of you will…"

He looks around the city, at the tall towers surrounding the square, and takes a deep breath, sucking in the air that was once so familiar to him.

"I used to love this place," he says. "I thought I'd live here forever. But I've learned all too well that things change, and not everything is meant to last forever. And like your lives, Eden is about to come to an end…"

A see people among the crowd looking at each other. A few words and whispers begin to chatter. I look at my allies and they, too, appear confused.

And yet it's President Alber's voice that rings out loudest.

"But, Baron Reinhold…I was told that I'd continue as President. What do you mean this city will come to an end?"

"Oh, I mean exactly that, Mr President," says the Baron, smiling. He clips his fingers and two soldiers swing their weapons at Alber's chest and head, one aiming at each.

"But…what is this?!" bleats Alber. "I did everything I was asked to do…I got you access to the city…"

"And for that, I thank you," says the Baron coldly.

And with a smile, and a tiny nod, two single shots ring out, one penetrating Alber's heart, and the other his head.

Once more, the crowd shriek and gasp at the sight, while the members of the Cabal merely look on as if it's nothing. I turn to my allies and in our eyes we tell each other that we have to do something…that we can't just stand here and wait to be killed.

And yet, disarmed and surrounded by soldiers and Seekers, there's absolutely nothing we can do…

Then, beneath my feet, I feel a deep rumbling. It comes from nowhere, an alien feeling for anyone who's stepped foot in this city. This isn't like the mainland, where an earthquake from miles away can cause the ground to rattle and shake. Here, nothing can impact the city's rigid motion, not even the most violent storm or terrible tornado. There's no feature of the natural world that can cause even the faintest of ripples through these streets.

But nothing about this rumbling is natural. It happens once, and then it happens again. And several more times, the platform rocks a little, vibrations rolling up through everyone in the square.

All eyes hunt for the Baron again, who looks down on us, watching as we react with confusion. But there's no confusion in him, or the allies standing to his left and right.

"What is this? What's going on?" calls out a voice from the crowd.

More voices shout with fear and bewilderment,

looking for answers even with their deaths so imminent.

It's not the Baron, however, who offers an answer. It's Athena, wincing through the pain in her arm, sweat beading on her forehead.

"You heard what he said," she calls out. "They're not taking this city back…they're going to destroy it."

"Yes…yes we are," laughs the Baron. "And all of you, my friends, will have front row seats."

"And that's what Knight wanted, is it?" I call over the growing clamour, drawing the Baron's eyes to me. "He wanted his great city destroyed?!"

"Theo…I told you before, not so long ago when we first met. I told you, didn't I, that if Augustus cannot have this city…then no one can. We'll see your world burn, and build our own from the ashes."

As he speaks, the rumbling sounds again, this time more aggressive, the ground shaking beneath us. Off in the distance, up on the deck level, the sound of explosions begins to echo down the streets, and I see the glowing flames of chaos once more appearing around us.

"And that, my friends, is my cue to leave," says the Baron loudly. "I bid you all a fond farewell. It's such a shame that you refused to turn…"

With those words, he begins moving away, descending from the stage with the rest of his men, his Seekers flanking him for company. I see the lighter haired one looking once more at me, his eyes then sweeping towards my mother. For a second, he stares at her before being called into the waiting hovercar, disappearing once more from sight.

From the cordon, a couple of the crowd try to rush through and escape, the soldiers momentarily distracted as the Baron and his convoy begin moving off. Their eyes are quick to see the attempt, however, several more dignitaries given the most undignified of endings.

The guns roar out, snapping bullets into innocent bodies, and I feel my arms tensing harder and harder, trying to rip open my restraints. I look at Ajax, muscles bulging beneath his bodysuit as he tries to do the same, the metal wrenching and grinding but refusing to break.

A couple more people attempt to flee in desperation, but they too feel the sting of the mercenaries' bullets. I swing my eyes to Athena, her teeth gritted as she watches things unfold, eyes searching for some means of escape. Then, I look to my mother, and note that she's doing the same. She stares forward, and I see her pick something up, see her sense something coming.

She swings her view over to the side, and my eyes follow. There, standing surrounding us, a dozen soldiers point their weapons, ready to fire as the city continues to grow louder with explosions, drawing ever closer.

And as I watch, I see them suddenly drop, one after another, legs giving way as they sink to the floor. Heads click back, red dots appearing in their centre, as the rest of the soldiers begin searching the skies.

And in that moment of confusion, we all see our chance. As the dignitaries cower and duck, the Watchers stand tall, the world now filling once more with little lines of white as bullets pour from all sides.

My eyes flash left and right and I see, hidden among the streets high and low, my father's strike force, sniping expertly as they've been trained to do. And among them, other figures appear.

Jackson. Ellie. Link.

Heroes, together again. Fighting once more for freedom.

31
The City Falls

The world roars with the sound of battle. Explosions. Gunshots. Screaming.

Burning buildings glow around us, the ground beneath us continuing to rumble and shake. And in that moment, I see the flash of one of the visions I had many days and weeks ago. Eden was going to burn all along.

Taking cover from the sudden attack, the Baron's mercenaries start firing back, their attention no longer on the crowd. I see one, however, who's got an eye for the kill, a look that tells me he's desperate to take as many lives as possible before his own is lost. He's the one who mowed down the innocent men and women only minutes ago. One of the Baron's fanatics, a worshipper of Knight, keen to be rewarded in the next life.

I promised myself I'd kill him first…I won't let myself down.

As he hides from fire, I refuse to let him act out his egregious intentions. With my hands bound, I begin stepping through the mess of cowering bodies, making a beeline towards him.

I see the white lines of bullets cross ahead of me,

firing at the mercenaries, about to slash through and seek them out. I see one right ahead, but don't duck under it. Instead, I lift my restraints ahead of me, place the connecting chain in front of the white trail, and wait.

A moment later, the errant bullet comes cruising, cutting straight through the chain and setting my hands free. A smile of freedom lights on my face as my pace now quickens, the murderer ahead about to spray a clip into the crouching crowd.

I don't let him. Bounding ahead, he sees me coming, but has no chance at all. Lifting his machine gun to my chest, he opens fire. But I'm no longer there, sliding left and reaching him in a flash. I take a grip of his head and twist, turning his neck backwards with a loud crack. I drop him to the earth, and feel nothing as I glance at his broken frame.

Instead, I lean down and scoop up his weapon, running from mercenary to mercenary as I take them out. From the shadows, Link does the same, his many wounds heavily taped, but his body tightly bound in a supportive suit similar to what we're wearing. As he marches through, terminating the remaining mercs, Ellie and Jackson arrive from other alleys, releasing the others from their bounds.

Soon enough, the chattering gunfire has been subdued, the Baron's soldiers taken out.

I rush over to the others, words already pouring out.

"What the hell happened?" shouts Cyra over the

din, looking at Jackson.

"It was Link and Ellie," he says. "They'd seen this coming, and managed to save me and my strike force back in the hanger. There's no time to explain. We have to get these people out of here…"

"Right," says Cyra, looking around. "What's the best way?"

"The docks," calls Ellie, running to join us with Link and Ajax. "The hangers are crawling…we'll never escape that way."

"OK, make for the docks right away," says Jackson. Then he turns to me. "Professor Lane," he says. "We have to get her."

"Where is she?!"

"Down in her lab," shouts my father, the city growing ever louder. "I won't let her stay here and die…"

"OK dad…OK."

He turns to Cyra once more, working to usher the leaders out of the square. "Cy, we'll meet you at the docks. Get as many there safely as you can."

She looks to her husband and son. "Where are you going?"

"I have to get Winifred."

"It's too late, Jack. The city is dead."

"And I won't let her die along with it. I need Theo's eyes. We'll be safe, I promise."

They kiss, briefly, a moment of tenderness amidst

the madness, before she lets his hands slip from hers.

"Be safe," she says, hugging me tight, before moving off to help the others.

Alone with my father, we begin running from the square, diving inside a waiting hovercar. I push my father away and get behind the wheel, my ability to see into the Void essential. It proves to be so as we spin around streets, crumbling bits of debris raining down from on high. Around us, people pour out of buildings, waking as the city is besieged from within.

We call out as we go, shouting out of the windows.

"GET TO THE DOCKS! GET OUT OF EDEN!"

Those who hear us turn in the right direction, moving North to the city docks. Those who don't continue to panic, not knowing what to do or where to go.

We can't help them, though. There's nothing more we can do.

Soon, we're approaching the wall, and tumbling from the car as a large chunk of debris caves in its roof. We take no notice of it, hurtling towards the lifts and praying they still work.

They do.

In we get, sinking into the fiery depths of the sea city, the entire platform still shaking and rattling as we descend. I keep my focus, searching the Void, as we step out onto Underwater 3 and begin rushing down the corridor.

As we go, the sight of water comes pouring in from the distance, cracks in the outer perimeter straining as seawater comes leaking in. Our feet splash as the lights come and go, the power threatening to go out as the entire structure groans and grinds, moaning in pain.

Ahead, in the darkness, the sight of Professor Lane's lab appears, the security door fastened shut. As we gallop, Jackson lifts the keycard from his pocket, ready to insert it. When he does, the door flashes and lifts, but only half way, forcing us to duck under it to get inside.

Immediately, our voices fill the air.

"Winifred!" calls Jackson.

"Professor Lane!" I call.

Ahead, the room flickers, the usually glowing screens ahead cracked and broken. Machinery lies everywhere, tables and cabinets tossed about by the violent shaking. We move in, calling her name, separating as we search the lab.

And then, I see her, lying on the ground, caught under a large monitor that's fallen to the floor. She lies there, motionless, her withered old frame crippled and broken. From her mouth, blood trickles, her eyes tightly bound shut.

"DAD! SHE'S HERE!" I shout.

Jackson's with me in a flash, sliding to the sloshing wet floor, cupping his hand to the Professor's cheek.

“Winifred,” he whispers softly. “Winifred, it’s me…it’s Jackson.”

As the city continues to collapse from within, everything seems to go quiet in my ears. I move forwards gently, listening as my father softly speaks to the woman who has done so much for him.

“Winifred,” he says again. “Can you hear me, Winifred?”

Slowly, I see her eyes flicker, and he speaks her name again. Then they open a crack, and then a little wider, before resting on Jackson’s face. A smile rises on her bloodied lips.

“Jackson…” her voice croaks. “You need to get out of here.”

“Not without you, Winifred. Now on your feet, soldier.”

He makes a move to try to lift her, but she merely shakes her head.

“My body is broken, Jack. It’s OK…I’m ready to die.”

“No, we can get you out of here. We’ll go walking in Petram, up in mountains…”

Her eyes smile at him, and a wrinkled hand lifts to his face. And for the first time in my life, I see a tear roll down my father’s cheek.

“You go walking with your wife and son. Live long for me, my dearest boy.”

Her eyes sweep over to me, and she gestures for me to come closer with her finger. I move in, leaning down, trying to stop my own tears from falling.

"I've found one more thing for you," she whispers. "In the file…"

"What is it?"

"There's no time," she says, her voice weakening with every word. "My notes…on…the desk…go…"

I see her eyes flicker as my father calls her name again. And then, slowly, they begin to lock, half open and fading away, staring right up to the ceiling. Empty.

My father looks at her for a moment longer, the room shaking violently.

"Goodbye, Winifred," she whispers, kissing her cheek. "And thank you…for everything."

Up onto his feet he goes again, me along with him. His eyes firm up and he looks to me.

"Grab the notes," he says. "We have to get to the docks…"

32
A Final Secret

I rush over to the Professor's desk and see a little notebook sitting upon it, before sweeping it up and running to the door. My father waits for me, ushering me under as he follows. Then back down the corridor we go, our feet splashing once more as the entire level continues to fill with water. It's deeper now, pouring harder, the leaks becoming floods as the dams threaten to burst.

We reach the lifts just in time, a wave of water rushing towards us as we rise up again through the city. When we hit the summit, and step onto the deck, we see the devastation continue to evolve before us. More buildings burn. More bodies line the streets. More booms and explosions ripple and burst, echoing around the great dome as it fills with smoke.

With our hovercar crushed, we rush to find another, but find it impossible. Most are destroyed or locked or otherwise unusable.

"We have to run," shouts Jackson. "As fast as we can…the city is coming down."

Our jog turns to a gallop as we dash through the city, moving around the perimeter towards its

Northern edge. I constantly search for danger, deviating our path around falling detritus and sudden explosions, staying right next to my father so I can thrust him to one side if I need to.

Other people that we pass have no such luck. I can see their fates sealed but am unable to help. All I can do is shout a warning as a block of broken building comes clattering down from above, or a sudden flame pours out of a window, burning those beyond it.

Most don't hear me. Many don't listen. Only the few who heed my warnings survive, only to be caught by the next attack.

It matters not. Soon, the entire city will be crumbling into the depths, and anyone left within will go with it.

Some stragglers have the wit to follow us, staying close as they realise who I am and what I can do. By the time the docks come into view, I've gathered a bit of a tail, a dozen or so canny survivors moving in my slipstream.

I scan the docks ahead but see no sign of our people. We gallop to the edge, the wall of the city opening out to reveal the sea beyond. Here, up eight levels from the waves, only the largest ships are visible. At other levels below, smaller vessels gather, some commercial but most used for transport and trade, huge merchant vessels designed to ship produce to and from the city.

Over the railings, we see one such ship being loaded. Not with produce, but with people. And among them, leading the charge, I see my mother, and Athena, and Ellie and Link, all of them working to get as many people aboard as possible.

We shoot towards the stairs, dropping down a level, then two, until we come around the corner and see them ahead.

My mother's face bursts open with relief as she sees us, but there's no time for anything else. We join them as I spy Ajax and Velia among the throng, and Leeta too, already on board, guiding people to the back.

Clangs of metal sound as the stairs begin to grind and bend, the entire structure of the city now twisting out of shape. I hear Link calling for the boat to start as the last of the city residents continue to rush from the platform. Some, on the stairs, get caught as they collapse, tumbling to their depths many levels below.

We stand as a troop of Watchers, just off the boat, looking ahead for anyone else we can save. From the shadows more come, the last few, screaming for us to wait. The boat slowly begins to drift off, a small gap opening up as it starts sliding out to sea.

And then, we all see it together. The whole section in front of us, several levels of the city all crumbling down. And suddenly, the screams of those running at us are cut short. They're all crushed before our eyes.

"There's no one else," calls Athena, staring at the carnage. "We've done all we can."

We move back, jumping onto the boat as it continues to drift away, only a few hundred saved from the city. They all gather on the deck, every single set of eyes watching in horror as we slowly float from the docks. The grand structure, so long the centre of our nation, pours fire and smoke, groaning a deafening roar as it takes its final few breaths.

I watch, unblinking, as it droops and sags, many square miles of metal slowly being consumed by the waves. Tens of thousands of lives inside, ended by the whims of a madman, seeing out the wishes of an even more callous mind.

For a long while, no one says a word. We just stand there in silence and watch as we move further from the city, and it moves deeper into the waves. The water boils and froths around it as the fires are quenched by the unstoppable force of mother nature, only a twisted metal husk still remaining above the surface that will continue to send a spiral of smoke into the sky for many days.

Tears are shed. Wounds are seen to. And already, plans are made for what to do next.

Because that's what war is all about. You pick yourself up, and you go again. Just like Athena taught us in the training cave of Petram. When you hit the floor, defeated, you rise up and come back stronger. And that's the only thing we can do.

But not now. Now, I stand alone, just staring at the sea city, barely able to commit such an act to reality. I consider for a second whether I'm in a terrible nightmare. Whether these visions, these powers, have twisted my mind like the city before me. Whether I'll wake somewhere safe and calm, all of this just an awful dream.

But I don't consider it for long. Because I know that this is what my life is now. And until I die, it always will be.

And as I stand alone at the front of the boat, staring over the railing as we drift away, I feel my fingers dipping into my pocket, and pulling out Professor Lane's notepad.

I flick inside, and right at the front, see her words, scribbled by her own hand.

It reads:

All the Seekers show identical DNA except one.

One is unique, separate from the others. A mixture of two gene donors, cloned from two sources...

I think again of the four clones, all identical but one. One with his fairer hair and blue glint to his eyes. One who's stronger and more powerful than the others. One's who's unique.

I continue reading, but already I know what her words are going to tell me.

One source is as the other three...Augustus Knight.

The other, however, is one of our own.

I turn and look at my mother, working to fix wounds and console people. The most kind-hearted, good-natured woman you could ever hope to meet.

And as I look at her, I read her name in Professor Lane's hand.

The other source comes from Cyra Drayton...

THE END

The story will continue in Book 3!

To hear about the author's latest discounts and new releases, sign up to his newsletter at www.tcedgebooks.com

Made in the USA
Las Vegas, NV
20 December 2023